To Love

and to

Cherish

D0011815

Lauren Layne

To Love and to Cherish

POCKET BOOKS

New York   London   Toronto   Sydney   New Delhi

Pocket Books
An Imprint of Simon & Schuster, Inc.
1230 Avenue of the Americas
New York, NY 10020

First Pocket Books paperback edition November 2016

POCKET and colophon are registered trademarks of Simon & Schuster, Inc.

For information about special discounts for bulk purchases, please contact Simon & Schuster Special Sales at 1-866-506-1949 or business@simonandschuster.com.

The Simon & Schuster Speakers Bureau can bring authors to your live event. For more information or to book an event, contact the Simon & Schuster Speakers Bureau at 1-866-248-3049 or visit our website at www.simonspeakers.com.

Interior design by Devan Norman

Manufactured in the United States of America

10 9 8 7 6 5 4 3 2 1

ISBN 978-1-5011-3517-0
ISBN 978-1-5011-3518-7 (ebook)

For Kristi.
Because . . . Logan.

Prologue

Eight Years Earlier

WHAT CAN I GET you, miss?"

Alexis settled at the barstool, unwinding the scarf from around her neck and placing it on top of her warm puffy coat before smiling at the bartender. "Pinot grigio?"

"You got it. Which one? We've got two by the glass."

"Um . . ." She glanced down at the menu, scanning for the wine list. "I had one the other day . . . I think it was four dollars?"

"Ah, yup. That's our happy-hour white. I can still give it to you, but it'll be eight fifty now as it's past seven."

"Oh," Alexis said, trying to hide the stab of dismay. "That's fine."

She'd just have to drink it slow, make it last.

"Food menu?"

"Yes, please," she said. "You mind if I work on my laptop here at the bar?"

The bartender shrugged, her blue eyes completely disinterested. "Fine by me. Tuesdays in January are slow. You could pretty much sleep here, and nobody would notice or care."

A few days ago, the offer might have been somewhat tempting, but as of yesterday morning, Alexis was officially a New York resident.

Well, sort of. Did subletting count? She'd signed a three-month sublease on a two-bedroom place in Harlem with a sweet, if slightly ditzy, roommate named Mary.

It wasn't quite where she wanted to be, but it beat the cheap hotels she'd been staying at before now, at least budget-wise. Enough so that she was fully intending to eat something with protein in it tonight.

She flipped open the menu and winced as she saw the price of a cheeseburger. *Or not.*

Even hole-in-the-wall pubs were pricey in Manhattan. Alexis thought she'd been prepared, but she was running through her allotted spending money a hell of a lot faster than she'd expected. Especially considering she hadn't made any traction on a potential investor in her business idea: an elite, full-service wedding-planning agency.

Alexis glanced at the bartender, hoping she wasn't too late to cancel her wine order, but the bored-looking redhead had already poured her wine and was heading her way.

At least the glass was filled to the brim. Alexis must have looked like she'd needed it. Still, she'd have to offset the wine price with the cheapest food item. *Again.* Just a few months ago, she wouldn't have thought it possible to be sick of French fries, but she'd passed that point about a week ago.

"You know what you want to eat, or need a few?" the bartender asked.

"Still deciding."

"No prob." Her attention was on her phone. "Just holler when you're ready."

The bartender wandered away, still typing on her phone, and Alexis opened up her laptop and pulled out the ever-present file folder where she kept a printed copy of the most recent proposal.

Generally speaking, the electronic version of her business plan was more practical, but you never knew when someone who mattered was going to ask you for more information, and she wanted to be ready.

Alexis was *always* ready.

Her stomach rumbled in hunger, and hard as she tried to ignore it, it wasn't the first time a tiny part of her wished that she'd taken her father up on his offer of a loan. Then her company would be a reality instead of a dream, and maybe she'd be able to eat something other than cereal and ramen.

But though she had a reasonably good relationship with her sometimes-cold father, his stipulations had just been too much.

For starters, the loan came with a location requirement. *Stay in Boston.*

That wasn't the dream. New York was the dream.

The other stipulation had been even harder to swallow.

You could hire your sister, you know . . .

Yeah, no.

She didn't want to hire her sister. She loved Roxanne, but her sister wasn't the type of person she was looking to bring on to help get this business off the ground. Alexis needed someone with drive and business acumen. Roxie, while smart and savvy, was easily bored when it came to her career choices. Alexis needed someone who'd be in it for the long haul.

Plus, there was the bigger elephant in the room—it was just too damn hard to be around her sister right now.

The wound would heal, eventually. Alexis knew that. It was just a little too fresh, and Boston was just a little too painful.

She took a sip of wine as she opened her spreadsheet. The potential investor she'd spoken with today had been polite and shown token interest but was concerned with her growth model, specifically with the size of her team.

It was a valid point—a tiny number of employees would mean they could only support so much business. Still, Alexis was hesitant to change it. What the company would lack in scalability, it would make up for with consistency. Perfection every time, even if there were *fewer* times.

She left the column as is. Alexis knew it was unrealistic to think she wouldn't have to make some compromises, but she kept holding out hope that someone would *get* it. That someone would hear her, see what she was trying to do, and understand.

"Hello."

The sexy British accent startled Alexis out of her thoughts, and she glanced up, both alarmed and intrigued to find that the face that awaited her was every bit as appealing as the voice.

The man was about her age—early, maybe mid-twenties—and ridiculously cute. His hair was dark and maybe just a touch too long, as though he intended to get a haircut but kept forgetting. The eyes were brown and friendly, accented by trendy black-framed glasses.

The chunky cable-knit sweater with elbow patches—*for real*—bordered on dorky, but then, Alexis had always had a soft spot for dorky. He had a bit of the Clark Kent thing going on, which had always been far more her type than the overrated Superman.

"Hi," she replied quickly, realizing that she'd been staring.

His smile grew wider as he extended a hand. "Logan Harris."

Darn. Even the name was good.

"Alexis," she said.

"Does that come with a last name?" he teased, lowering himself to the vacant barstool beside her.

"Not to strange men," she retorted.

"I could buy you a drink. Get rid of the 'strange' part."

Alexis's smile slipped as she remembered that romance, even flirting, wasn't part of her plan. She'd learned the hard way that she could have one or the other—her own business or a boyfriend—not both. *And even if she wanted the latter, the latter didn't want her back*.

"No thanks; I'm fine," she said, letting the slightest amount of chill enter her voice. The ice-princess treatment, Roxanne called it.

Logan shrugged, undeterred. "All right then. May I borrow your menu?"

She nodded, and he picked it up, perusing it for several moments and paying her no attention.

It was both a relief and also a bit of an insult, if she was being entirely honest, to be given up on so easily.

Alexis tried to turn her attention back to her laptop but watched out of the corner of her eye as he finally shut the menu, waiting patiently to catch the bartender's eye.

"Hi there," he said, when the bartender ambled back over. "I'd like a Stella, and maybe a bite to eat?"

Alexis didn't miss the once-over that the bartender gave Logan before the curvy redhead leaned over the bar, displaying perky boobs as she clicked her pen and pulled a notepad out of her back pocket.

"Shoot," the bartender said flirtatiously, looking a good deal friendlier than she had when she'd spoken to Alexis.

Not that Alexis blamed her. A cute Brit could do that to a girl.

"All right then," Logan said. "I'd like the burger, medium, with Swiss. Fish and chips, extra tartar, and . . . how's your chicken club?"

The bartender blinked. "It's good. But you want all that?"

"I do. Thank you."

"Suit yourself," she said, scribbling Logan's order on the pad.

"Hungry?" Alexis couldn't resist asking after the bartender moved away.

Logan gave a sheepish smile. "I'm a recovering

student. I sometimes get so wrapped up in my day that I forget to eat."

"A *recovering* student. What does that mean?"

He turned slightly toward her. "Someone's showing plenty of interest in a *strange* man."

She bit her lip. "I'm sorry if I was rude before. I'm just not really in the market for . . . you know."

He gave her an easy smile. "Everyone's in the market for a friend, Alexis."

She opened her mouth and then shut it as she realized he was right. She *could* use a friend. She'd spent her entire life in Boston and knew almost nobody in New York. This guy seemed nice and nonthreatening enough—what would be the harm in a little conversation over dinner? It had been too long since she'd had somebody to share a meal with.

Logan seemed to know the moment she capitulated, because he turned more fully toward her. "A recovering student, Alexis, is a recent graduate. One who hasn't quite absorbed that there will be no more finals, no more requisite all-nighters, and no more dorm sex."

Alexis laughed. "Undergrad, then?"

He gave her a wry look. "How young do I look, darling? MBA from Columbia. Just finished up end of last May."

She felt a little stab of relief that he wasn't twenty-two.

He leaned toward her slightly. "Twenty-five next month, just in case you were wondering. *As a friend.*"

She tried to hide her smile and failed. "Columbia, huh? You're a long way from home."

"Noticed that, did ya?" He winked. "I came over here for undergrad, also Columbia. Always figured I'd go back to London and maybe someday I will, but . . ." He shrugged. "Seems I have stuff to do here first."

"Such as?" She took a sip of her wine, dismayed to see that it was half-empty.

"Well, this will probably shock you, given my vast amount of brawn, but I'm an accountant. Or at least I will be, once I get my business up and running."

Alexis was impressed. "Your own business?"

Most twentysomethings, even those with an entrepreneurial bent, opted to get a few years of work under their belts for someone else before branching out on their own.

He nodded. "I'm working out of my flat for now, but I'm hoping to lease some office space soon, get some legitimacy. If nothing else to get my father off my back."

"He's not a fan of your plan?" Alexis asked.

Logan's shoulder lifted, and for the first time he seemed a little sad. "Both parents have had it in their heads that I'd come home. Run the family business in London."

"Which is . . . ?"

He spun his beer glass idly. "Financial consulting firm. My father's the CEO, Mum's the COO."

"Wow, that's . . ."

"Scary?" Logan supplied.

"I was going to say impressive. That they work together—without killing each other, I mean."

"They're in love. It's atrocious," he said with a wink. "What about your folks?"

Alexis laughed. "*Not* in love. They divorced when I was in high school. Dad's remarried and happy now, I think. Mom not so much."

"And you?" he said. "Are you happy, Alexis?"

She pursed her lips, surprised and yet not entirely unsettled by the personal question. "It's been a while since anyone asked me that. Since I even thought about it, really."

"Think it out. I'll wait," he said with a wink.

She didn't have to think that long. "I'm *almost* happy."

"You sound quite confident on that."

She shrugged. "Let's just say that I need a few things to fall into place in my professional life, but once that happens . . . yeah. I'll be happy."

She'd make sure of it.

"You're starting your own business."

Her head whipped around. "How'd you know that?"

Logan reached over and tapped her laptop. "I can spot an Excel spreadsheet from a mile away."

"Is that why you came over here?"

"No, darling. That would be your smile."

"I don't remember smiling."

He burst out laughing. "You're unusual. I like that. And you *did* smile. At the bartender, when you ordered your wine."

"You were watching me," Alexis said, eyebrows lifting. "Rather creepy for a *friend*."

Instead of acknowledging her comment, he nodded his chin at her laptop. "What are you working on, if you don't mind my asking? Dare I hold out hope you're also an accountant and we can have darling, glasses-wearing babies together?"

"My eyesight is twenty-twenty," she retorted.

"So that's a maybe, then?"

Alexis couldn't help the laugh, a *full* laugh, the first in a long time, and his eyes crinkled a little at the corners as he watched her. "Tell me about you, Alexis, my new best friend."

Damn, he was charming.

"Well," she said slowly. "I'm not an accountant— sorry to break your number-crunching heart. But I, too, am a 'recovering student.' "

"Do tell."

"I finished up my master's program at Boston College end of last May. Marketing and business administration."

"Boston," he said, the word sounding ridiculously appealing in his clipped accent. "And what brings you to New York?"

Alexis waved a hand over her laptop and the folder holding her business proposal. "This."

"And *this* would be . . . ?"

She shoved the folder his way and took another sip of her wine—a big one.

He pulled it toward him, opening it and beginning to read.

Having the entire thing memorized, Alexis's mind couldn't help but "read" along with him inside her own head.

The Wedding Belles is a boutique wedding-planning company committed to providing carefully curated weddings for the discerning bride . . . The Wedding

Belles ensures the perfect combination of classic elegance and innovative modernity, promising a wedding that's both timeless and contemporary . . .

Logan turned the page, and Alexis expected him to lose interest once he was past the marketing fluff, but to her surprise, he read every last page, analyzed every last chart she'd painstakingly built.

His food arrived and Logan gestured with one finger for another round of drinks, before absently pulling a fry off one of the plates and shoving the plate in her direction.

She bit her lip. She couldn't. She *shouldn't*.

But the smell of the chicken club, with melted cheese and ripe avocado between buttery, toasty bread, was too much to resist. She picked up a knife and cut off a quarter of the sandwich.

"Oh my God," she whispered around the first heavenly bite.

Out of the corner of her eye she thought she saw him smile, but he never looked up from her proposal, careful to wipe his fingers between fries and turning her pages.

Finally, he'd read the entire thing, and Alexis was mortified to realize she'd eaten half his chicken sandwich, a quarter of the burger, a good two-thirds of the fish, and more than a few fries.

Logan didn't seem to mind as he picked up the remaining half of his chicken sandwich and took a thoughtful bite.

He chewed slowly, methodically. Took a sip of beer. Then turned toward her once more. "Where are you with this?"

"How do you mean?"

"You need funding, yes?"

She nodded, reaching for the second glass of wine the bartender had brought along with Logan's beer. She couldn't afford it, but . . . what the hell?

"Yes. I'm envisioning a three-story, multiuse brownstone that could serve as both office space for the team, reception, as well as my living quarters. It'll be more money up front, but I've done the math, and it makes more financial sense in the long run when you factor in the cost of moving, inflation, lease renewal."

"You want to start it off right," he said. "From the very beginning."

She nodded, grateful that someone finally understood. "I know conventional wisdom suggests that I should start it out of my home and sort of build up, but the entire brand of the Belles is elite. The clients I want aren't the ones who will meet in the living room of my Harlem apartment."

"Any nibbles?"

She lifted a shoulder and pulled another fry off the plate, long past the point of playing coy about being desperately hungry. "I've had a few meetings. Nobody's laughed me out of the conference room yet—just a lot of noncommittal 'We'll be in touch.' "

He nodded. "You have a location in mind."

She smiled, loving that it wasn't a question so much as a statement. As though he knew the way her mind worked, putting the cart before the horse and touring Manhattan real estate when she couldn't even afford a second glass of eight-dollar wine.

"Aha," he said, with an answering smile.

"Okay, fine," she said. "It's on Seventy-Third between Broadway and West End, and it's just . . . perfect."

"Upper West Side," he said in surprise.

"Yes. It feels right for the Belles. Classic but up-and-coming, upscale but not stuffy, expensive but not too expensive . . ."

"You really have thought it all out." Logan was studying her.

"Since I was, like, twelve," she admitted.

"Never wavered?"

Alexis shook her head. "Nope. The vision became more precise over time, not less."

He turned away, watching his beer glass as he spun it idly on the bar top. "I had a great-aunt. Margaret. Great old lady, great sense of humor. She passed away a few months back."

"Oh," Alexis said, a little confused by the change of subject but sympathetic all the same. She touched his arm consolingly. "I'm sorry."

"Thank you," he said. "Although she was ninety-two and passed in her sleep. Definitely the way to go, don't you think?"

"Can't say I've put too much thought into dying. Quite the opposite, actually."

"Yes, I can see that about you, Alexis," he said thoughtfully.

She liked the way he said her name, embracing all the syllables. *Uh-lex-iss.*

"Aunt Margaret left me some money. Quite a lot of it, actually," Logan said, still not looking at her.

"Um, congratulations?"

Logan's shoulders didn't move, but he turned his head, resting his chin on his shoulder as he pinned her with an intense gaze. "I'd like to make you an offer, Alexis Morgan."

She stilled. "What kind of offer?"

He used his elbow to indicate her proposal. "I'd like to fund the Wedding Belles."

Her breath caught in her throat. "Why would you do that?"

Instead of answering, he turned to face her more fully, and all traces of the casual postgrad vanished, and she realized she was seeing the accountant version of Logan Harris—the shrewd businessman.

"There's a catch."

She tried not to let her deflation become visible. Of course there was a catch. There always was.

"I don't want to just offer you a loan. I want to be part owner. Fifty percent."

She was already shaking her head. "That's not in the plan. It's *my* business."

He smiled. "That won't change. I won't tell you how to run it. You'll do things your way. But this business plan is legit, and I want to be a part of it."

"I'd pay you back every penny with interest," she said. "I expect I can be profitable in two years, I already have a handful of socialite connections, all engaged or *almost* engaged, and—"

"No deal," he said. "I own fifty percent or I'm not involved at all."

Fifty percent.

This complete stranger wanted to own fifty percent of her business. Fifty percent of her *dream*.

She shook her head. "I can't. Thank you, but no."

His gaze shuttered just for a moment before his smile returned, just slightly more restrained than before. "Fair enough."

Logan shifted his weight, and she felt a little bite of disappointment when he pulled his wallet out of his back pocket. He was leaving.

The urge to tell him to stay was strong, and for the life of her, she couldn't figure out if it was for personal or professional reasons. She didn't know what she wanted from Logan Harris, but she wanted *something*.

The thought scared her, and was exactly what had her biting her tongue.

She watched as he put several bills on the counter, saw immediately that it was more than enough to cover all of the food, plus her drinks and a hefty tip.

"No, Logan, please." She reached forward to pick up some of the bills and return them to him, but he caught her hand.

Alexis gasped at the contact. His thumb found the center of her palm, his long, strong fingers closing around the back of her hand.

"Let me, Alexis." It was a command.

Her first instinct was to scratch back at his high-handedness, but she couldn't seem to think when he was touching her, didn't want to do anything other than what he wanted her to do.

Not like her at all.

No doubt about it, this was a man she needed to guard herself against.

She slowly nodded. "Okay. Thank you."

"There," he said softly. "That wasn't so hard, now, was it?"

"Actually, it nearly killed me," she grumbled.

His smile was slow and intimate. "I know."

Logan's gaze dropped to their joined hands, and his thumb brushed against her palm, lingering as though reluctant to release her, before he finally let go.

He pulled something else out of his wallet, set it purposely in front of her. A business card. *His* business card.

"You'll call me if you change your mind." Again, it was a command. She was starting to gather that beneath the quiet smile and charming accent was a man accustomed to exercising control in all things. *Much like her.*

Alexis picked up the card. It was heavy white card stock with nothing but his name, phone number, and email. The card suited him. Simple and to the point, but the midnight-blue font rather than the expected black belied just a hint of unconventional that appealed to her far too much.

"I can't," she whispered again, eyes locked on his card.

She felt his gaze on her profile but didn't meet his eyes, and he finally gave up, pulling on his heavy wool coat.

"It was lovely meeting you, Alexis."

She finally looked up, met his piercing gaze. "You, too."

He opened his mouth as though to say something but then shook his head and slowly started to walk away. Alexis felt something twist inside her at the thought of him leaving, and she gave in to the urge.

"Logan."

He turned around, hands shoved into his pockets, eyes unreadable.

"Why?" she asked, lifting his business card slightly. "Why would you offer this?"

He jerked his head in the direction of her folder. "It's a good plan. Worth the risk."

She shook her head slowly, searching his face. "No, it's something more than that. Another reason. I'd like to know what."

The outer corners of his eyes crinkled a bit, and he gave a fleeting smile before walking back to her, crowding her against the bar.

For a moment she feared—hoped?—that he would kiss her, and from the way his mouth dropped to just inches from hers, she thought maybe he wanted to.

Then his face turned, his lips brushing against her cheek instead. "Say yes to my proposal, Alexis. Say yes, and maybe someday I'll tell you the other reason."

Logan pulled away, held her gaze for a heartbeat.

Then he stepped back, gave her a sly wink, and walked away without a backward glance.

Alexis sat there for a long time after, his card in her fingers, her heart in her throat, and her life in the hands of a stranger who somehow didn't feel like a stranger at all.

Chapter One

S O LET ME ASK this—how many layers in a wedding cake is excessive?"

If there was anything Alexis Morgan had learned in nearly a decade of wedding planning, it was that you never told a client that her vision was excessive. You simply *guided* her to that conclusion.

"How many layers are you thinking?" Alexis asked her client in a practiced neutral tone, defaulting to the answer-a-question-with-a-question technique that she'd found worked exceedingly well with indecisive brides.

"Twenty?"

Wow. Okay, yeah—that's excessive.

"We can do twenty," Alexis lied smoothly. "But keep in mind that the nine-course meal we're planning will already include two dessert courses. We don't want to minimize the specialness of those."

Especially at five hundred bucks a head, just for the food.

Extravagant, even for a Wedding Belles client.

Nathalie Sorrel was an example of how far Alexis had come in the eight years since starting her company from this very same office.

Nathalie was an international supermodel and the very definition of the elite clientele Alexis had always dreamed of. Her latest modeling contract had been in the high six figures. Add in the fact that she was marrying Eric Hill, an NBA superstar whose contract was in the seven figures, and, well, if anybody could afford a twenty-layer wedding cake, it was these two.

Still, much as it was Alexis's job to create dream weddings, it was also her *brand* to draw the line between tastefully extravagant and completely ostentatious.

"You don't think I should do the big cake?" Nathalie said, pursing the pouty lips she was known for.

"I think it doesn't fit the vision of the wedding you originally talked about," Alexis said, skipping the fact that none of her bakery contacts would undertake something so ridiculous. "When I asked you to describe your dream wedding in three words, you told me lavish, unique, and intimate."

"A big cake is lavish."

"Yes, but it's not intimate," Alexis said. "Part of what makes your wedding so wonderfully special is the fact that you're capping it at fifty people, even though hundreds would kill for an invitation. You're creating something small and special. You want lavish, not gauche."

It was just the right thing to say, as Alexis had known it would be. There was no dirtier picture to paint for the Manhattan elite than the notion that something they did might be considered *gauche*. Knowing this was the Belles' specialty, and Alexis's own brand of genius, if she did say so herself.

Alexis had made a name for herself by knowing how to walk the fine line between opulent and gaudy.

After all, who better to know how to avoid gaudy than one who'd grown up swallowed in it?

"You're right," Nathalie was saying as she nodded enthusiastically, her azure-blue eyes widening as though a lightbulb had just gone off inside her head. "You're so right. Eric and I have really been priding ourselves in restraint with this wedding, and I don't want to jeopardize it with a cake."

Alexis's smile never slipped, but inwardly she maybe rolled her eyes, just a little. Any notion of restraint in this wedding had come from Alexis herself. But then that, too, was part of the job.

It's not that she made the weddings her own. With every single contract, Alexis was committed to creating the exact experience the bride envisioned. It was just that sometimes they needed a little help implementing that vision and not getting sucked into bridezilla land.

They all thought they wanted a twenty-layer cake when *really* what they wanted was a small, elegant cake with dark chocolate truffle and Bavarian cream filling and a single pale pink ribbon around the base to match the sashes of the bridesmaids' dresses.

And it was Alexis's job to help them see that.

Five minutes later, a small chocolate cake was exactly the conclusion that Nathalie came to as they finished up their meeting. The model rose from one of the ergonomic chairs in the conference room, stretching out her limbs-for-days as she pulled on the same Burberry trench coat she'd modeled in their latest catalog.

"Enjoy Milan," Alexis said as she escorted Nathalie to the door of the Belles' Upper West Side headquarters.

"Ugh, the only thing worse than a last-minute trip is a last-minute trip on a red-eye," Nathalie said, checking her Cartier watch. "Thanks again for seeing me last minute. I really appreciate you squeezing me in after-hours like this."

"That's what I'm here for," Alexis said, refraining from saying that it's not like she had other plans to get to.

Alexis liked to keep up the guise that she was a woman on the go for the benefit of her clients, who were firmly entrenched in the lifestyle of the high-flying glam and fab, but the truth was the Belles was her life. Her workday rarely started later than seven and never ended before eight, and Alexis liked it that way.

Mostly.

Alexis waved good-bye to Nathalie and closed the door, feeling the same sense of relief she always felt when she was done with client work for the day.

Working with people was a part of the job—obviously. But as a fierce introvert, Alexis's favorite part of her day was always the recharging moments late in the evening when she'd sit at her little kitchen table in her apartment upstairs with a glass of wine and her planner.

"You know, I was just starting to think my diet was going well, but seeing Nathalie Sorrel makes me realize I have, like, *such* a long way to go." This from Jessie, the Belles' longtime receptionist and Alexis's most recent right hand now that her previous assistant, Heather, had been promoted to full-time wedding planner.

Alexis gave Jessie a distracted smile. "Take it from someone older and wiser: comparing oneself to supermodels never ends well."

Jessie punched a button on the phone, switching it over to voice mail. "You're thirty-three. I'm twenty-six. Not that much older."

Alexis rubbed at her forehead. It certainly felt that way.

"Plus," Jessie was saying on a long-suffering sigh, "you wouldn't get it. You're a size two, and I officially just Ben and Jerried out of my size eight."

"Ben and Jerry's is a verb now?"

"It is when it has the power to make your hips explode."

Alexis paused at the unusually glum note in her receptionist's voice. Jessie was a bubbly extrovert whose personality was every bit as vibrant as her bright orange curly hair and sparkly green eyes.

"Everything okay?" Alexis asked, watching as Jessie pushed away from her desk and started to pack up the Tory Burch purse Alexis had bought her as a Christmas present.

Jessie glanced up. "Ugh, was my pity party coming out? Sorry."

"No need to apologize. Want to talk?"

"No, it's okay. I mean, yeah, but . . . okay, whatever—do you ever get tired of being single?"

Alexis didn't so much as blink, and she *certainly* didn't flinch. She was very sure of this. If Alexis had mastered anything over the years, it was hiding her feelings.

Especially feelings related to her nonexistent love life.

"I find I enjoy the solitude," Alexis said slowly.

Jessie laughed. "Yeah, I forgot who I was talking to. I, on the other hand, like someone to listen to my constant chattering. It's been three months since that prick dumped me to get back with his ex, and I haven't had a single decent date. I thought maybe losing a few pounds would do the trick."

"You already know what I'm going to say to that," Alexis said with a little smile.

"That any guy who doesn't like me with extra padding on my hips isn't worth having?" Jessie said. "Yeah, yeah. Doesn't mean I'm not stopping at the gym on the way home."

"Just make sure you're doing it because it makes you feel good, not because you just saw Nathalie Sorrel's tiny butt wiggle out of here."

"Yes, Boss," Jessie said, saluting. "You need anything before I head out?"

"All good," Alexis said. "Heather and Brooke gone for the day?"

"Yup. Brooke is at that new restaurant soft opening to see if their private event space is worth going on the list, and Heather . . . not sure, but I'm thinking she's doing the newlywed thing?"

Jessie wiggled her eyebrows playfully, and Alexis forced a smile. It wasn't that she wasn't happy for Heather Fowler, now Heather Tanner. Heather was her longtime employee, formerly as assistant, now as a wedding planner in her own right, and a good friend. One of Alexis's best friends, in fact, although strictly speaking, Alexis wasn't really a BFF kind of gal.

Heather had found herself in a whirlwind romance with her sexy neighbor that had ended in a very spontaneous, and very romantic, wedding several weeks earlier.

Alexis was thrilled for Josh and Heather. Heck, she was also thrilled for her other wedding planner, Brooke, who'd recently gotten engaged to a ridiculously handsome hotel tycoon, Seth.

And if she was a tiny bit jealous, she didn't think about that. Didn't have time for it, really.

"Your groceries were delivered while you were meeting with Nathalie," Jessie was saying as she pulled on her bright green jacket. "I put your eggs and stuff in the fridge."

"Thanks, you're great," Alexis said distractedly as she picked up the pile of mail and began flipping through. Bills, bills, and more bills. She set them aside to be dealt with tomorrow when her longtime accountant, Logan Harris, came in for their twice-weekly appointments.

"I know," Jessie said in a singsong voice, all trace of former glumness gone. "See you tomorrow, Boss."

Alexis locked up behind Jessie, gathered her planner, iPad, and laptop, and headed to the stairs to climb to her third-floor apartment.

Despite the fact that all of her favorite girl-boss blogs had been on a kick about not working where you live and vice versa, throwing down a massive downpayment on her Upper West Side brownstone had been the best decision of Alexis's life.

From the very beginning, she'd envisioned her home and office exactly as it was now: a classy reception and conference area to serve as a place for excited brides to discuss their dream weddings, a second-floor office space for her team to have room to spread out and work, and a third floor just for her to live.

Well, not *just* for her.

That was the one part of her life that hadn't quite lived up to expectations; when Alexis had bought the property all those years ago, she'd had visions of being married by now. Maybe a baby. Or two. Finishing up her workday and bounding upstairs to relieve the nanny of her little bundle of joy, getting in a cuddle or two before bath and bedtime, and then relaxing with her husband over a nice glass of wine as they discussed their respective workdays.

Funny how some dreams came to be and some stayed just that. *Dreams*.

Alexis pushed the thought aside as she opened the door to her apartment. She smiled upon seeing that Jessie had arranged the white tulips Alexis had added to her grocery delivery in her favorite Anthropologie vase. She absently rearranged them to her liking before carrying the vase to the small sideboard. She lit a scented lavender candle and slowly exhaled the stress of the day.

Alexis loved her apartment. Loved the dark

hardwood floors, the crisp white cupboards of a newly renovated kitchen. Loved the way the big tree out front let just the right amount of filtered sunlight through on a Sunday morning, loved the way the muted gray of her living room walls kept it cozy on snowy winter nights and serene on spring evenings such as this one.

Alexis changed her color scheme every couple of years to keep the apartment from feeling stale, and most recently, she'd gone with grays and purples, which suited her mood lately.

Calm and just a little bit melancholy.

Not for the first time she wondered if maybe a cat wouldn't be a good investment. She'd prefer a dog—a big, dopey golden retriever like the one she'd longed for as a kid, but she had neither the space nor the schedule for a dog.

A cat, though . . . a cat could do its business in a litter box, would probably prefer for her to be gone as often as it would for her to be present.

A cat would be someone to talk to at the end of a long day.

A day like this one.

Alexis went to the fridge, pulling out a bottle of the Grüner Veltliner she'd opened last night. She pulled down a crystal glass from the cupboard where all of her stemware sat neatly lined up, polishing the glass with a paper towel before pouring some of the crisp white.

Small pleasures, she reminded herself as she took a sip. Savor the small pleasures, and the empty parts won't seem so bad.

Alexis's cell phone rang just as she was opening her

laptop, and she picked it up, glancing at the screen and bracing for a frazzled bride or a panicking vendor.

Her glass froze halfway to her lips when she saw it was neither.

Her thumb hovered over decline. Oh, it was ever so tempting.

But like she always did, Alexis sighed and answered the call. "Hi, Mom."

"Lexie. How are you, dear?"

Lexie. She'd always hated the nickname, but she'd learned at an early age to pick her battles when it came to Cecily Morgan.

Alexis took another sip of wine. "I'm doing well. How are you?"

She winced as she asked it, knowing it was the expected and appropriate thing to say and yet dreading her mother's response all the same.

For Cecily Morgan, *How are you?* was never met with an *okay* and certainly never a *good*. Not since Alexis's father had committed the ultimate of all clichés and left her mother for a much younger woman. And then—to add insult to injury—Alexis's father had actually gone and *married* Tawny. Alexis suspected the fact that her father had at least seemed to find a second shot at true love rankled her mother more than if Tawny had just been a passing flavor-of-the-month, garden-variety sort of fling.

"Did I tell you that *she* came by the club the other day?" her mother was saying.

Another cliché: her mother's refusal to say Tawny's name. At least she'd moved on from *that woman*.

"Oh yeah?" Alexis asked, refusing, as she always

did, to play into the she-devil routine. She liked Tawny. Her stepmom could be a little crass, sure, but she had a good heart and liked to laugh. Tawny was *fun*. Alexis's mom . . . not so much.

"Yes," Cecily said in disgust. "Tossed back three chardonnays before four o'clock. I wouldn't be surprised if your father's driving her to drink."

Sort of like you're driving me to drink? Alexis deliberately put the glass of wine to the side.

"How are things otherwise?" she asked, trying to steer her mother to non–Jack Morgan–related topics.

"Oh, *well*," her mother said, emphasizing the last word with a combination of weariness and impending gossip. "Have you talked to your sister lately?"

Alexis stiffened ever so slightly at the mention of Roxie. She was almost to the point where mention of her sister didn't sting. *Almost*.

But not quite.

"I called her last month on her birthday," Alexis said quietly.

"*Well*, I saw her just the other day, and . . ." Her mother's voice had dropped to a whisper. "I think she's expecting."

Alexis's world tilted, just for a moment, and then righted itself. "What?"

"Well, she wouldn't eat a thing, even though we were at that little French bistro she loves. Just kept picking at the bread basket, and well, dear, you know how judicious I've always encouraged you girls to be about unnecessary carbs. And any time Adam tried to encourage her to eat something else, she looked positively ill, had to leave the table. I thought she was going to be sick at the sight of my tuna tartar salad. Then I started thinking and I recalled that the other week, she didn't have a single sip of that Chablis I opened. When have you ever known Roxie to turn down a good glass of wine?"

Alexis swallowed. Once. Twice. *Nope*, her mouth still felt dry. "Maybe she's not feeling well."

"Well, of course she's not feeling well if she's expecting a baby!" her mother snapped. "First trimester was the worst for me, especially with you."

Alexis's eyes closed. "But she hasn't confirmed anything?"

"No," Cecily said. "Which is why I'm calling."

"I already told you I haven't talked to her. I certainly don't know if she's pregnant."

I don't want to know if she's pregnant.

"I think she's keeping it quiet because of you," her mother said, not pulling any punches. "She's protecting you. Your feelings."

Alexis wanted to argue. She wanted so badly to open her mouth and tell her mom that that was crazy, but the thing was . . .

It felt true.

If Roxanne were pregnant, she was no doubt in agony about Alexis finding out. Despite the fact that they'd had nearly a decade to work through the tension between them, Alexis couldn't exactly claim that she had healed.

And Roxie knew it.

"What do you want me to do?" Alexis asked, reaching once more for her wineglass. Might as well. *She* wasn't pregnant with Adam Hogan's baby.

But she might have been. Had things gone very, very differently, she'd have been the one declining her mother's wine, she'd have been the queasy one at the little French bistro, pulling off chunks of a baguette as her insides roiled against her because she was in the process of creating new life.

It hurt more than a little that her mom didn't seem to understand this. Then again, she and her mother had never seen eye to eye. Cecily had always been *barely* tolerant of Alexis's entrepreneurial tendencies, gently reminding her all through high school and college that nice boys liked nice girls, not smart ones.

Not an exact quote, but the sentiment had certainly been clear.

Turned out her mother had been right. Guys liked the girls who were sweet and giggly, not the ones who were ambitious and quiet. *Or at least Adam did.*

Pregnant or not, Alexis was suddenly starting to feel a little queasy herself.

"I think you should talk to her," Cecily said. "Tell her it's okay if she's pregnant."

Alexis's eyes closed once more, and this time she squeezed them shut, tightly.

What if it *wasn't* okay?

What if the fact that her sister was pregnant with the child of the man Alexis once loved would never be okay?

Chapter Two

WHEN LOGAN HARRIS HAD come to New York nearly a decade and a half earlier to attend college from across the pond, he'd fallen quickly and thoroughly for the city.

Staying had never been the plan.

Logan had been born and raised in London, his stint in New York due more to an itch to "see the world" before taking over the family company than it had been a burning desire to relocate permanently.

So at eighteen, he'd hopped on a plane for New York, for what he'd always imagined to be a short stopover to pick up his business degree.

But something had happened when he'd stepped out of that cab on that crisp fall day fifteen years ago outside the formidable gates of the Columbia campus.

It'd felt like coming home.

It had made no sense.

Home was back in England where he'd had a perfectly happy upper-middle-class upbringing, parents he respected, a younger brother he actually liked, a girlfriend at the University of London.

But by the time he'd graduated four years later, there'd been no denying the facts: he wasn't going back to England. Not yet.

To visit, *yes*.

Logan enjoyed his annual holiday trips back to the UK to see his family (he and the college girlfriend were over, their lusty teenage promises not nearly strong enough to survive a bicontinental courtship).

But as much as Logan enjoyed catching up with his parents and brother, spoiling his nieces, and getting a decent cup of tea, there was always a sense of relief when he stepped into Heathrow at the end of his holiday, and even more so when he stepped off the plane in JFK.

Logan's friends back in the UK often asked him what it was about New York that kept calling him back, and in college, the answer contained a rambling description of the city's energy and its people, Central Park in the fall, the way the Village didn't really come alive until eleven p.m.

Passionate, but vague.

But when Logan was twenty-four, just graduated and looking for his first real foot in the door of his career, his reason for staying in New York had become less vague, doubly passionate, and 100 percent secret:

A woman.

Eight years ago, Logan had walked into a bar and fallen hard for a prim woman in a cheap suit, and that's simply all there was to it.

Would Logan still be living in New York at age thirty-three if not for Alexis Morgan?

Perhaps. *Maybe.*

Probably not. He had responsibilities back home. A small Harris-family empire to take over, as his parents reminded him during every phone call.

But he wasn't going anywhere yet. There'd be no leaving as long as she was here. Even if sometimes he wasn't all that sure she even registered his existence.

Times like now.

Logan gave up on trying to keep her attention, pulling off his glasses and tossing them on the desk as he rubbed at his tired eyes. "Alexis, you're not listening."

"Yes I am," she said automatically.

He smiled a little at that. It was very her. Never wrong, even when she was.

Logan respected it. Alexis's fake-it-till-you-make-it methods had turned her from a wide-eyed girl with loads of ambition into the shrewdest businessperson he knew, man or woman.

She was sharp, had good instincts, and was marvelously driven.

Not to mention drop-dead gorgeous with a rather perfect arse.

But nobody knew Alexis Morgan like he did, and he'd bet his favorite three-piece suit that she hadn't heard a word he'd said all morning.

Strictly speaking, as the Wedding Belles' accountant, he didn't *have* to meet with Alexis twice a week. Hell, he didn't even need to meet *once* a week. He met with his other clients once a month, if that, and did the rest over phone or email.

But Alexis and the Belles had always been different.

Not only were they his first client, not only was he the silent part owner of the company, but Alexis was . . . Alexis.

And so every Monday and Thursday morning at seven a.m., he took the 3 train from his high-rise apartment in the financial district up to the Seventy-Second Street stop on the Upper West Side and walked the few blocks over to the Belles.

Monday morning, he brought coffee; Thursday mornings, she made coffee. He wasn't quite sure how or why it worked out that way, but for eight years now, that had been their routine.

That's how it was with Alexis and Logan. Everything was routine, everything in its place.

And Logan's place was as her accountant.

Perhaps that wasn't fair. He knew on some level that Alexis thought of him as a friend. They'd known each other too long, saw each other too often to be anything less.

But was Alexis aware of him as a man?

No. Certainly not.

Did that bug him to all hell? Of course. Did he frequently have the urge to peel away her layers—and clothes—to show her just how fucking *right* they could be? Absolutely.

But Logan Harris was a patient man.

It wasn't time. He knew, perhaps better than anyone, that Alexis was on a crusade to take over the world, and that crusade did not involve relationships. At least not yet.

The only thing that made her obliviousness to him

even remotely tolerable was that Alexis didn't really seem to register *any* men on her romantic radar.

And it's not like Logan had been a monk in the meantime. He took women to bed when it suited him, sometimes even tried to make a go of it with the best of them. But it never went anywhere.

Sometimes a month would go by, maybe several, and then Logan would figure out how to wriggle his way out of it. And if some distant part of his brain registered that this pattern was a product of the fact that they were all stand-ins for the one he really wanted, he could deal with that.

How much longer, he didn't know. But damn it, he was trying.

Waiting.

And getting damn tired of it.

"All right then," he said, sliding his glasses back on his face. "So I'll sell the Belles to the hot dog chap over in Central Park, yeah? Maybe throw in the deed to your flat?"

"Hmm?" Alexis said, looking up at him with the same vacant expression that had been on her face all morning. Her peaches-and-cream complexion turned slightly pink as she registered what he'd said. "I'm sorry," she said, resting her elbows on the wooden table of the small upstairs conference room above the Belles' main reception area. "I'm having a hard time keeping my head in the game this morning."

He frowned. It was unlike her. To say that Alexis never gave less than 100 percent was an understatement.

"Everything all right?" he asked, adjusting his glasses.

She hesitated, and when she opened her mouth, he thought for sure she might confide in him—*trust* him. Instead she shook her head and forced a smile. "Yes, fine."

Fine, my arse.

He took a closer look at her. She appeared the same as she always did. Gray trousers and a white blouse. Luscious brown hair tamed and pulled into a tidy knot at the nape of her neck. Pearl earrings and the small diamond necklace he knew she'd bought for herself the day the Belles had turned profitable, one year and two months after opening.

As always, she looked neat and crisp and positively *begging* to be mussed a bit.

But a closer look showed something else. A tightness around her full pink mouth, shadows in her golden-brown eyes.

Something was wrong. And *damn*, but he could tell from the resolute way her jaw had just shifted in stubbornness that she wasn't going to tell him what.

He knew he should let her be—he'd always been good at that. Giving her the space she needed. Hell, he was pretty sure that was the only reason he was still around.

But something had been shifting lately. In him? In her? He wasn't sure.

Whatever it was, it had him opening his mouth when he'd previously have kept it shut.

"You're not fine," he said, reaching for his coffee cup and studying her.

She looked at him in surprise, and maybe a touch of irritation.

Too damn bad.

"It's personal," she said with a dismissive smile.

"I reckon most things are," he said casually. "But whatever it is, it's impacting your work, which makes it my business."

She smoothed a hand over her hair and sighed. "You're right," she granted. Alexis was nothing if not logical. "I'm sorry, Logan."

"No need to apologize," he said, still studying her. "But perhaps today isn't the best day to tackle taxes?"

She let out a tired laugh. "Certainly not. That's more your arena anyway."

Logan took a sip of coffee to stifle the unfamiliar urge to defend himself. She hadn't criticized him—not even a little bit. But sometimes he couldn't help but see himself through her eyes, and he felt . . . dull.

It was obvious that in her eyes, she could brush him off whenever it suited her, and it seemed to frequently suit her.

Most of the time he let her. But this morning he felt like pushing her, just a little, and seeing where it got him.

"Tell me what's wrong," he said.

It wasn't a request, his voice just a touch commanding in the way he frequently was with other clients but rarely with her. Again, her gaze flickered in surprise.

"I'm—"

"Fine, I know," he said, impatience making his tone clipped. He'd pushed, she'd pushed back, and that was pretty much all he could take first thing on a Thursday. Logan stood and began gathering his files and placing them back in his briefcase.

"You're leaving?" she asked in surprise, glancing at her watch.

"I am." He clicked the snaps on his briefcase closed. It was an old-fashioned briefcase, a hand-me-down from his late grandfather that he'd asked his parents to ship over once he started working in the States. He'd always liked it. Logan had respect for the classics, for the way things had always been done.

But for some reason today, it didn't feel classic so much as old, didn't feel dignified so much as fuddy-duddy.

Bollocks. What was going on with him?

He pulled his briefcase off the table and turned. "I'll see you Monday."

"Logan." Alexis's voice was surprised as she pushed back her chair and stood. "Is everything okay?"

"I'm fine," he said, deliberately mimicking her own phrase.

Her eyes narrowed. "Wait—"

Logan felt an unfamiliar surge of anger. At her and himself.

Maybe I'm done waiting.

He turned toward the door, ignoring her plea, and she moved toward him, reaching out and touching the sleeve of his suit. Even through the fabric, it felt like a brand.

Damn her. Damn her and this hold she had on him.

"What, Alexis?"

She blinked, looking momentarily stung by his sharpness. "What's going on with you?"

He rolled his shoulders irritably and straightened his glasses. "You're not the only one who has personal things going on right now."

Her gaze studied him carefully. "Okay. I can respect that. But if you do want to talk about it, know that I'm always here."

"I don't. Want to speak about it," he clarified.

He gently removed his arm from her touch and headed quietly and deliberately out the door and down the stairs.

Logan felt her gaze on his back, knew she was confused. Hell, *he* was confused. It was unlike him to be so impatient, especially with her. He was her accountant and part owner in her business. Nothing in that description required her to confide what had her all tied up in knots this morning.

For a long time, it had simply been enough that nobody else got to know what tied her up in knots, either.

But something was shifting. Logan trusted his instincts more than anything else in his life, and his instincts were telling him that change was on the horizon.

Coming from her?

From himself?

Both?

He didn't know. All he knew was that he was far from satisfied with what Alexis Morgan was offering him.

He wanted Alexis to talk to him, yes, but the real problem was that he wanted more than that.

He wanted everything.

And she wasn't offering.

Chapter Three

WELL. THAT HAD BEEN weird.

Alexis had known Logan for over eight years, and she'd never known him to storm out of one of their meetings like that.

Of course, *storm* was a strong word.

Logan Harris didn't storm anywhere. He was like her in that way. Calm. Controlled.

But as she watched him walk away, hearing the front door slam a moment later, she had the strangest sense that Logan's calm control wasn't as natural as hers.

Almost as though he kept something hot and fierce bottled within.

She shook her head to dismiss the notion. *Nah.* She knew Logan. The guy was as tame and likable as they came.

And she liked him. She had since that very first day when he'd approached her in that divey pub all those years ago.

It had taken her all of five minutes to see that there

was so much more to Logan than the accent. He was smart. Funny, in an offbeat, dry-as-a-bone kind of way. Kind.

Of course, it had taken her a bit longer to decide to take him up on his offer of funding the Belles. But not much. One week after he'd handed her his business card, Alexis had called him.

She'd accepted his offer, right down to his insistence that he own half the company—a provision made tolerable by his slightly puzzling demand that he remain a *silent* partner.

The rest was entrepreneurial history.

Logan Harris had been her very first friend in the city, but he was a hell of a lot more than that.

He was half her company.

And Alexis's company was *everything*. It was the one thing in her life that she could control. The one thing that never let her down.

That never broke her heart.

Logan Harris was a part of that company, and as such, the safest thing she knew. Logan was her rock. Her stability. Her *center*.

Which was why it was so jarring to have him walk away like that.

She picked her phone off the table, tempted to call him and ask him to come back. He'd been absolutely right to chastise her about her lack of attention. Alexis prided herself in separating personal from business, but today she'd failed him. And herself.

Today, she'd been utterly wrapped up in the bomb her mother had dropped last night about her sister's potential pregnancy. She'd been so hopeful that sleep would ease some of the sting, maybe unloosen the knot in her stomach.

Nope.

She'd woken up this morning feeling every bit as off as she had last night after hanging up with her mother. And it wasn't Roxie and Adam that were bothering her—at least not *just* them.

It was herself.

Alexis had the strange, wildly unfamiliar sensation that something was wrong with *her*.

The life that had seemed so tidy and perfect yesterday now felt rigid and wrong.

The five-year plan she'd set for herself on her thirtieth birthday felt stodgy and uninspiring.

All because, what—her sister was maybe having a baby?

Snap out of it, Morgan.

She set her phone down without calling Logan, not because she didn't want to talk to him, but because she had a somewhat urgent need *to* talk to him.

Alexis wasn't an idiot. She knew what the other Belles and most of her other friends thought about her and Logan. Half thought they were either hooking up or on the verge of hooking up. The other half thought they were secretly in love.

Neither was even remotely true.

She hadn't so much as kissed the man in the eight years she'd known him. He'd never made a move, and *she* certainly hadn't. He was a colleague and owned half her company. She'd worked too hard to build the Belles to risk it all with someone who was nearly as invested in her company as she was. Logan was an excellent, careful business partner, the very best she could have hoped for, and she wasn't going to jeopardize that for a careless hookup.

But if she was honest, there were times when she *wondered*. Wondered if things had gone a different way that first night in the bar, had Logan not shown an interest in her business ambitions, had he not patiently and intently coaxed her into sharing her whole passionate dream about starting a wedding-planning company . . .

Would she have gone home with him that night?

And if she had . . . what would have come of it?

It was a thought she didn't explore often. Whenever she did, she felt . . . confused.

Alexis picked up her and Logan's coffee cups, taking them into the small second-story half kitchen used for the Belles' business. Logan had barely touched his, and she felt a little stab of regret. Usually it seemed like he found a reason to linger, finishing his last sips even after the work was done.

Today he hadn't been able to leave fast enough.

Absently she washed the mugs, putting them away before going to retrieve her laptop and phone, intent on getting started with her packed day before the other Belles arrived around nine.

As she picked up her cell phone, she bit her lip, although this time not with the urge to call Logan but with the urge to call her sister.

And yet even as Alexis's thumb scrolled through her contact list to Roxie's name, she envisioned what that conversation might look like.

Mom thinks you're knocked up with Adam's baby. True?

Oh me? I'm fine, just fine. No, no boyfriend. Not even so much as a date on the horizon.

Alexis locked her phone without making the call. She would call her sister eventually. She had to. Even through her own pain, it killed her a little to think that her only sister was keeping a secret this big out of fear of how Alexis would react.

But there was the not-so-tiny matter of Alexis's pride.

So her sister might be pregnant? Alexis would figure out how to deal with that in her own time, in her own way. But if the reason for keeping it a secret was pity for poor, lonely Alexis . . .

No. Just *hell no.*

For years now, Alexis's love life had taken a backseat to, well, *everything*.

She hadn't been on a good date in—God, she didn't even want to think about it. Sure, she'd had the occasional hookup with a couple of discreet men who understood and respected her no-strings-attached boundaries, but when was the last time she'd gone out to dinner with a man and let herself consider the possibility of caring, or at least having fun?

Over a year. Good Lord, it had been over a year since she'd had a decent date.

It's time, Alexis told herself quietly. *You're thirty-three. It's past time.*

Okay, now she just sounded like her mother, and that was no good. Alexis loved her mother fiercely— she loved her entire family, obviously. But truth be told, she'd always prided herself on being different from her mom. Cecily Morgan had based her entire self-worth on being Jack Morgan's wife. When Jack had left her, Cecily had simply . . . crumbled. She hadn't bothered to develop an identity outside of wife and mother, and now she was wildly unhappy and let everyone know it.

Alexis wanted to be a wife and mother, too, but if that didn't happen, she refused to let herself break because of it.

Still, that didn't mean that maybe she didn't need to step up her efforts a bit. It didn't mean she didn't have to *try*.

Alexis paused on the way to her office, stopping to assess herself in the mirror.

She ran a hand over her smooth chignon, took in the pink, barely there lip gloss, the subtly smudged brown eyeliner.

She looked . . . fine. She always looked fine.

But she wanted to do better than fine.

She'd always been so concerned with being taken seriously, with not being perceived as ditzy or flighty, that she'd let herself become a bit *blah*. Serious, yes, professional, definitely.

But somewhere along the line, had she forgotten that she was also a woman? That she had wants and needs that had nothing to do with being featured in *Fortune* magazine or the 40 Under 40 list.

Alexis's fingers lifted, brushing along the starched collar.

When had she started to look so *hard*?

No wonder she hadn't had a date in way too long. Alexis was a little ashamed to admit it, even to herself, but she wanted to be a woman that men looked at. More specifically, she wanted to be one they looked at twice. The one who got a second date. Then a third.

Alexis needed to be a different type of woman. She needed to be the woman who wasn't single while her sister played house with her ex.

Alexis didn't have the faintest idea where to start.

But that was the benefit of owning a small all-women company where your employees were also your friends.

Alexis might not know what to do. But she was willing to bet the Belles would.

Chapter Four

"YOU DO REALIZE WHAT time it is here, yes?" Logan groaned as he picked up his cell phone, rolled onto his back, and dropped his arm over his eyes. He had spent his entire adult life in New York City. Well over a decade now.

And yet, his father had never quite seemed able to master the tiny little concept of the five-hour time difference.

This morning, he beat Logan's five a.m. alarm by four minutes.

"Morning, son." James Harris's polished, posh voice came over the line crystal clear, as though he were next door rather than halfway across the world. Logan's father was a touch stodgy, a bit formal, and not at all prone to hyperbole or theatrics—all qualities that could make for a trying personal relationship but had guaranteed his father's professional success as the longtime founder and CEO of Harris Services, a tony financial services firm based out of London.

"Barely," Logan muttered. "It's *barely* morning here."

"Yes, well, what I have to say couldn't wait."

Logan's eyes flew open and he sat up. "Is everything all right?"

"It's about your mother and myself," James said without preamble.

Logan's heart beat a little faster.

Divorce? Had decades of working side by side finally broken them? They'd always seemed to be the perfect partners, both in life and work, but Logan supposed there could be plenty going on that he didn't know about.

He was a grown man. He could handle his parents splitting up. As long as they weren't sick or—

"I'm retiring."

Logan blinked, then ran a hand over his face, trying to comprehend. "Retiring?"

He had . . . not seen that coming. Sure, he'd known that *some*day they'd finally call it quits, but they'd shown no sign of slowing down in recent years. He'd always figured his father would start thinking about it at sixty-five. *Maybe.* And he was only sixty-two now.

"We've been discussing that we're not getting any younger and that there are things we want to do."

Since when? Logan wanted to ask. This was news to him. His parents were good people. They'd been supportive, if not exactly *warm* parents. They were smart, driven, kind.

But Logan couldn't remember them so much as taking a vacation that didn't somehow relate back to Harris Services. Couldn't remember a dinner conversation or even a Christmas Day without some mention of The Company.

"Such as?" Logan asked after a few beats of silence.

"Travel. Hobbies. The things we haven't been able to indulge in given our commitment to the company and to raising a family."

Ah. There it was. The guilt trip.

Logan leaned over and flicked on the lamp before reaching for the glasses on his nightstand.

His father was a master of the subtle guilt trip, and Logan was the recipient of most of them. Logan's younger brother got fewer. Partially because Charlie had married and promptly produced three well-behaved grandchildren. Partially because Charlie had always leaned toward academia over business. There'd never been any pressure on *Charlie* to take over the family business. Charlie was protected by Oxford and his quest for tenure as a professor of literature.

Logan, on the other hand . . .

Well, Logan had a pretty good sense of why his father was calling.

"It's time for you to come home, Logan," James said.

Logan shoved the covers back irritably as he stood and adjusted the string of his blue pajama pants before heading into the kitchen toward the coffeepot.

"Son? Did you hear me?"

"Yes," Logan said, scooping beans into the built-in grinder of his machine.

"Well?"

Logan punched the button with more force than was necessary, relishing the way the loud grating noise probably drove his father mad.

It wasn't that Logan was a rebellious son. It was just he was damn resentful that his father seemed to think that an early morning phone call was all that was required for Logan to turn his back on the last fifteen years of his life and dash home to a country that hadn't been home in a very, very long time.

And yet it wasn't as simple as telling his father *no* outright.

Logan wasn't sure that he wanted the family company.

But neither was he sure that he *didn't* want it.

Truth be told, he thought he'd have a few more years to figure it out. Just his luck that his professional life would get ahead of schedule just as his personal life fell even further *behind* schedule.

"I can't," Logan said quietly when the coffee machine stopped its grinding and began the slow methodical drip of the brewing process. Logan still enjoyed a nice cuppa, which in his house, had always referred to tea. But his time in the US had given him an equal appreciation for coffee.

"What do you mean you can't?" his father asked irritably, as though Logan were twelve instead of thirty-three.

"Because I have a life here," Logan grated out. "My own business. *Businesses*," he corrected.

"And that's exactly your problem," his father said. "You've got your finger in too many pies, son. You're not making anything of any of them, because you're spread too thin. Flitting from one thing to the next."

Logan laughed incredulously.

Flitting. As though his business acumen was nothing more than a glorified hobby.

His accounting business alone was more than

enough to keep him in custom tailored suits and a top-of-the-line flat on the fiftieth floor of a high-rise just steps away from Wall Street.

Every penny of his not-insubstantial profits from the Wedding Belles went into a fund that would allow him to retire by forty if he wanted to.

But he didn't want to, because in addition to all that, there was NumberSync—Logan's latest endeavor with Heather's husband, Josh Tanner. NumberSync was Logan's brainchild that would see a marriage of accounting know-how and technology. On-the-go accounting for the entrepreneurial set; accounting that could be maintained on your smartphone via an app rather than a phone call with some nerd in a rented office space.

The company was barely off the ground. He couldn't leave it *now*.

Could he?

Logan silently cursed the thought. Then he cursed his father for even allowing it to pop into his head. That was the trouble with *playing the field* in your professional life. You were always looking for the next big challenge. The next chance to stretch your brain to try something different.

Taking over his family's business, while something that was apparently expected of him, was nonetheless exactly the kind of *different* Logan craved.

Logan had done the safe and old-school thing with the accounting business. He'd done the angel-investor thing with the Belles. He was trying the risky start-up path with NumberSync.

But he hadn't yet held the reins of a big business.

Hadn't yet exercised managerial muscles, nor had he embraced the challenge of improving upon someone's brainchild rather than birthing his own.

Taking over Harris Services would be a whole new kind of endeavor, and the challenge appealed to him. To say nothing of the fact that Logan wasn't *entirely* immune to the allure of a family legacy. Independent as he was, he liked the thought of carrying on the family torch in some way, of passing it along to his own daughter or son someday, if they wanted it.

"Well?" his father asked impatiently.

Logan smiled, feeling a little surge of fondness for his dad's unreasonable and yet oddly endearing way of attempting to get his way. He could almost see his father checking his Rolex, tapping a tasseled shoe as he calculated the time it would take to finish up this conversation and get to his next meeting.

"I'll need time to think about it," Logan said quietly. "You're catching me a bit by surprise here."

There was a moment of silence. "Of course," his father said. "You'll need time to make arrangements. But son, I hope you know, I hope you realize . . ."

Another awkward pause.

"Your mother and I miss you. Charles does, too. And the kids barely even know their uncle Logan."

Logan winced. He didn't know if his father was intending to twist the knife, but he was most certainly making Logan's chest ache. Lately, he'd been all too aware of just how alone he was. He'd always thought he'd have a wife and kids by now, but things had gotten in the way of his timeline.

Alexis Morgan had gotten in the way of his timeline.

"We're a family," his father said, the roughness of his voice sounding strange around the clipped upper-crust British accent. "Your family."

"I know," Logan said. "I miss you guys, too."

"So what's keeping you? I've done my research on all of your business endeavors. All of them can be done just as easily from here as from there. You can . . . Skype. Or whatever it's called."

Logan smiled a little at his dad's attempt to be up on the times, but there was little joy in the smile.

Because Logan was realizing there was no good way to explain to his father that what was keeping him in New York wasn't work so much as a woman.

A woman who barely registered his existence, even after eight years of him being right there in front of her.

He couldn't explain it to his father.

Because he could barely even explain it to *himself*.

Chapter Five

"WAIT, SO YOU'RE TELLING me that whether or not I meet the man best suited to be the father of my future children is dependent on which way I swipe my finger on my iPhone?" Alexis asked, frowning down at her screen.

"Future children?!" Jessie said, snatching the phone back out of Alexis's hand. "Give me that. Slow your ovaries."

Alexis made a grab for her phone, but Brooke had just wrapped a strand of Alexis's hair around the barrel of a curling iron, yanking her back into position with a little squeak of pain.

"I *did* tell you to sit still," Brooke said unsympathetically. Alexis shot her a dirty look that Brooke pointedly ignored as she reached for another section of hair. Geez, give the normally laid back, sunny woman a can of hair spray and a curling implement and she suddenly morphed into a drill sergeant.

Alexis rubbed at her head. "How are we not done yet? Am I going to look like Shirley Temple?"

"Yes, definitely!" Brooke chirped sarcastically. "Why? Was that not what you wanted?"

Brooke set the curling iron aside and came around to face Alexis, her blue eyes scrutinizing her handiwork on Alexis's hair. Alexis liked to think she had a decent amount of self-confidence, but it was difficult not to feel entirely dowdy next to Brooke Baldwin.

The blonde was one of those effortlessly pretty people with wide blue eyes, a big smile, and lots of shiny golden hair. Brooke had moved from LA to New York a year before, but she hadn't lost her California-girl allure. Something Seth Tyler, rich-as-God hotel magnate, had definitely noticed. And put a ring on, tout de suite.

The wedding date was set for December, and Alexis had felt no small amount of shock when Brooke had asked her to be a bridesmaid. She was the woman's boss, and they'd known each other a little over a year.

But then Brooke had pointed out that Alexis had played a rather instrumental role in helping Seth and Brooke get together. Alexis supposed that was a nice way of saying she'd *meddled*.

Alexis's makeover session was going down in the veritable *palace* where Seth and Brooke now lived, the restored and updated Hamilton House, complete with a built-in bar, a screening room, a small gym area, two home offices, and a gourmet kitchen to weep for.

The women had set up camp in one of the small, cozy seating areas, complete with two cream-colored love seats and a classy gold bar cart currently completely covered in cosmetics.

"So, when I suggested that I might want to glam

up my look a bit, exactly how many Sephora stores did you guys raid?" Alexis said, counting at least twenty lipsticks.

Jessie raised her hand. "Hi, my name is Jessie, and I'm a beauty junkie."

Alexis glanced at her in surprise. "You hardly seem to wear any."

"Um, that's because I'm skilled in application," Jessie said with a wink. "But also, being a beauty junkie doesn't mean you *use* all the makeup. Just that you *have* it."

"It's true," Brooke said with a nod, waving her hand over the makeup selection. "A fair amount of this is mine, and yet mostly I rely on one lipstick and black eyeliner to get my look."

"Black eyeliner," Alexis said thoughtfully, leaning forward to study her friend. "Is that how you always look so sexy?"

"Nah, that's genetics." This from Heather Tanner, who came back into the room armed with two bottles of wine and several glasses, her dark blond curly hair up in its signature unruly bun. "Sorry it took me so long. Brooke, I was hitting on your fiancé. You've seen his biceps, right? Yum."

Brooke lifted her eyebrows. "I have. I've also seen your husband's biceps."

Heather gave a happy sigh at the mention of Josh. "*Oh* yes."

"Oh man," Jessie said, flopping back on the couch. "I want that."

"Want what?" Alexis asked. "Josh's biceps? Or Seth's?"

Both Heather's husband and Brooke's fiancé *did* have nicely sculpted upper bodies. Alexis mentally added it to her "wish list."

Jessie shook her head. "No, I mean I want the dopey love expression."

Heather blinked. "Um, dopey love expression? That is so not me."

Alexis held out her wineglass so Heather could fill it with a lovely white. "It is, though, a little bit, dear."

Alexis lifted her hand to the hair Brooke had worked on for twenty minutes, then held out a hand. "Mirror."

"No, not yet," Brooke ordered as she took a sip of wine. "We have more work to do."

"I feel like a project," Alexis muttered.

"But you love projects," Jessie said, patting Alexis's shoulder.

"Sure. When I'm the one working on them," Alexis replied.

"So," Heather said, plopping onto the opposite love seat. "Are we going to talk about what prompted your little summons getting us together for all this?"

"What, the dating app or the makeover?"

"Both," Heather murmured, her eyes narrowing slightly as she studied Alexis. It was . . . unnerving.

Alexis knew her role in this group—in *life*—and she was usually the one doing the studying. The one who knew what everyone else was up to, their issues, their problems and how to fix them.

Relying on other people, even if they were her friends, was uncomfortable. But then, this whole thing was. Asking for help. The makeup. The dating.

The whole thing felt both wrong and necessary, and for the life of her she couldn't figure out how to reconcile that. Alexis trusted her instincts. It was how she'd gotten to where she was. Business owner. Apartment owner. Dream job.

But for some reason, that one single exchange with her mother—that one stupid phone call—had left her reeling.

Alexis Morgan, wedding planner extraordinaire who could troubleshoot a wedding during a Category 4 hurricane, who could find a bride her dream wedding dress same day, who'd planned a wedding for the president's daughter, and Hollywood starlets, and the third richest man in the world, had been thrown off course by her younger sister's pregnancy.

No, not even pregnancy.

Her *maybe* pregnancy.

It was as humiliating as it was alarming.

"Alexis." Brooke's voice was gentle as she sat on the coffee table and set her hand over Alexis's. "Is everything okay? You know we were all thrilled when you suggested a girls' night, and if you want to dip your toe in the dating scene, we're right there with you. But you don't need new lipstick and curled hair to do it. You're beautiful."

Alexis gave a small smile. It was such a *friend* thing to say. Alexis considered herself attractive. Her features were in the right place, she was well coifed, she knew her way around an eye shadow palette, even if it was just the one and always the same mélange of subtle colors.

But beautiful? No.

And that was okay. She didn't need to be beautiful to the world. Not to the world, not even to that one special person, or whatever.

She just wanted to get outside of herself for a little bit. She had the nagging sense that she was missing something in her life but didn't know what. And until she knew, how was she supposed to chase it?

Alexis broke eye contact with Brooke and held out her hand to Jessie. "Give it. Teach me this Tinder thing."

"Well, Tinder's just one of them," Jessie said hesitantly. "And to be honest, I haven't had the best of luck. I've met some nice guys, and a bunch of weird ones, but I haven't really clicked with any of them."

"There are a lot of people in this city," Alexis said carefully. "It's statistically unlikely that any of us will find someone that we click with, at least not right away."

"Brooke did," Jessie said defiantly. "So did Heather."

"So did Alexis," Heather muttered into her wineglass.

Alexis looked over at her friend with narrowed eyes. "What?"

Heather stared back at her. "You heard me."

Alexis let out a weary sigh. "This isn't the Logan thing again, is it?"

"Well, there's a reason it keeps cropping up," Heather said. "If you want to start dating, why not start there?"

"He's a friend," Alexis said, the words rolling off her tongue without thought. "And more important, a colleague. He's my accountant. Nobody dates their accountant."

"They do when he's hot and has a British accent and a name like Logan," Brooke chimed in.

"Logan and I would never work," Alexis said, taking a sip of her wine.

"Does Logan know that?" Heather asked.

"Of course," Alexis retorted.

"Really."

"Yup."

"So you've told him you're going to start dating other people?"

Alexis hesitated, hating the way the question gave her pause, as though the thought of telling Logan about her dating life seemed wrong somehow. "It's not his business."

"But you *did* just say he was a friend," Jessie said lightly.

Alexis groaned and looked at her receptionist, who, of all of her employees, tended to be the least prying. "You, too?"

Jessie shrugged, orange curls bouncing. "I love Logan. We all do."

"Well, I don't," Alexis snapped.

They all looked at her.

"I *like* him," she explained. "I just don't think he's my grand romantic match like you guys do."

"No chemistry?" Brooke asked, sounding disappointed.

Alexis opened her mouth to respond, only to realize she didn't have a good retort to that.

She only knew that going there with Logan, even in her thoughts, meant complicating things.

Complicating things meant risk.

And she couldn't risk losing Logan. She *wouldn't*.

Alexis tilted her head to one side then the other in a futile effort to ease the tension in her shoulders. "Can we not do this? Please. Tell me about these lipsticks. And then I want someone to take a picture of my new fabulous self for these weird apps."

She saw the look exchanged between Brooke and Heather but pretended not to. She knew what they thought. That there was a perfectly good guy right in front of her for the taking.

They were right.

Logan Harris was a good guy. *The best*.

Which is exactly why she wasn't going there.

Logan was . . . everything. He was her friend and her business and her future all wrapped up into one admittedly yummy package.

And Alexis's careful, practical heart, even at its most vulnerable like it was now, just couldn't handle the potential of losing everything.

Chapter Six

HARRIS. COME IN, MAN. Beer?" Josh asked, stepping aside to let Logan enter and holding up the bottle in his hand.

Immediately, Logan felt a bit of the tension in his shoulders ease, which was often the case around Josh Tanner.

Hell, he was pretty sure it was the way everyone felt around Josh. The two of them had met several months earlier through Heather Fowler (now Heather Tanner). Heather and Josh had one of those nauseatingly charming love stories, and Logan couldn't be happier for them, even if he was a bit . . . jealous.

Here he was waiting for his woman for the better part of a decade, where Josh had won his in a matter of months.

But no matter.

Heather had gained a husband, and Logan had earned a friend and surprise business partner.

"A beer would be great," Logan said, setting his briefcase by the front door and shrugging out of his jacket.

"Long day?" Josh asked as he went to the fridge. Josh's "uniform" of jeans and a Henley were a far cry from Logan's own preference for suits, but Logan never felt stodgy around the other man, just more relaxed.

"A bit," Logan admitted. "Not unpleasant, just back-to-back meetings, a few unplanned."

Josh nodded, his blue-green eyes studying Logan as he handed over the beer. A month ago, Logan wouldn't have even realized that he was being studied, but he was getting to know the other man better—knew that he was being assessed.

"There's something else," Josh said, his eyes narrowing just slightly in a way that reminded Logan that Josh had been a Wall Street shark before he'd quit the corner office.

Oh, you mean like that I've been summoned back to England, and I'm both tempted and annoyed by it? You mean like the fact that I've wasted eight years waiting on a woman who can't even tell me what's bothering her?

"Yes," Logan was surprised to hear himself say. "There's something else."

Josh tilted his bottle back and took a sip. "Talk about it?"

Logan set his own beer on the big table that had once been Josh's kitchen table. What had used to be Josh's apartment was serving as the temporary headquarters of NumberSync.

Josh and Heather had been neighbors when they met, and after getting married, they'd torn down a couple walls, turned the two apartments into one big one. Half was for living, the other for working. Logan considered himself lucky that he was invited to both halves of the apartment on a regular basis. Lucky to have friends like this.

"I received a call from my father the other day," Logan said slowly, lowering to the chair.

Josh's eyebrows lifted. "You don't talk much about your folks."

"We're not close. I mean, we have a good relationship, but we drifted a bit once I moved to the States. I don't get back as much as I should."

"Ah. So this was a 'we're not getting any younger, visit more' talk? I get those all the time, and my parents live in Jersey."

"They're looking for more than a visit, I'm afraid. They want me to move back. Take over the family business."

Josh whistled. "Should have offered you something stronger than the beer. You thinking about it?"

Logan met his friend's eyes. "Whatever happens, I'm still one hundred percent committed to Number-Sync."

Josh rolled his eyes. "Dude. I'm hardly worried about that. Plus, we're a company committed to helping people work from anywhere. I'd certainly hope that'd allow our *founder* to work from anywhere."

Logan gave a distracted nod. Josh was right. And really, Logan wasn't terribly concerned about the prospect of having to advance the company from the other side of the pond. It wasn't ideal, but it was doable.

Josh dug his hand into a bag of open potato chips

on the counter, munching them as he continued to study Logan. "So you are thinking about it."

Logan shrugged. "I admit I'm intrigued. I always thought I might go back someday; I've just been . . ."

"Yes?" Josh prodded when Logan trailed off.

"Nothing," Logan said, adjusting his glasses. "How's the search for a developer going?"

"Good, actually," Josh said, wiping his hand on his jeans to get rid of chip crumbs and picking up his beer once more. "Maybe. Found a guy with potential. Full interview's not until tomorrow, but he's got a great resume and I didn't want to blow my brains out when we talked on the phone, which is more than I can say about our other boring candidates."

"Most excellent," Logan said, picking up his beer and taking a drink.

"Come on, man. I get that the British thing means you're more restrained, but sort of thought you might be a little more excited. Can I get a *fuck yeah*?"

"Fuck yeah," Logan said distractedly.

Josh pointed the bottle at him. "Your head's still on your parents' guilt trip."

"It's a big decision," Logan said a trifle impatiently.

"It is," Josh agreed, hooking his foot around the leg of the chair across from Logan and pulling it out so he could sit. "So let's play a pro-con game. I'll go first. Pro: you're closer to your family. That's cool. Con: you're further from your new buddy Josh. That sucks."

Logan smiled a little.

"Your turn," Josh said, leaning back in his chair.

Logan rolled his eyes at the ridiculous game but

played along. "Pro: a part of me has always wanted it. Con . . ."

Josh's eyebrows lifted in challenge.

Logan sighed. "A part of me has always wanted something else more than I wanted to take over the family company."

"Something in New York," Josh said.

Logan nodded.

"Some*one* in New York," Josh pressed on.

Logan picked up his bottle and took a drink. He didn't respond. He didn't have to. Logan knew Josh had been around their group long enough to pick up on . . . whatever it was that was ongoing between him and Alexis. And whatever he hadn't discovered on his own, Logan was sure Heather had filled him in by now.

"Shit, man. Does she know you're thinking of moving?"

"No," Logan said sharply. "Nobody does. And I'd appreciate if you'd keep this between us. Or if you must tell your wife, at least tell her not to tell Alexis."

"Sure," Josh said. "But she'll find out sometime. If not on the personal front, then on the work front. You're her accountant and partner."

"Silent partner," Logan corrected, out of habit.

Eight years ago, when he and Alexis had been drawing up paperwork, it had been his idea to ensure that his involvement remain between them and their attorneys.

At the time, it had seemed prudent. He hadn't wanted anyone on his accounting side to think his energy was divided. He might have been funding Alexis's dream, but he was trying to launch his own at the same time.

Alexis had protested, insisted that it wasn't *fair* that everyone assume she was doing it on her own when she really wasn't.

Logan had reassured her that accepting his money hadn't made the Belles any less hers. As if there were any doubt in anybody's mind. The Belles was hers. Had always been hers.

It was all she'd ever wanted.

As far as he knew, she'd never told anyone about his real involvement in the company. He was fairly certain the other Belles didn't know. At least they'd never mentioned it.

He hadn't told anyone besides his family, and now Josh, mainly because as his business partner, he thought Josh deserved to know. Logan thought it was probably the one thing Josh actually kept from Heather, since it was his private business information.

"Something's up with Alexis," Logan said cautiously, watching Josh for his reaction.

Other than the slight pause as Josh took another sip of his beer, there wasn't much to go off of.

"Oh yeah?" Josh asked at length, after a few prolonged moments of silence.

Logan tapped his fingers against the table. "She's been quiet. Withdrawn."

"And that's different than normal?" Josh asked, resting his elbows on the table.

Josh had a valid point. Alexis was hardly the heart-on-her-sleeve type of woman. She was guarded even on the best of days, but he knew her. Knew that this was something more than her usual cautiousness.

"It's something more," he mused out loud. "I

noticed it last week, though perhaps it was just a bad day. But I noticed it at our meetings this week as well."

"You ask her about it?"

"Yes," Logan muttered. "Went over about as well as expected. She shut me down, I got . . . irked. I suppose I may have overstepped. Not many people appreciate their accountant prying into their personal lives."

"Bullshit," Josh said. "You're more than her accountant and partner. She knows that."

Did she? Logan wasn't always sure.

"Has Heather said anything?" Logan asked, hating himself for asking but needing to know all the same.

Josh looked away, just for a moment, and Logan's eyes narrowed. "Tanner."

Josh ran a hand over his face. "How'd we go straight to here? We didn't even pretend to get any work done."

Logan sat forward, pinned his friend with a hard gaze. "Tell me."

"You know that I think—hell, pretty much everyone does—that you and Alexis should be a thing."

"Everyone except Alexis," Logan muttered.

"Right. So, dude, help me understand why you haven't just asked her out already. She's obviously your woman."

Logan was already shaking his head. "She's not ready. Alexis has deliberately made no room in her life for anything but the Belles. She will. I'm confident that she will, and when she does, I'll be waiting. But if I push too soon, she'll block me out entirely."

"And how exactly are you measuring when she's 'ready'?"

Logan shrugged. "Alexis is a planner. Everything is calculated, so when she decides it's time to cultivate her personal life, she'll approach that the same way she does everything else: rationally, in steps. I wouldn't be surprised if she puts together a project plan. And when she's ready to date . . ." Logan shrugged. "She'll see me."

"And what if she doesn't?" Josh said slowly.

"She will."

Josh sat forward slightly, his expression going serious. "No, I'm serious. What if Alexis has decided it's time to start seeing someone, and that someone isn't you?"

Logan froze, searching Josh's face. "You know something."

Josh hesitated. "*Heather* knows something. I just get the high-level version, so you should really take it with a grain of—"

"Tell me," Logan interrupted, his mind racing. "Tell me absolutely everything."

Josh sighed and went to get another beer. "It's pretty much like you said. She's neglected her personal life, realized that, decided to fix it, complete with a plan, and . . ."

"And?" Logan said, feeling the sudden urge to punch something in anticipation of what Josh was about to say.

His friend's expression was sympathetic. "And that plan doesn't seem to involve you. It does, however, involve"—he let out an uncomfortable cough—"a Tinder profile."

Logan very slowly sat back, stunned, even though he'd been bracing for it.

Tinder? Really?

Alexis Morgan was ready to date. Was *planning* to date. And it didn't involve him.

He shook his head. *Wrong, Alexis, darling.*

This change of events absolutely *did* involve him.

Logan reached for his cell phone and stood. "Excuse me for a second, would you? I'm going to step outside to make a private phone call."

Josh shook his head. "Don't be dumb. I'll go in the other room, give you privacy. You calling Alexis?"

Logan snorted. "So much for privacy. But not Alexis. I have plans for her far more deliberate than a phone call. No, I'm calling my father."

Josh's eyebrows lifted. "You've made a decision."

"I have not," Logan said, as he hit dial and lifted the phone to his ear. "I'm going to tell him I need a month to decide."

"What happens in a month?"

"In a month I'll know." For years, Logan had been waiting for the right time. Been waiting for the catalyst that would signal it was time to make his move. To claim his woman.

Now was that time.

Alexis was his woman.

And it was long past time she saw him as a man.

"Know what?"

Whether or not I have something to stay for.

Chapter Seven

ALEXIS GLARED DOWN AT the YouTube video on her iPad. Brooke had insisted that all Alexis would have to do was follow the vlogger's instructions on how to curl her hair to re-create the soft, voluptuous waves Brooke had created out of thin air the other night.

Yeah, not so much.

The twentysomething vlogger did indeed have a head full of bouncy, volumized curls. Alexis, on the other hand, still had her usual flat head of fine, straight hair, except now the ends looked sort of crimped and fried for her efforts.

Alexis took a scrutinizing look in the mirror. At least her makeup was on point. Cosmetics were easier than hair. You didn't have to worry about things like straight-hair genes getting in the way of your goals. Makeup was all about the right product and lots of practice. And in the week since her makeover session at Brooke's house, Alexis had gotten in lots of practice.

Not for work, of course. By day she still did her usual understated look. The bun, the brown liner, the swipe of neutral lipstick. But every night, Alexis had come upstairs to her little apartment, poured a glass of wine, and experimented with the makeup haul she'd purchased herself from Bergdorf's.

She wasn't quite ready to start her own beauty blog or anything, but the results were better than good, if she did say so herself. Tonight, for her first Tinder date (wow, so *that* was happening), Alexis had gone for a classic smoky-eye look and pale lip. Not too smoky as to cross the eye into edgy rocker, but just enough blend of dark colors to make her feel a little mysterious.

The makeup update even made her dress feel different. The basic Chanel sheath was one Alexis had worn dozens of times before. Usually it signaled "timeless classic," and it still did tonight, but paired with the pink stilettos and amped-up cosmetics, it now looked downright sexy.

That hair though . . .

Alexis sighed and reached for a hair band and bobby pins. Here was hoping Todd McDowell liked a nice chignon.

She was just about to go about her usual business of pulling her hair back when the intercom buzzed.

Her gaze widened. *Crap*. Todd was early. Or was she late? A quick glance at the clock showed that he was indeed fifteen minutes early. She tried to tamp down the surge of irritation. One of her pet peeves was people who thought the earlier the better when it came to social calls. If it was work-related, by all means get there an hour early. But to Alexis's way of thinking, it was the ultimate faux pas to show up more than five minutes before the agreed-upon time for social events.

"Be open-minded," Alexis muttered to herself as she trekked down the stairs to let him in. Hadn't Heather been reminding her of that all day? She repeated her friend's words in her head. *Promise me you'll give the guy a chance. Unless he screams serial killer or has a toupee, you must make it through the entire date.*

Still, the guy would just have to wait downstairs until she was ready. No way was she giving up control this early in the game.

Alexis paused before opening the door, rolling her shoulders and pasting what she hoped was a relaxed, friendly smile on her face.

It wasn't Todd.

She slumped just the tiniest bit in relief, her smile relaxing.

"Oh," she said, stepping aside just as Logan entered. "Hi. What are you doing here?"

He stepped into the reception area like he had hundreds of times before, and as his arm brushed hers just slightly, Alexis registered that though he was wearing his usual Burberry trench (a Brit all the way, this one), there was no sign of the usual suit. Instead he was wearing a long-sleeve black shirt and gray slacks.

"Sorry. Forgot my key. You look nice," he said in his usual polite, semi-disinterested tone.

Alexis felt a strange flicker of disappointment. She

wanted to look better than nice. She wanted to look *beautiful*.

"I have a date," she said, lifting a hand to her hair with a nervous laugh she barely recognized. Alexis didn't *do* nervous.

"Oh yeah?" he asked, tilting his head slightly.

Belatedly, Alexis realized she'd seen Logan a couple of times since hatching her dating plan but hadn't mentioned it to him. She'd been trying to tell herself that it had been an oversight—that it simply hadn't come up.

But seeing him now, Alexis knew that she'd withheld the information deliberately. Which didn't make sense. Logan was a friend. She shared nearly as much with him as she did Heather, sometimes even more so.

But telling him that she was dating had seemed . . . wrong, somehow.

Clearly Heather and Brooke's insistence that there was something between Alexis and Logan was getting to her head. Not that she wanted them to be right. And from the disinterested look on his face now, it was obvious the other Belles couldn't have been more wrong.

Which was a good thing, she insisted to herself. A very good thing.

Logan lifted a hand, pointed upward. "I think I forgot one of my client folders here the other day. You care if I run up and check?"

"No, of course not." Alexis waved distractedly toward the stairs.

Too late she realized that these few moments spent talking with Logan meant she wouldn't have time to do anything elaborate with her hair. She'd just have to bank on the fact that all the women's magazines were right when they said that guys really didn't notice your hair so long as your other, um, *assets* were attracting the proper kinds of attention.

A glance at her watch showed she had just enough time to quickly fix her hair, grab her purse, and be back down here to wait for Todd.

Alexis was just coming back down the stairs from her apartment, hair pulled into a hasty low bun, as Logan came out of Brooke's office. "Found it under a pile of Brooke's stuff. She's not nearly as tidy as you. But then, most people aren't."

"You are," Alexis said, as she paused at the top of the stairs and waited for him.

"True. Perhaps that's how we've survived each other all these years."

"Is that what we've been doing?" Alexis said with a little laugh. "Surviving?"

"What would you call it?"

Alexis had started to take a step down but paused at the unexpected question. "What do you mean?"

Logan wasn't smiling back. "Our relationship. How do you define it?"

"We're business partners," she said. "And friends. Of course."

"Of course," he murmured.

Alexis narrowed her eyes at him. "You're being odd. What's going on?"

This time he did smile. "No, I'm just not saying what you think I'm going to say. I'm being *unexpected*, and you've always hated that."

Her eyes narrowed even further. She *did* hate that, but she didn't appreciate being called out on it.

"What are your plans tonight?" she asked, deciding to ignore his weirdness altogether, heading back down to the ground level to wait for her date.

"Nothing major."

"No date?"

He gave her a curious look and she realized what her words had betrayed.

"No," he said. "No date."

His voice was light and easy, and Alexis searched his face for censure, but his expression was unreadable to her. Guarded, even.

Since when was Logan Mr. Mysterious?

He was just *Logan*.

He glanced at his watch. "This chap *you're* dating. He's picking you up here?"

"Yes. At six."

He lifted his eyebrows. "Mighty old-fashioned for a first date."

"How do you know it's a first date?"

He gave a slight smile. "Isn't it?"

"Yes," she admitted. And then, even beneath all the oddness and very slight tension between them, he was still her friend, and she needed a friend right now. "I'm nervous."

His expression softened just slightly. "Yeah? Why?"

"I don't know." She licked her lips nervously, tasting the unfamiliar pale pink gloss. "It's been a long time since I've done this."

"What triggered the change?" he asked, his expression going slightly more intent.

Alexis looked away. It wasn't that she didn't want to confide in Logan; it was just that she felt so silly. It felt ridiculous to say out loud that your reason for going out on a dinner date with a total stranger was because your younger sister might be pregnant and you didn't want to be left behind, that you didn't want to be single when that bomb dropped.

"Okay then, Alexis," he said quietly, resignedly, when she didn't respond. "Enjoy your evening."

He turned and took a step away.

"Wait, Logan—"

He turned back around, his gaze sharp, but before she could beg him not to be frustrated with her, there was a knock at the door.

Neither moved for a moment, and finally he tilted his head toward the door. "You going to get that?"

"Yes. Of course." She took a deep breath, straightened her shoulders, and opened the door.

Todd McDowell looked exactly like his picture, which was both a relief and also . . . underwhelming.

Todd was thirty-nine and divorced, a consultant who traveled frequently. According to their message exchange, it was his travel schedule that had led to the dissolution of his marriage.

He also had a wide, easy smile, a friendly gaze that promised a skeleton-free closet.

Todd McDowell was exactly as he'd seemed to be, and exactly what she wanted.

So what if there wasn't any belly flip or catching of her breath when their eyes met? She was out of practice. Maybe the spark was just out of practice, too.

"Hi, so nice to meet you," Alexis said, stepping forward and extending her hand.

"Likewise," he said, shaking her hand.

Darn. No spark there, either.

Todd's gaze shifted curiously to her right, and Alexis realized how strange it must seem that there was a man in her home when her date came to pick her up. "Todd, this is Logan, my accountant."

"Ah," Todd said, extending his hand to Logan.

"A pleasure," Logan said.

Alexis felt a strange sort of pang at seeing the man she was about to go on a date with shake the hand of the man she . . . cared for.

"Ah, you're English!" Todd said.

Alexis almost winced. People who pointed out the obvious were one of her pet peeves.

Give him a chance.

"I am," Logan said evenly.

"How long you been in the States?" Todd asked, making polite conversation.

"Since I was eighteen."

"Here to stay, then."

"It would seem so, although my family's still in London, so never say never."

Alexis gave him a startled look. Logan had considered moving back to England? That was new. And . . . *wrong*.

Perhaps she wasn't the only one keeping secrets.

"Well, I'll let you two get to it," Logan said with a slight smile, stepping aside so that Todd could enter.

Alexis felt panic claw at her throat. This was a

mistake. The thought of Logan walking out of her life so that a stranger could walk into it . . .

Calm down—it's just one date.

"Bye, Logan," she blurted out, taking an unintentional step forward as he stepped onto the porch.

He turned back and she saw understanding in those brown eyes, as though he could see right through her.

"Alexis," he said with a perfunctory nod. Then he stepped back toward her, bending his head and softly kissing her cheek.

From the outside, it would seem like a formal good-bye from a formal Brit, but he lingered just for a second.

"Don't be nervous," he whispered directly in her ear. "You look beautiful."

Beautiful. Not *nice. Beautiful.*

Logan stepped back, nodded politely to Todd, and then walked away, leaving Alexis with the strangest urge to call him back, to ask him to *stay.*

"I'm really looking forward to our dinner," Todd said politely.

"Me, too," she said automatically, gathering her purse and her keys and giving her brightest, glossiest *fakest* smile.

But her eyes were locked on Logan's retreating back as she said it.

Chapter Eight

THE MONDAY MORNING AFTER he'd watched another man take Alexis to dinner, Logan let himself in the Belles' front door the way he always did, with two coffees in hand: sugar-free vanilla latte for Alexis, Americano for himself. Like clockwork.

But as he climbed the stairs to the conference room, there was no sign of Alexis. *Not* like clockwork.

He frowned and checked his watch. He was right on time. Two minutes late, actually, given that the Starbucks barista had been in training.

Logan shrugged and settled in to wait for her. He was feeling slightly pissed over the fact that he hadn't heard from her all weekend. Not that he'd expected to, really, but he'd spent two long days wondering how that date with the boring, all-wrong-for-her guy had gone.

Wondering if the other man—Todd?—had touched her. Kissed her.

Logan hadn't needed to get that file on Friday night, obviously. It could have waited until Monday.

But he'd needed to make sure that Alexis *saw* him. It had felt important, somehow. Vital. Logan couldn't stop her from dating, but he could make damn sure she was thinking of him while she did so.

He wasn't above a little strategic manipulation.

Not with the clock ticking.

His father hadn't loved that Logan hadn't had a ready answer about taking over the company, and had nearly blown his top—as much as one's buttoned-up British self could blow one's top—when Logan had said he'd need a few weeks to make a decision, but that was too damn bad. Logan wasn't about to turn his life upside down just because his parents snapped their fingers.

Not until he'd made one final play here.

When Alexis didn't show after five minutes, he texted her.

Okay?

Her response was almost immediate. So sorry. Overslept, running behind. Come up?

Huh. All right then.

It certainly wasn't the first time she'd been running late, nor was it the first time they'd met in her apartment rather than the office, but it was hardly a regular occurrence. Maybe the fifth time in eight years.

Still, since it didn't particularly make a difference to him where he drank his coffee and discussed tax returns, he texted her back.

Be right there.

The front door to her apartment was ajar. "Alexis?" he called as he pushed it open.

She was standing in her kitchen, bare feet, yoga pants, damp hair, and a spatula in hand as she scrambled eggs on the stove.

His heart got caught in his throat just for a moment at the sight of her. She looked . . . damn, she looked perfect.

Logan had meant it when he said she'd looked beautiful on Friday night. It had been jarring to see her all made up, her eyes moody and secretive, her slim body hugged to perfection in that little black dress, her heels tall and sexy.

He'd wanted her, even as he hated that she was all dolled up for another man.

But *this* Alexis, casual, just a touch rumpled . . . *this* Alexis was even more beautiful to him, because he knew he was one of the few people allowed to see her this way, even if it was a privilege seldom bestowed.

"Ugh, hi," she said, glancing over her shoulder. "I'm really so sorry. I don't know what happened. I always set three alarms, but every now and then I just sleep through all three."

"Not a problem," he said, setting his briefcase down and coming to the stove to hand her the coffee. "Late night?"

"Not really," she said, reaching out for the drink and nodding in thanks as she continued to stir at the eggs with the other hand. "I mean, I went to bed the same time I always do, but I couldn't sleep."

Tell me about it, he wanted to say. But since

nudging her to talk to him had been doing him little good lately, he stayed quiet.

Apparently that was the right thing to do, because out of nowhere, she opened her mouth and blurted, "My mom thinks my sister's pregnant."

Well then. That was . . . random.

"Oh?" he said.

He knew Alexis had a sister. Younger, if he was remembering correctly, but he'd never met her. A bit odd, come to think of it, seeing as he knew most of Alexis's other friends and her entire inner circle, had even once had the displeasure of meeting both of her parents.

She nodded and took a sip of her latte. "I know what you're thinking. That I should just call her, ask if it's true."

Logan gave a little smile. "Actually, can't say I had much of a chance to formulate much of a thought about anything just yet, but I suppose that's what *you're* thinking?"

She looked up at him, and there was a vulnerability in her wide-set brown eyes he was unaccustomed to. "Do you think I should call her?"

Logan sensed he was on dangerous ground, although he couldn't quite identify why.

"How about you tell me why her maybe pregnancy bothers you?" he asked.

She gave the eggs one last stir and flicked off the burner but didn't move to scoop them onto the two plates she'd set aside. Instead she stood there, staring down at the skillet.

Logan set his cup on the counter and very gently nudged her aside. "Go sit."

To his surprise, she obeyed, going to sit at the small kitchen table. Logan scooped the eggs onto two plates. He wasn't hungry, but she'd made enough for two, and he didn't want her to eat alone.

He found her silverware drawer on the second try and, after grabbing two forks, joined her at the table.

"How was your weekend?" she asked, not touching her eggs.

"Pleasant," he replied. "And your date with . . . ?"

"Todd."

"Right." Not that he'd actually forgotten the other man's name.

"It was nice."

Nice. Damn it—that told him nothing. On one hand, it was hardly high praise, but she had that thoughtful tone in her voice, as though she was perhaps considering a second date.

"You seeing him again?" he asked, forcing himself to take a bite of the eggs, even though his stomach was in knots.

"I don't know. It's just . . ." She fiddled with the fork, still not touching her breakfast.

"Just what?"

"This whole dating thing. It's not like I thought it would be," she said glumly.

Logan resisted the urge to do a victory fist pump.

Exactly as he had hoped for.

And planned for. He *knew* this woman.

Josh had argued for something bigger and ballsier than stopping by on Friday night before her date.

Specifically: *pin her up against the wall and kiss her.*

Josh's idea certainly held plenty of appeal.

But Logan had known it wasn't the right first move. Logan needed to reposition himself in Alexis's life, yes, but he needed to do it slowly. So slowly that she'd wonder if she was imagining it at first.

It had worked.

Logan had seen the confusion on Alexis's face on Friday. He'd *felt* it in the way she'd watched him as he'd walked away, although damn if that hadn't been the hardest moment of his life, leaving this woman to be wooed by some other man.

As for what was next though, he wasn't entirely sure. Not when she was all unbound and rattled as she was now.

He watched her for a moment before reaching across the table and tapping a finger against the back of her hand. "Eat, Alexis."

She glanced up.

"You get irritable when you're peckish," he said gently.

Alexis surprised him by laughing and scooped up some eggs. "Too true."

She wasn't herself, and best he could tell, there were two players at work. One was whatever had been bothering her since last week—her sister's maybe pregnancy, it would seem.

The other appeared to center around her disappointing date on Friday.

They ate in companionable silence, both lost in thought as they finished their breakfast.

"So this Todd guy wasn't the one, hmm?" he asked, picking up her empty plate after she pushed it away and taking both plates to the sink.

"You don't have to clean up."

He ignored her and waited as he ran the water, knowing her tendency to buy time to think before addressing a question she didn't have a ready answer for.

"He was a nice guy," she said finally.

Logan allowed himself a smirk since he had his back to her. The poor guy had gotten the word *nice* applied to him twice in under five minutes. He didn't stand a chance.

"He kissed me," Alexis added.

Logan's smirk vanished, his grip on the plate he was rinsing so firm he wouldn't have been all that surprised if it snapped in two.

He carefully placed the plates on her drying rack and turned back around to face her. "Oh yeah?"

She let out a long sigh and stood. "I shouldn't be talking to you about this. You don't care, you're my accountant, and we're supposed to be reviewing my tax return, right?"

"I feel confident it's where it needs to be, but we can review it if you'd like," he said slowly, resisting the urge to demand more details about the kiss, even though he wasn't at all sure he wanted to hear them.

"No, I trust you," she said, taking a sip of her coffee then setting it aside on the table. "But I should be getting ready. My nine a.m. canceled, which is nice, but—"

Logan touched her arm lightly as she went to brush past him toward her bathroom. "Alexis. You know you can talk to me about anything."

"I've always thought so, but we've never really talked about this," she said, meeting his eyes.

"*This* being . . . ?"

"Our romantic life. Our respective romantic lives," she rushed to clarify.

"True. But you wouldn't have brought it up if you didn't have something you needed to talk out. You're the last person to speak for speaking's sake. If you mentioned it, it's weighing on your mind; as your friend, I'd like to help."

She sucked in her cheeks and glanced down at where his hand touched her arm. He reluctantly withdrew his fingers, but she didn't move away.

"The kiss was sort of a letdown," she said quietly, wrapping the fingers of one hand around the wrist of the other and twisting in an idle, nervous motion.

"They often can be," he said.

"Really?" Her eyes were begging for reassurance, and it damn near killed him how insecure she was about this.

"Sure. All the time. It's a chemistry thing. There are more bad kisses to be had than good, I'd say."

"Like, *all* kisses are a letdown? Is kissing overrated?"

He gave a little laugh. "Well, I don't know that I'd say *all* kisses. Some can be quite compelling."

Her shoulders slumped. "Yeah, that's exactly the problem. *All* my kisses are in the 'meh' category. I thought Friday night's must have been bad because I was out of practice, but then I got to thinking, I haven't had a good one in a long, long time. And I've been telling myself that maybe I was just picking the wrong guys, but last night I had this thought . . . what's the common denominator here? It's me. What if I'm the bad kisser, and . . . oh God, I'm babbling. I never babble."

It was quite true. Alexis Morgan never babbled, but damn if it wasn't the most endearing thing he'd seen in a long time.

"Alexis—"

She held up both hands and backed away. "Wait. Don't say anything. I'm feeling horribly embarrassed, and I just . . . can we do this later? I mean, not this talk, but our meeting. Will you hate me if we reschedule?"

"Yes," he said dryly. "I've been invested in the Belles for more than eight years, but this is going to be the thing that makes me walk. You making me eggs instead of reviewing a tax return."

She smiled. "You're the best."

I know.

"I'll see you Thursday, then?" she asked, running a hand through her hair.

She turned away without waiting for a response, heading into her bedroom to finish readying herself for the day.

Two weeks ago, he'd have let himself out without a second thought. But two weeks ago, she hadn't been out kissing other men—hadn't been babbling about being a bad kisser.

Logan stood leaning against her kitchen counter for several moments, sipping his coffee as he debated.

He could leave. Head to his office and regroup, figure out his next move.

Or . . .

Or . . .

Before he could rethink the wisdom of plan B, Logan set his Starbucks cup aside and followed the sounds of dresser drawers opening and closing.

He was walking into her bedroom just as she was walking out, and she collided against his chest in a startled exhale. "Oh! Logan, I thought you'd—"

His hands wrapped gently but firmly around her elbows. He pulled her closer until their chests bumped softly, her small breasts soft and perfect against him.

He kissed her.

It wasn't how he'd envisioned his first kiss with Alexis Morgan happening. And yes, he'd envisioned it plenty.

In his fantasies, he alternated between the types of kisses. In some fantasies, he was claiming her mouth and pouring every ounce of unspoken emotion into a kiss that was as hot and ardent as his fantasies.

In others, his fantasy allowed *her* to kiss *him*, and it was the sweet benediction he'd been waiting for for nearly a decade.

This kiss though—their *actual* first kiss—was a different animal entirely.

She was surprised. He could tell by her soft gasp, the stiffening of her body. But she didn't immediately shove him away, and he took advantage of her moment of shock to ease slightly closer, one hand lifting to the back of her head as he slowly deepened the kiss.

His lips moved over hers, nudging them open as his tongue slid inside. He swallowed her soft gasp, stroking his tongue against hers, and it was both ecstasy and torture finally having her this close and yet not nearly close enough. He wanted all of her. He wanted her naked and panting and arching for him.

But for now he settled for a kiss. A kiss that she was starting to respond to, her fingers finding his shoulders and digging in, her tongue meeting his, a little shy, a little unabashed.

His hand on the back of her head pulled her even closer as he took the kiss to a more carnal level, a place where it was only the two of them and the promise of unimaginable pleasure . . .

She pushed him away.

Not roughly, just a subtle shove of his shoulders, a little sound of panic.

He released her, still breathing hard as he met her bewildered gaze, trying to remember why he'd started this here and now, of all the times . . .

"You're not a bad kisser, Alexis," he said softly, brushing a thumb over her bottom lip.

She only shoved him harder, taking a step backward as she did so. "Don't."

He blinked at the sharp finality in her tone.

"Don't ever do that again. Promise me," she said, her voice cold as ice.

"Alexis—"

She turned away without another word, going into her bedroom and closing the door with a calm, quiet click that was so much more damning than a good slam.

He closed his eyes and swore softly as he dragged both hands slowly over his face, trying to register just how much of a mistake he'd made.

It had *felt* right. A part of him *still* thought it was the right move.

But then, far from her kissing him back right now, urging him to the bed, there was a door separating them. And probably a lock.

He was left to . . . leave.

Which he did. Slowly. Unhurriedly, he gathered his jacket, his briefcase, and his coffee. But as he closed the door he made her a silent promise.

This wasn't over. Not by a long shot.

Chapter Nine

ALEXIS STEPPED INTO THE elevator that led to Brooke and Seth's apartment and pressed the button with a slightly shaky finger.

She was nervous, which was stupid.

It was just a dinner party with friends. Good friends.

Good friends plus Logan.

Alexis wasn't quite sure how it had happened, but over the past few months, the Belles had moved rather dramatically from a group of cordial colleagues to friends. The sort of friends who got together for boozy brunches and Friday-night dinner parties.

It had taken some getting used to—she was really good at being a boss, not quite as good at being a friend, she'd realized.

But she was getting better at it. So much so, in fact, that she'd actually begun to look forward to the times when she could hang out with the girls and not have to be *in charge*.

She didn't mind that Logan had found a niche within the little group. He'd always been friendly with Heather, and he'd hit it off almost immediately with Brooke, so she supposed it made sense that they'd include him.

Alexis had even been happy about it.

But that was before The Kiss.

It had been four days since their disastrous kiss in her apartment, and she hadn't seen him since.

He'd canceled yesterday's regularly scheduled Thursday meeting due to a "conflict," which he'd communicated over text, and she'd been torn between relief and dismay.

Relief that she wouldn't have to face him. Dismay that they had some serious damage control on their hands now that he'd gone and messed everything up.

Still, she supposed she should *thank* him. It had been that moment of pure terror in her chest when he'd touched her that had motivated her to call Todd and ask him to lunch on Wednesday.

A mistake. Date number two with Todd had been even more lackluster than date number one.

And Alexis couldn't shake the feeling that it was all *Logan Harris's fault*.

The elevator door opened and Alexis took a deep breath and stepped into the apartment. Brooke and Seth's place took up the entire top floor of the building, so she was standing directly in the foyer.

Another deep breath. *It's just a dinner party with friends like you've done dozens of times*.

She was clearly the last to arrive, because a wall of sound hit her. Happy laughter and animated voices were coming from the kitchen, the universal gathering spot for just about every house party.

Alexis took off her jacket and hung it in the coat closet. She'd been here enough times to know the drill.

"Alexis!" Brooke's happy voice rang out as she walked toward her.

"Sorry I'm late," Alexis said.

"Everything okay?" Brooke asked, lowering her voice a little and frowning as she studied Alexis. "The girls and I were just saying how we've hardly seen you all week."

Alexis forced a smile. "Just busy. Everyone here?"

"Yup. Come on. Let's get you a drink, get rid of the stress that's causing all that tension."

Alexis's hand flew to her forehead, and sure enough, she felt the telltale crease between her brows. Her mother had been lecturing her about her "frown lines" since about the third grade.

She followed Brooke into the kitchen. The group, as expected, was the Belles plus significant others, as well as Seth's younger sister, Maya, and his best friend, Grant.

Maya and Grant were actually dating, although there was nothing simple about *that* story since Brooke and Seth had met while Brooke was planning Maya's wedding—to another man. That relationship had gone up in smoke for a number of reasons, but the silver lining was that it had led Maya and Grant to finally admit their feelings for each other. They'd been blissfully happy ever since.

Alexis's eyes kept scanning the room until she found . . .

There.

Though she'd been mentally gearing up for this moment for days, her brain did exactly what she ordered it *not* to and went back to the memory of right before his mouth had claimed hers—that moment of sheer terror and sheer anticipation.

And then even more troublesome, her brain started to dwell on the moment that *followed.* The way his hands had been so warm and firm as they'd held her against him, even as his mouth was gentle, his lips fitting hers perfectly . . .

It all came rushing back to her, except not to him, apparently.

Logan didn't even seem to register that she'd entered the room, what with the stunning redhead by his side. Wait. Who was this woman?

And the more pressing question—why did Alexis care?

All of a sudden, Logan's eyes flicked to hers, dark brown and intense, and Alexis sucked in a breath as his gaze latched onto hers.

What was this? Since when had she been so aware of him?

She looked away.

"Alexis, this is LeeAnne," Brooke said, gesturing to the redhead.

"Hi there," LeeAnne said with a warm smile, and she stepped forward and shook Alexis's hand. "Thanks so much for letting me crash your little group."

The woman really was stunning, Alexis realized with a pang. She was five nine, at least, her dark red hair was long, even in its high pony, trailing almost halfway down her back. Her eyes were wide and dark blue, her lips Angelina Jolie–esque. Logan's date or not, how would he not notice and want her?

"LeeAnne and I met at the salon," Maya was saying. "We were sitting next to each other and got to talking after we noticed we had identical handbags."

"I just moved here from Philadelphia," LeeAnne explained, "and have, like, zero friends. Maya took pity on me and invited me here."

Huh. Alexis loved Seth's pretty blond sister, but not so much at the moment.

Alexis felt someone press a glass of wine into her hand, and glanced up, smiling gratefully at Seth.

She'd always liked Brooke's fiancé. The man was taciturn on a good day, and a bit of a control freak, which is perhaps why they got along so well. Seth Tyler would do anything for the people he cared about, and Brooke was at the very top of that list.

Alexis took a small sip of wine to wash away the taste of jealousy. Not jealousy over Seth. She had absolutely no inclinations toward him like that.

But jealousy that someone loved Brooke as desperately as Seth did.

What would it be like to warrant that sort of love? A fierce and *lasting* love.

Alexis was pretty sure she'd never know.

"So what spurred the relocation?" Alexis asked LeeAnne politely, realizing that she'd been awkwardly silent since entering the room. "New job?"

"No. Well, I mean, yes, I do have a new one here in New York, but that wasn't really the catalyst. Bad breakup. Needed a fresh start." LeeAnne wrinkled her perfect nose.

"LeeAnne's a doctor," Heather said, sounding very impressed as she dunked a red pepper slice into hummus. "An oncologist."

Wonderful. Beautiful, friendly, and a doctor, which meant she was bloody brilliant.

Bloody?

Obviously Logan was rubbing off on her. Which wasn't half as fun as the thought of Logan rubbing up *on* her. His body on hers, his hands everywhere . . .

Oh hell.

Alexis set her wineglass carefully on the counter, hoping nobody would notice that her hand shook just slightly.

"Excuse me for a moment," she murmured to nobody in particular, as the group had resumed inane dinner-party chatter about which sort of cheese was the right option for a Philly cheesesteak sandwich.

Heather stopped her before she could exit the kitchen. "You okay?"

"Yeah!" Alexis said in a bright voice that sounded nothing like her. "Of course."

Heather's eyes narrowed, and she opened her mouth as though she wanted to press but realized it wasn't the time or place. "Later," she mouthed.

Yeah, no, Alexis thought as she left the kitchen. She loved Heather like a sister, but she wouldn't be telling Heather or anyone about her and Logan's kiss, and certainly not the terror it had inspired in the moment.

Nor the dirty fantasies it had inspired since.

Needing a minute to give herself a pep talk, Alexis headed toward Seth and Brooke's powder room.

She was about to close the door when it was pushed open again.

"What—"

Logan crowded her into the bathroom and shut the door, enclosing them both in the small space.

"What are you doing?" she hissed.

"Something's wrong. Tell me," he said, crossing his arms and looking down at her in that steady, penetrating way he had when he was working through a problem.

Rarely was the problem her, though, and she didn't like being under the Logan Harris microscope.

"Nothing's wrong."

"Alexis."

"Logan," she snapped. "Get out of the bathroom. This is odd. What will everyone think?"

"I suspect they'll think you're doing your girl thing in here and that I'm doing my guy thing in the other loo."

"You followed me," she protested. "They'll think something's going on."

He leaned down slightly. "First of all, I don't think anyone even registered we left—they're still all arguing about cheese and sandwiches. Second, what does it matter what they think? The only people who should be worried about something 'going on' is us, so just forget about them."

She pursed her lips, not enjoying his calm logic that was usually *her* card to play.

"LeeAnne's pretty," Alexis said, hating that the words were out before she could think through them.

What was going on with her? It was like she was unraveling, and it was all his fault.

He lifted his eyebrows. "She is."

"So you noticed." She pushed her index finger against his chest.

Logan let out a small laugh. "Yes, of course I noticed. I'd have been blind not to."

The admission bugged her more than she cared to admit, and she closed her eyes.

"Alexis." His tone was just a trifle impatient. "Would you please talk to me?"

Her eyes flew open. "Oh sure, *now* you want to talk. You who've been avoiding me."

"I was giving you space! Last I saw you, you looked ready to slap me," he snapped.

"You kissed me! It was out of line and I was mad."

He took a step closer. "Mad because I did it or mad because you liked it?"

Both.

Her chin lifted in warning. "If I liked it, why would I have called Todd and asked him out for another date?"

It was meant to get him to back off, and for a second, she'd thought it worked, because his own chin snapped back slightly as though she'd struck him.

But then he moved in again, not touching her, but he may as well have been, because she *felt* him. Felt his body heat.

"Did he kiss you again?" Logan asked, his head dipping just slightly closer to hers. "Did you like it?"

She wanted to lie to him. Wanted to say that yes, Todd had kissed her again, yes she'd liked it . . .

Because the truth . . .

The truth would destroy everything she'd worked for.

The truth was that that kiss with Logan was unlike any she'd ever had.

Utterly epic.

She smoothed a hand over her hair and fought for composure. "Look, Logan. I don't know why you did what you did on Monday, if it was a rare lack of impulse control, or you were proving some sort of point, or maybe you just lost your damn head, but I'm not looking for anything romantic with you."

"You're not looking for anything romantic with me," he said slowly. "But you are looking for it with someone else?"

"You're my colleague," she said a little desperately. She reached out before she could stop herself, starting to lift her palm to rest lightly, shyly against his chest. "You're my friend."

To her utter shock, he shoved her hand aside, shifting them both so her back was against the wall, his hands on either side of her head as he caged her in. "Why not me, Alexis? Why when you finally decide to stop living in a shell, why some random chap off the street, *and why not me*?"

Alexis couldn't speak. Couldn't breathe. She'd never seen Logan like this, and this unknown side of him both terrified and exhilarated her.

In the distant part of her brain, she registered that her friends had been right. Logan *did* seem to want something more than what she was willing to offer him, and the temptation and the impossibility of that made her angry.

And sparked something else in her she couldn't even begin to decipher right now.

She shoved at his chest, but he didn't move. "So what, Logan? You decided that you should get first dibs? Is your ego smarting because I didn't immediately fall at your feet the second I decided I wanted to get laid? Is that the problem here?"

His face went lethal and he pressed into her all the way until they were chest to chest and she could feel his heart beating against hers, the hard buckle of his belt digging into her stomach.

"Tell me that kiss on Monday wasn't hot as hell and I'll back off," he said huskily. "Tell me you didn't enjoy it every bit as much as I did. That you haven't been thinking of it every second since it happened. Tell me that, and I promise to leave you alone, and I'll ask the pretty doctor out, see if *she* enjoys my kisses."

Everything in her rebelled at the thought, and yet the alternative was unthinkable. Logan Harris owned half her company . . . he was her sounding board, her confidant, her business partner . . . if they tried and failed . . .

"Don't think," he said, lifting a hand to her hair and tangling his fingers in it. "Whatever you're thinking, stop, and for once in your damned life, just feel, Alexis. What do you *want*?"

"I want us to continue on as we've always been," she whispered. "Friends."

As long as you're my friend, you'll never leave me.

"Friends," he repeated.

She nodded.

He bent his head slightly so they were nearly

cheek to cheek, his breathing fast and maybe a little defeated.

Or maybe not, because when he pushed back, there was fresh determination in his eyes, and for one thrilling moment, she thought perhaps the determination was toward her—that he was going to kiss her again, claim her as his.

But instead he offered her an easy old-Logan smile and eased away, his hand going for the doorknob.

"All right, Alexis," he said in that cool, composed British voice he used when they were discussing business. "Have it your way, then. Let's see how you like *friends*."

Chapter Ten

Damn, but he was fed up.

Yes, it had only been a few days since he'd gone from docile accountant to seducer, but Alexis was being obtuse and stubborn.

It would be one thing if she were immune to him. It would have burned, but he'd have respected it.

She wasn't immune to him.

She'd *wanted* that kiss. Just like she'd wanted him when he'd cornered her in the bathroom.

She wanted him now, too. Logan knew it in the way her eyes tracked his every move at the dinner table.

But right now, he wasn't sure that he cared. Not when he'd gotten a teary phone call from his mum that afternoon.

A true stalwart Brit through and through, Anna Harris didn't cry.

Except, apparently, when her eldest son didn't obey his summons and return to the motherland. They'd been quiet, tortured tears that she'd tried to hide, and that had just made it worse.

I don't understand, Logan. What's there for you in New York that's more important than your family?

A classic parental guilt trip, yes, but a legitimate one in this case.

What *was* more important here in New York than family?

Certainly not a woman who was too scared to follow her own heart.

Logan's time was running out, and he was feeling damned irritable about it.

He knew he was playing with fire. Knew it in the way he let his eyes linger on Dr. LeeAnne Valentine longer than he actually wanted to. Long enough so that a certain someone would surely take notice.

Then again, maybe it was time he did consider a woman that actually seemed interested.

LeeAnne was drop-dead gorgeous and wonderfully intelligent. It wasn't her fault that she wasn't Alexis Morgan.

"So Logan," LeeAnne said around a bite of Seth's perfectly cooked chicken. "How did you come to be part of this group? You're the accountant, right?"

Logan set his fork down and sat back in his chair, picking up his wineglass and taking a generous sip of the dark red, oaky liquid. "Alexis and I met at a bar several years ago before the Wedding Belles was formed. I've been around since the beginning."

Jessie leaned forward toward LeeAnne, saying in a loud mock whisper, "Logan here is the only one of us who knew pre-Belles Alexis, and he's, like, super stingy on details about what our girl was like."

Alexis's face never lost its calm, careful mask, but

she did flick him the tiniest of glances that couldn't have been more clear in meaning: Be. Quiet.

Nope.

"She was about like you'd expect," Logan said. "Quiet. Contemplative. Deliberate."

Beautiful.

"What did you do before you started the company?" LeeAnne asked Alexis.

Alexis placed a bite of roasted carrot in her mouth. "Planned the company."

LeeAnne laughed. "And before then?"

"Went to school so I had the know-how to start the company."

"You're so scary," Heather said fondly.

"You are, rather," Josh said. "You know, right, that the rest of us spent our early twenties making stupid decisions?"

Alexis merely smiled. "I don't know what to tell you. I've just always known what I wanted."

"Alexis, love you like a sister, but that's . . . weird," Josh said.

"Not so much," Logan said, swirling his wineglass. "I've always known what I wanted."

He said it casually, not even looking at Alexis as he said it, but he saw from the slight stiffening of her shoulders out of the corner of his eye that she suspected it might have something to do with her.

There was a moment of silence at the table before Grant leaned over toward Maya, showing her his knife. "What do you think, babe? Sharp enough to cut the sexual tension?"

Brooke gave a high-pitched nervous laugh before

hosting instincts took over and she changed the subject. "So, one of my clients offered me a box at the
Mets game next Saturday. Anyone interested?"

As Brooke no doubt expected, this launched the
requisite and good-natured Mets-versus-Yankees debate, and the rest of the meal passed without Alexis
so much as looking at him.

Which, oddly, Logan didn't mind. Just a few weeks
ago, she'd have made eye contact half a dozen times if
there was a reference to an inside joke, or if she was
directly throwing conversation his way. Heck, they'd
probably have been sitting by each other, he'd have
refilled her wineglass as necessary, she'd have passed
him the pepper knowing his tendency to put it on just
about everything.

The couple who wasn't a couple.

And though he didn't particularly relish this tension between them, he knew that it was necessary—
necessary for Alexis to see him as something other
than good old Logan.

So instead, he refilled LeeAnne's wineglass, asked
her to pass the pepper, joked with her over the merits
of tea versus coffee.

As a reward, he felt Alexis's gaze boring into his
forehead.

"So LeeAnne," Logan said, as everyone was finishing up last bites of dessert and sips of coffee. "Do you
plan to be in New York long-term?"

The pretty doctor pursed her lips. "You know, I
think so? I mean, not that we ever plan these things.
I certainly hadn't intended to leave Philadelphia,
honestly. But I like it here. I've got a great job, I love

my apartment, and if you guys are any indication, the city's got some pretty great people."

Maya leaned forward and gave a conspiratorial smile. "We've got some pretty great guys, too."

"Guys, plural?" Grant asked idly, setting an arm around the back of his girlfriend's chair and lifting one eyebrow.

She blew him a sassy kiss and turned back to Lee-Anne. "Seriously, have you met anyone since you've been here, LeeAnne?"

Logan noticed that Alexis had gone rather still in the process of helping Brooke clear plates.

LeeAnne fiddled with her coffee cup. "Not really, but I can't say I've been looking."

Maya smiled. "Well, if you do decide to venture into the New York dating scene, seriously let me know. I know a bunch of amazing single guys."

"One of whom's right at this very table," Brooke said in a teasing voice as she picked up Logan's plate.

Logan met Brooke's sparkling blue eyes, and he could have kissed her right then, because he knew full well what she was up to—knew that in her own way, she, too, was goading Alexis.

"No lady friend for you, hmm, Logan?" LeeAnne said, far too confident to be coy.

"Oh I have plenty of lady *friends*," he said, leaning toward LeeAnne slightly with a conspiratorial smile, even as his entire being was focused on Alexis as she went around the table refilling coffee mugs.

This time he saw Alexis roll her eyes. She was aware of what he was up to, obviously, but it was also working. He saw it in the tension around her eyes, the way she was spending a hell of a lot of time looking at him and LeeAnne.

"Well, I may not be in a dating place now, but maybe in a few months . . ." LeeAnne said with a little laugh in a friendly, semiflirtatious tone.

Alexis's hand faltered in the process of refilling their coffee cups, and not too long ago, Logan would have been all over himself to reassure her that she had nothing to worry about. That he was hers.

Tonight though . . .

Logan smiled back at LeeAnne, slow and deliberate. "I'd very much like that."

Logan was at a point in his career that he no longer needed to carry around a business card case, hungry for new clients, but he still kept a couple in his wallet.

He pulled one out, sliding it across the table to LeeAnne, letting his fingers brush hers. "You'll give me a call if you change your mind."

It was a long shot, but when he heard Alexis's sharp intake of breath, he knew it had paid off. Knew that she remembered their first meeting with the same clarity that he did.

He put his wallet back in the pocket of his sport coat, idly meeting Alexis's eyes as he did so, taken aback by the swirling emotions there.

But just as he was ready to cave, ready to tell her that he'd wait for her for fucking *ever*, the shutters slammed back down again and she turned on her heel, marching into the kitchen without a backward glance.

LeeAnne gave a quiet sigh. "I'm sorry. I didn't know that it was like that."

"I'm not sure that it *is* like that," Logan said, his eyes still on the doorway where Alexis had disappeared.

LeeAnne gave a feminine snort. "You can invite me to the wedding."

A half hour later, the table was cleared and people were saying their good-byes.

"Thanks, love," Logan said as he bent to kiss Brooke's cheek. "Appreciate you including me."

"Stop," she chided gently. "You're a part of the Belles family. Hell, you're the *patriarch*."

He shrugged. "Don't let Alexis catch you saying that."

"Still. You're more than an accountant. You know that, right?"

He lifted his eyebrows and searched Brooke's face, wondering if she knew about his real role in the Wedding Belles.

She winked. "Josh told Heather, who told me. I told Seth, who told no one, but it doesn't matter, because all the important people now know . . . you're a silent partner."

He sighed. "Does Alexis know that you know?"

Brooke shook her head. "Was it her idea to keep it a secret?"

"No, mine."

Brooke frowned. "Why?"

He ran a hand over the back of his head. "I don't reckon I even know anymore. I told myself it was to protect my own business interests early on, but I think perhaps it was more about putting her at ease."

"Letting her think she's in control," Brooke said knowingly.

Logan gave a slight smile. "You know her well."

"And you know her better."

"Do I?" he murmured, glancing over to where Alexis shrugged on her coat while talking with Jessie.

He'd been so damned careful with her, and now he was wondering if it had been a serious error in judgment. If he had been *too* careful.

If he had left her alone for too long, allowing her walls to grow too high, her defenses too strong.

Damn it, she wouldn't even look at him.

And suddenly, Logan was very, very tired.

As Brooke moved away to say good-bye to Heather and Josh, Logan was a little surprised to find Seth studying him. Brooke's husband had quite a stare on him, and Logan lifted his eyebrows in response. "Yes?"

"Don't give up on her," Seth said quietly.

Logan didn't pretend to misunderstand. "Spoken like someone who didn't give up on his woman?"

Seth shook his head. "No. Spoken like someone who wasn't given up on."

Logan stilled. *Interesting.*

He nodded as he shrugged on his coat, clamping Seth once on the shoulder in thanks, lifting his hand in farewell and giving a generic bye to the group before exiting.

Not so long ago, he'd have waited for Alexis out of habit, but he couldn't expect her to break her habits if he didn't break his.

Still, he couldn't help himself from lingering a bit once outside, pulling out his phone to email back a panicked client who'd managed to lock himself out of his online banking portal.

When there was still no sign of Alexis, he turned and headed in the direction of his apartment. Logan lived a good ten blocks or so from Seth and Brooke's place, but it was a nice night. Clear, with just the barest of chill that came from early spring evenings.

Plenty of time to gather his thoughts and to figure out his next move. He needed to woo the woman, but he was out of practice in all but the most surface of flirtations. He smiled at the irony—the very *reason* for his rustiness in the art of romance was now the same reason he wanted to overcome it

As with most things in Logan's life, it always came back to Alexis Morgan.

He paused on the quiet sidewalk, shoving his hands in his jacket pockets and turning his face toward the sky, taking a deep breath.

Logan forced himself to think about the situation logically. Was it worth it, really? Was *she* worth it? Objectively speaking there were a hell of a lot of women in the world. More importantly, there were plenty of women in *London*.

And he doubted a single one could be as complicated or as difficult as the one he'd chosen.

What would it be like? he wondered. What would it be like to move on, to *truly* allow someone else in, rather than just biding his time with stand-ins?

Could he do it?

Did he want to?

"Logan!"

His head whipped around at the sound of his name. Alexis was walking toward him in her usual quick pace, her even steps and stiletto shoes paying no mind to the uneven sidewalk as she made her way to him.

A strand of hair had pulled loose of the knot at her neck, the jacket belt at her waist knotted more haphazardly than he was used to seeing.

Her eyes were wide and clear as she got closer.

Logan sighed. Ah hell. No. There was no moving on, not yet.

There was only *her*.

But he was wary, all the same. Alexis wasn't the type to go chasing after someone. If she was following him now, it was either quite good or quite bad.

She stopped in front of him, adjusting her purse strap on her shoulder. "You didn't wait."

He lifted his eyebrows. "Why would I?"

She looked away. "I thought you might have waited for LeeAnne."

"You heard what she said," he said softy. "Not on the market at the moment."

"And when she is?" Alexis asked, looking back at him.

Logan shook his head. "You don't get to do this, Alexis. You don't get to tell me you hate my kiss, and then in the same evening get upset at the thought I might kiss someone else."

"I never said I hated it," she whispered.

He took a step closer. "No?"

She blew out a frustrated breath. "Logan. I don't understand you like this. I don't get what you want from me."

He stared into her eyes. "Yes. You do."

He turned away, but Alexis reached out, grabbing his sleeve.

Logan opened his mouth, but before he could tell her to figure her shit out, she went on her toes and pressed her lips to his.

Alexis Morgan was kissing him.

Logan froze the second her lips melded against his, both in shock and sheer pleasure at the way her mouth fit his perfectly, the way one hand slid around the back of his neck, pulling him down to her.

His hands lifted immediately to her waist, sliding around her back and tugging her in closer. Logan deepened the kiss, and she let him, giving a soft, breathy sigh as his tongue nudged her lips apart.

If this was her experiment, she could experiment on him any old day or time. For all the days.

Alexis pulled back slowly, and he reluctantly let her, instinctively knowing that she needed to be in control of this particular kiss.

She stared up at him.

"What was that?" he asked, his voice coming out a little ragged.

She shook her head. "I don't know. *I don't know.* I need . . . I need to think."

He closed his eyes in frustration. It wasn't a surprise, of course, but he didn't have time for this shit.

"About the kiss?" he asked, opening his eyes and meeting hers.

"About everything."

"Alexis—"

She held up a hand. "I'm leaving; I just need to say one thing."

"Okay . . ."

"*Damn you*, Logan," she said, pushing at his chest. "Damn you for ruining everything."

She turned on her heel, and Logan let her walk away.

This time.

Because if they kept having kisses like that, *one* of these times she wouldn't walk away.

Chapter Eleven

THE DAY AFTER SHE stupidly kissed Logan on the sidewalk, Alexis was darn lucky her bride was an easy one, the wedding a breeze, because for perhaps the first time in her career, her head wasn't in the game.

Sure, she made certain that the cake was delivered to the correct room in the hotel, that the hungover DJ had the first-dance song ready to go, that a slightly oblivious bridesmaid added a strapless bra to fix a headlights situation, but it took *effort*.

Every step of the way, Alexis was reminding herself to focus—that it was Haley and Mike's special day, and they deserved her attention, not a British accountant who had very suddenly, and very alarmingly, gotten far too sexy for his own good.

Alexis had been planning and facilitating weddings for a good eight years now, and though she'd never be so cold as to say she was used to them, she had, over time, developed a certain amount of immunity to the intense emotion of the vows.

Tonight? Not so much.

Tonight she'd felt her eyes water as the father of the bride had walked his youngest daughter down the aisle. She'd heard herself laughing softly with everyone else as the groom had been staring so besottedly at the bride that he'd had to be reminded twice to repeat his vows. She'd barely bitten back an *awwww* when the bride had surprised the guests and the groom with a sweet song she'd written herself.

Alexis tried to tell herself it was a function of a really lovely wedding, and of course that was true, but she was no more attached to this bride and groom than to any of her other clients. She liked them, but this wedding wasn't more personal than any other wedding.

Instead, she was all too afraid that her sentimentality came from something much more dangerous. The combination of her sister's potential pregnancy, her mother's constant voice mails asking if Alexis was going to bring anyone to dinner when she was in New York next week, and then Logan, it had all left Alexis, well . . . *wanting*.

She wanted to be the woman that the guy couldn't stop looking at because he was so damn in love. And though she wasn't musically inclined enough to write a song, she wanted someone to care enough to listen if she did.

Alexis wanted . . .

She just wanted.

Period.

The feeling was as liberating as it was unnerving. For so long she'd kept herself bound in this tight little knot of efficiency. Everything in its place, always in control. Kissing Logan last night had been a mistake, but it had also been out of control, and out of control had been wonderful.

Also, dangerous.

Because if Alexis was really honest with herself, as she tried to be, she wasn't so sure that this new sense of longing was as vague as she wished it were.

She was afraid that it was specific. That she wanted Logan. But to what end? To kiss again, just to get that high? To sleep with? And then what?

What happened when he got bored?

What happened when he realized she'd never be the perfect wifey content to put his career ahead of her own, to have babies at the expense of the Belles? She wanted it all. The career and the family. And as far as she could tell, guys didn't want women who wanted it all.

They wanted the one who was smart enough to have a career, but who also wanted to be the superstar, hands-on mom.

Alexis would be an awesome mom. But she'd also be the one with the nanny, the one who sometimes went with store-bought bake-sale goods, and who'd miss soccer games because she had to work a wedding.

What man signed up for that?

Would Logan?

Alexis pushed the thought aside.

It was just after midnight when she headed home, this wedding being a relatively tame one. She was glad. All she wanted was a bubble bath with her favorite orange blossom bath oil, a scented candle, and the delicious Regency romance waiting on her Kindle.

Alexis slowly walked down Seventy-Third Street, begging her feet in their stiletto-clad misery to hold on just a little longer, when she saw them.

White tulips. Three dozen of them at least, and beautiful.

They were her favorite.

Alexis treated herself to white tulips every now and then, when they were in season, and when she needed a pick-me-up.

But other than her birthday, when the Belles or her dad got her a bouquet, nobody ever gave them to her. And somehow she knew they were for her. Not for the Belles, not a decoration for the lobby.

For *her*.

She all but dashed up the steps, dropping her oversized bag to the ground as she grabbed the card.

Alexis was sprawled across the white envelope in boring, indifferent handwriting. The florist's, no doubt.

And though the inside of the card had the same impersonal handwriting, the message itself was very personal.

For you, Alexis. In hopes that you'll be thinking of me as often as I'm thinking of you. Always.
        —Logan

Alexis ran her hand over the sharp corner of the card. She'd known the flowers would be from him, even as she hadn't wanted to let herself hope. She smiled a little, tapping the card once against her palm before slinging her bag over her shoulder and carefully gathering the lavish vase as she opened the door.

They were playing a dangerous game, she and Logan, and though her brain protested in fear, warning her that things could go so terribly wrong, her heart?

Her heart was being ridiculous, all warm and fluttery and irrational.

Because Logan Harris wasn't just out to seduce her. He was out to *woo* her

And though she'd hardly admit it, even to herself, Alexis Morgan was a woman who very much wanted—*needed*—to be wooed.

Chapter Twelve

"D AD, I TOLD YOU. A bit more time. Please."

"How long does it take to realize that your place is home with your family?"

Logan gritted his teeth as he took a sip of tea. The tea had been meant to soothe his agitation over Alexis, but that had been before he'd gotten the phone call from his father. Had he known about the incoming call, he'd have gone with something a bit stronger. A lot stronger.

"Respectfully, you forget that London hasn't been *home* since I was eighteen," Logan said quietly.

"Nonsense," his father said in a clipped voice. "Home is where your family is. Your family is here."

"A year ago you were just fine with the status quo. Hell, a *month* ago you were fine. You don't get to snap your fingers and expect me to do your bidding."

"Of course," his father said impatiently. "Your parents are handing you the reins of a multimillion-dollar corporation. It must be quite the hardship."

Logan rolled his eyes at the sarcasm as he lowered

himself into his favorite leather chair—an expensive Italian designer piece he'd bought for himself five years ago when he'd realized he had a bit more money than he knew what to do with. Logan had always enjoyed the making of money more than the spending of it, and even now he wondered if he wouldn't have been just as happy in a chair with imitation leather for a fraction of the cost.

He'd have traded every piece of overpriced furniture in his flat for company right now—and no, his irritable, commanding father didn't count.

He wanted a slim brunette. One who favorited no-nonsense hairstyles, but would let him pull the pins out one by one until her chestnut waves fell over her shoulders, over his fingers.

Better yet, he wanted that hair spread out over his pillow, wanted to hear her gasps as he slowly, deliberately divested her of every ounce of that rigid self-control.

"I told you. I'm not saying no, I'm not saying I don't want it. I just want a month to think about it."

"I don't understand," his father said in a slightly defeated tone. "What's there to think about? What's going to change in a month?"

Logan took a sip of his Earl Grey. "It's my business."

"Then tell me as your father, not as a CEO itching to hand off the reins."

The request caught Logan off guard. It wasn't that his family was so cold as to not care what was going on in each other's lives, but the questions were generally relegated to holiday dinners, almost as though they were all following a script.

He spoke with his family on the phone at least a couple of times a month, but those conversations too often felt like they came with an agenda. Spontaneous *how are yous* were not standard Harris conversational fare.

Logan shrugged. What the hell?

"It's a woman," he said.

His dad let out an uncharacteristic laugh. "Your mother was right, then. Alexis?"

Logan's eyebrows went up. His parents knew who Alexis was, obviously. She'd been a part of his life for the better part of a decade, and they'd met her on a trip out to New York a couple of years ago.

But he'd never told them how he'd felt about her. Apparently he didn't have to.

"You're finally dating, then?" his father said.

Dating? No. Kissing, yes. Sending flowers to, yes. Wanting to sometimes strangle? Definitely.

"No," Logan said through gritted teeth. "We're not."

"You're staying in New York for a woman you're not even seeing?"

Logan dipped his head and ran a hand through his hair. "It's complicated."

"Because you have feelings she doesn't return."

Ouch. Leave it to his father to get to the heart of the matter.

"Thanks for that," he grumbled.

His father sighed. "I'm sorry, son. I know you've always had a tender spot for this woman, but it's been years now. Perhaps it's time to accept that she's not the one for you. Move on."

If only it were that easy.

Logan took a sip of his tea, but it was definitely no longer making the cut now. He stood to make himself a gin and tonic.

"Your mother and I only want you to be happy, Logan."

Logan smiled, because as usual, even the kindest words sounded irritable coming out of his father's mouth.

"And if I find that it's New York that makes me happy?"

"Damn it, that woman's not worthy of you!"

Logan's hand stilled in the process of adding tonic to the gin. "I'm sorry?"

There was a frustrated exhale, then a deep breath as his father fought for control. "She's a lovely woman, I'm sure, but how long are you going to let her lead you around by the nose? Don't you want more?"

Logan had been about to take a sip, but he slammed the glass back down on the counter instead. "Of course I want *more*, Dad. Why do you think I asked for a month? I'm trying my damned hardest to convince her to give me a chance."

"Don't you want a woman you don't have to throw yourself on the ground for? One who's not inclined to walk all over you?"

His father's words angered Logan because there was truth there. He *was* tired of waiting, and yet how could he possibly give up before he'd even tried? Sure, she'd texted him *thank you* for the flowers, and yes, she'd planted one on him the other night, but it wasn't enough—not nearly enough. He was ready to cannonball into the water and she was still dipping her toe in.

"Just a few more weeks," Logan told his father through gritted teeth. "If it doesn't work out, then . . ."

"You'll come home?"

Logan took a healthy swallow of his drink, trying to imagine what it would be like to leave New York and never come back.

To leave Alexis.

The thought burned, and yet Logan was starting to question which was more likely to destroy him: living without her, or living *with* her and not having her.

He wasn't quite sure.

One thing he *was* sure of: the next move would have to be Alexis's.

Chapter Thirteen

ALEXIS HAD A SECRET she kept hidden in plain sight: she *loved* weddings. It was why, as a little girl and later a precocious teenager, she'd always wanted the business she would one day build to revolve around them.

She didn't gush over them the way Brooke did; she didn't all but levitate with excitement over them the way Heather did. When it came to giddy brides, Alexis was careful never to overshadow their excitement with her own.

Most days, she let people think that weddings were her business, not her soul. But there were some days she gave in. Sundays, specifically. From the very beginning, Alexis had always carved out time on Sunday evenings to let herself look at weddings not as a wedding planner, not as a businesswoman.

Simply as a woman.

And so, every Sunday night, Alexis had a standing date with a glass of chardonnay and a pile of bridal magazines. Every now and then she'd stumble across something for her clients, but for the most part, Alexis perused the magazines for *her*.

She let her imagination wander and let her heart dream as she turned page after page, pretending it was her own wedding she was planning. She'd been at it for eight years now, and her preferences had evolved over time, from A-line dresses, to mermaid, to sheath, to ball gown, and back again.

In her early twenties she'd been on a pastels kick, her midtwenties she'd been all about the jewel tones, her late twenties it was monochromatic color schemes.

At thirty-three, she'd settled down a bit, content to ooh and aah over the latest trends, even as she began to wonder more with each passing year if she'd ever implement any of them in her *own* wedding.

Alexis's Sunday nights were sacred alone time—the centering point of every week that was just for her.

Which was why it was *highly* annoying to find that on this particular Sunday night, she couldn't seem to get to that soothing Zen place. Instead of focusing on a far-off wedding day in the future, her brain was persistently circling on a moment in the past.

Two moments specifically, both involving Logan Harris.

Both involving *kissing* Logan Harris.

Alexis slammed *Brides* shut in disgust and tossed it aside, glaring at the gorgeous tulips she couldn't seem to stop staring at.

Friday night's kiss had been a mistake. It was just that she'd been so sure, so hopeful that the preceding kiss had been a mistake. That it had simply been the shock and the newness that had made kissing Logan unforgettable.

Her experiment hadn't paid off.

They were now two-for-two in the *exceptional kiss* category, and for the life of her, she couldn't figure out how she felt about that.

On one hand, it would be easy to give in. To simply lean into the kiss, to lean into *him*, and see where it went. To see if their bodies would meld as well as their lips seemed to.

On the other hand, Logan wasn't like any other guy. You couldn't have a one-night stand with a man you saw several times a week. You couldn't simply not return the calls of your best friend if it didn't work out.

Alexis figured she could weather just about anything life threw at her, but losing Logan . . .

It was inconceivable.

Resolutely she opened up the magazine, determined to lose herself in the pros and cons of the latest trend—a gourmet ice cream sundae bar instead of cake.

She wouldn't think about Logan. Wouldn't think about the way he tasted, or the way he held her, or the way her heart had seemed to fall out of her chest when he'd handed his business card to LeeAnne Valentine just like he'd handed it to her all those years ago.

And then to kiss her (well technically, she'd kissed him, but he'd damn well kissed her back), and then send flowers . . .

What did he want from her?

And why now? Why, just as other areas of her life were beginning to fray, did he have to go start being all weird on her?

Alexis blindly flipped through six more pages of her magazine, absorbing none of it and giving a huge sigh of relief when she heard her cell ring from its charging station on her end table.

Normally she hated interruptions on Sunday night, but tonight she'd kill for one.

Any interruption would do, except . . .

Alexis froze as she glanced down at the caller ID. There was exactly one thing that could take her already precarious hold on self-control and send it spiraling.

This was it.

She squeezed her eyes shut, wanting so, so badly not to answer. But if she didn't answer, then she'd just keep wondering.

And wondering would be worse.

She swiped her thumb to take the call. "Roxie. Hi."

There was a heartbeat of silence, as though her sister hadn't been expecting her to pick up. "Alexis."

Roxanne had always been the one person in the Morgan family to respect that Alexis despised the name Lexie. Too bad she couldn't have respected other things.

Like staying away from my man, Alexis thought bitterly.

"How are you?" Roxie's voice was soft and a bit cautious. "It's been a while. A little over a month."

There was no censure in her sister's tone, only sadness.

She and Roxie had come a long way since those early days when Adam had dumped Alexis . . . for Roxanne.

It had been rough for a couple of years with them exchanging only the bare minimum of words at holidays. But *slowly*, they'd healed. Slowly they'd figured out a way to be friends again, if not exactly with the inseparableness they'd once shared.

Still, friends or not, that didn't mean Alexis was ready to hear what Roxie was about to say.

"I'm good," Alexis said in delayed response to Roxie's question. *Stalling*. "Things with the Belles are going great."

Roxanne laughed. "You know I love you, you know I love your whole career-woman thing, but that's not what I'm asking. How are *you*? Separate from the Belles."

"I don't know how to separate myself from the Belles," Alexis said slowly.

The statement slipped out, but the second she said it, she realized how true it was.

And how sad.

But maybe not, Alexis countered herself. There was nothing wrong with being a career woman and only a career woman.

If nothing else, it was smart. A business she could control.

A business wouldn't leave you for your sister.

"Okay, don't kill me for sounding like Mom, but any fun developments on the romantic front?"

Her sister's voice was light, but Alexis tensed anyway. From anyone else, the question was mildly annoying. From Roxie, it was almost unbearable.

Or rather, the *truth* was unbearable. That Roxie had Adam, while Alexis had . . . nobody. Her eyes flicked to the white tulips, then flicked away again.

"Maybe," Alexis lied, forcing a brightness into her tone. "It's early yet though; I don't know that I'm ready to talk about it."

"Alexis, that's wonderful! I'm so happy for you!" Roxanne squealed.

I bet you are. Eases your guilt.

Alexis winced at the uncharitable thought. That was unfair. Truth be told, Alexis couldn't really figure out where she wanted to be in her relationship with her sister. For years now she'd been wavering. One moment she'd be desperate to call her sister, to gab about *The Bachelor.* She wanted to get back to their BFF status.

The next moment she'd be reliving the moment her sister had hooked up with her ex, and wanting very much to never see either of them again.

The latter reaction was unreasonable. Alexis knew that, she did. But it didn't make the feeling any less real. Or painful.

"Okay, anyway, I'm boring," Alexis said. "Tell me about you."

There was a long pause that had Alexis moving back to her living room and picking up her wineglass as she slowly sat on the couch.

"Actually that's sort of why I'm calling," Roxanne said at last. "I have some news."

Here it comes.

"Yeah?"

There was another pause, and she heard her sister take a breath. "Adam and I are having a baby."

Boom.

As she expected, Alexis's world tilted, and she closed her eyes. She'd known it was coming. She'd had a couple weeks to get used to the thought.

And yet, how prepared could you *really* be for the bomb that your sister and your ex-boyfriend were expecting a child together? Even after all this time, how could you make it not hurt to know that the boy you'd once loved with your whole heart had fallen in love with your sister?

And now they were going to be parents.

Together.

"Alexis?"

"Wow. That's . . . congratulations," she managed.

"I can't believe I'm going to be a mother. And you're going to be an aunt!"

Alexis took a breath. *Right*. There was that.

She was going to have a niece or nephew. And more than that, in some deep, guarded part of her, she was happy to know that two people she cared about so fiercely were going to have a baby together.

"I'm really happy for you," Alexis said, meaning it, even through her own swirling emotions. "You're going to make such a good mom."

"Thanks, sis. I've . . . honestly, I've put off telling you. I know our whole situation is complicated, and I was afraid you'd be . . ."

Hurt? Devastated? Angry?

"I'm happy for you and Adam," Alexis said more firmly. "Really."

"Good," Roxie sighed in relief, "because there's another bit of news, sort of related, equally big."

Alexis stilled, unsure how much more news she could take.

"We're getting married."

Alexis must have been expecting this, because the second bomb didn't rattle her nearly as much as she would have thought. Of course they were getting married. They'd been dating for years, they were happy, they were having a baby.

"Wow, double congrats!" she said in a high, squeaky voice that sounded nothing like her usual cool monotone.

"Thanks," Roxanne said. "I'm, well, I'm really happy. Obviously. But here's the tricky part. I'm still first trimester, but I really want to have the wedding before I start to show. My childhood wedding dreams didn't involve a baby bump . . ."

"So it's happening quickly," Alexis said, her brain unable to stop from going into wedding-planner mood.

"Yeah, about that . . . Alexis, we're sort of thinking of doing a resort wedding in Naples. Daddy has connections with one of the fancy hotels down there, and they got us a really good deal on short notice. They have an opening, and if we miss it, it'll be *months*, and I just can't wait that long."

Alexis's eyes narrowed. "*How* short notice?"

A brief pause.

"Next weekend. And you're coming," Roxanne said in a rush, her voice breaking a little. "You have to come. Promise me you'll be there. I'm not doing this without my big sister."

Alexis slowly bent at the waist, curling into a small

ball as she faced the reality of having to watch her sister and Adam get married.

In a week.

Deep breaths. Really deep breaths.

She could say no, certainly. She wanted to, rather desperately. But what if this was her chance to heal? *All the way* heal?

"Alexis?"

"Yeah, okay," Alexis said, slowly sitting back up again. "I'll be there."

Chapter Fourteen

Can you come over?

It wasn't the first time that Alexis had texted him out of the blue on a weekend asking him to come over, but it was close.

There'd been the time when she'd been taken down by a particularly nasty stomach bug. Another when her bathroom had flooded and she hadn't been able to get ahold of a plumber. Another when a bird had gotten in through her bedroom window and she couldn't figure out how to get it out.

That was it.

Three times in the eight years they'd known each other.

Tonight's message had come right as he'd gotten out of the shower after his evening workout, and he'd meant to tell her no.

To tell her that he was done jumping through hoops for her when she didn't give a damn thing in return.

And yet somehow he'd found himself throwing on jeans and a sweater and hailing a cab uptown at ten thirty on a Sunday evening, simply because she'd asked him to. He could be frustrated with her, pissed at her, and it didn't seem to matter, because at the root of all that was something unshakable.

He cared for her.

And her for him. Through it all he knew that, and if she needed him . . .

Well, here he was.

And even with all that was between them lately, he knew that she'd have done the same for him. That she'd be there in a heartbeat if he called and asked her to be. You didn't find that sort of connection every day, and Logan wasn't ready to let go of it. Wasn't ready to give up on the chance that it could be more.

Not yet.

He pulled out the spare key that let him into the Belles headquarters. He'd let himself in dozens of times in the past but always for business reasons. But tonight as he climbed the stairs toward her third-floor flat, he registered that everything felt different. As though change was just around the corner.

And then Alexis opened the door and he realized what was different.

Her.

Over the years, Logan had only ever caught glimpses of versions of Alexis other than the perfectly composed, in-control version she wanted people to see. He'd seen tired Alexis, sick Alexis, frustrated Alexis, even panicked Alexis, in the early days, but he'd never seen *this* Alexis.

She rested one bare foot on top of the other as she leaned a cheek on the side of the door and smiled up at him slowly, sexily, and just the tiniest bit sloppily.

"Hiya, Harris."

Bloody hell. Alexis Morgan was utterly pissed.

It was both alarming and slightly adorable the way she swayed a bit, her eyes soft and a touch unfocused.

"Hullo, Alexis," he said, setting his hands on her elbows and nudging her aside so he could enter.

If he didn't know she'd been drinking before, he knew now in the way she didn't jump away from his touch. In fact, she seemed to be going out of her way to touch him as he entered her flat and shut the door.

A fact made all the more excruciating by the realization that she was wearing very tiny pajamas, the little camisole one quick tug away from easy removal.

"Want a glass of wine?" Alexis said, feet padding softly away toward the open bottle on the counter.

Logan rolled his eyes toward the ceiling to avoid looking at the shorts that barely covered her small, perfect arse.

"No, I'm fine."

"Suit yourself," she said, plucking her own wineglass off the kitchen table as she passed and refilling it with a healthy pour.

Oh dear.

"Alexis."

"Hmm?" She turned toward him, not quite unsteady, but her movements were looser than he'd ever seen.

Best he could tell, her level of drunkenness meant

a headache likely awaited tomorrow morning, but she wasn't *quite* pissed enough that she wouldn't remember tonight's events, which meant he had to tread carefully. Anything he said or did would be used against him, of that he was quite certain. This might be drunk Alexis, but it was still Alexis.

"How much of that have you had, darling?" he murmured, coming toward her.

"Of what, this?" she said, glancing down at the glass. "I don't quite remember. I finished off a bottle of white I had open in the fridge, and then I thought that some red sounded yummy. Doesn't red sound yummy? So then I opened this lovely cab franc. You're sure you don't want?"

"I'm quite sure," he said, his eyes on the glass as he contemplated the best way to switch it out for some water.

She took a sip, holding his eyes over the glass, her expression thoughtful.

He swallowed, having the strangest sense that in spite of being completely sober, *he* was the one in trouble.

Logan cleared his throat. "Did you need something?" he asked. "I thought perhaps you might want to talk, but . . ."

"But what?"

He smiled gently. "Respectfully, darling, I don't think you're in any condition to talk tonight."

She sighed and glanced down at her wine before setting it on the table. "You're quite right, Logan. As usual. I didn't call you here to talk."

The warning sirens in Logan's head grew even louder. He took a step back, but not fast enough.

Alexis launched herself at him, slim arms winding around his neck, soft breasts slamming against his chest, all in the span of a single heartbeat before she tugged his mouth down to hers.

Logan meant to do the gentlemanly thing and set her back gently. He really did.

But *damn*, she tasted good. Like wine, and familiarity, and maybe just a little bit of loneliness that he longed to banish.

Somehow his hands were sliding up her back, his mouth tilting to deepen the kiss.

She moaned at his response, her fingers tangling in the hair still slightly damp from his shower, as she kissed him back, carnally.

Logan felt his cock harden against her stomach, and she moaned again, this time rubbing against him at the same time she bit his bottom lip.

He let out a soft curse before nudging her head aside, lips traveling down her neck, his tongue soothing every spot that his teeth scraped.

They were both panting, and though he knew he should go slow—hell, he knew he shouldn't go at all—his fingers found the strap of her top, tugging it down so he could taste the soft, smooth skin of her shoulder.

It was as far as he meant to go. Just one taste and then put her to bed. Alone.

But Alexis had other plans.

She stepped back from him slightly, lips pink and glistening from their kiss, and without looking away from his gaze, lifted a hand to the other strap of her camisole, slowing pulling it over her shoulder.

With nothing holding it up, the silky blue top slid to her waist.

Logan couldn't find his brain.

Alexis Morgan had perfect breasts. Small and pointed, slightly heavier on the bottom, perfect pink nipples hard and beckoning him.

Logan shook his head and took a step back. "Alexis. We can't. Not when you're—"

"Not when I'm *what*?" she said, stepping forward and reaching for his hand.

He closed his eyes. "You've had wine. A lot of wine."

"I have," she said in a calm, no-nonsense tone that told him the practical Alexis was in there somewhere beneath the seductress Alexis.

But it was definitely Seductress Alexis that lifted his hand and placed it on one small, perfect breast.

She gasped as his palm made contact with her flesh, and Logan groaned.

She felt so good.

He silently hated himself, even as he moved his hand, his palm testing her weight before he let his thumb drift over the peak of her breast, finding that sensitive little nub already hard and ready for him.

Her eyes were closed, her breath coming in little pants of want.

He watched his thumb drift back and forth, torturing her nipple, even as its neglected companion begged for his other hand. Even as they both begged for his mouth.

Logan's gaze drifted down over her flat stomach, down to the tiny shorts she was wearing with their little bow. It would be so easy to slide a hand down, to slip fingers under her knickers where he knew he'd find her warm and wet for him.

He swallowed. Damn, he'd wanted her for *so long*.

His eyes drifted back up, found her watching him with desperate, slightly unfocused eyes.

But not like this. Not after all this time.

Slowly, and with so much reluctance he thought he'd choke on it, Logan pulled his hand away from her, reaching for her camisole and tugging it back up, reluctantly covering her breasts.

He saw that even through her wine haze she understood, and her eyes went wide a moment before she slammed her arms against her sides, trapping the fabric so it couldn't slide down again.

She tried to get her arms back in the straps, but her motions were jerky.

"Here," he said quietly. "Let me—"

"Don't touch me," she snapped, stepping back. "Not unless you're going to *touch me*."

"Alexis—"

"Don't," she whispered, keeping her head bent as she focused on sliding one hand into a strap, and then the other. "You'll only make it worse if you try to explain."

His eyes narrowed at the unfamiliar note in her voice. It wasn't drunkenness so much as . . .

Logan stepped forward, pressing his thumb gently to her chin and nudging her face up toward his.

What he saw there knocked him back a bit. She was *crying*.

He frowned. This was more than wine-induced

drama. There was something very, very wrong here, and he'd walked square into the middle of it. Something that didn't have anything to do with him.

"Alexis, what's the matter—"

She slapped his hand away and then swiped at the tears on her cheek. "Get out."

"Like hell," he growled, stepping closer to her. "You're upset—"

"Because you didn't want me!" she yelled, swiping again at her face. "You didn't *want* me."

"Don't be daft. Of course I *want* you, but not like this, Alexis. Not when you're half-pissed and likely to hate me for this in the morning."

Alexis was slowly shaking her head back and forth, arms wrapped around her waist.

She wasn't hearing a word he was saying, he realized.

"Get out," she said in a quiet, sad voice that tore at his heart. "Now."

"Alexis."

"Please leave. Please." Her voice cracked.

"I will," he said quietly, reaching out a hand. "But at least let me explain—"

"Never mind," she snapped. "If you won't leave, I will."

Alexis turned and walked to her bedroom, her posture remarkably prim for a woman who'd just consumed a glass too many.

The bedroom door closed with a final click, much as it had that morning a week ago when he'd kissed her.

Well, he'd done a good bit more than kiss her tonight, and though he couldn't quite say he regretted it, one thing was becoming abundantly clear: he'd just made a major misstep.

Logan stood still for several moments, staring at the closed bedroom door. Wondering what very key piece he was apparently missing to the Alexis Morgan puzzle and doubting whether he would ever figure it out.

Chapter Fifteen

I CAN'T BELIEVE YOUR sister is getting married in less than a week," Brooke exclaimed, plopping down in a leather-backed swivel chair next to Heather.

"Believe it," Alexis muttered as she wrangled with the Excedrin bottle. The three women had gathered in the second-floor conference room for their weekly status report where they shared client progress and other business updates, and damn if Alexis was going to make it through the meeting without some serious medication. Her morning dose had long worn off, and her headache was coming back with a vengeance.

The humiliation though? That had been going strong since the moment she'd opened her eyes this morning.

Too bad there were no pills to take the edge off of throwing yourself at your accountant.

And then being rejected.

"So wait," Brooke was saying slowly as she pulled her long hair into a casual knot at the top of her head. "Your sister calls you yesterday, tells you she's pregnant and getting married in Florida *in a week*. And you're just . . . good with that?"

Alexis rubbed her temples. *No.* No, she was *sooooooooo* far from good with that. "I don't know that I have a choice," she said quietly.

"There's always a choice," Heather said in a calm, matter-of-fact tone.

"Says the only child," Alexis retorted just the slightest bit tartly.

Heather nodded thoughtfully. "Touché. Neither Brooke nor I have siblings, so I suppose we don't get it, but respectfully, I've never gotten the impression that you and your sister are close."

There was a quiet question in Heather's voice. An invitation to talk if she wanted to, and Alexis was a little surprised to find that she did want to.

"We used to be," Alexis replied, picking up her coffee cup and washing down the pills.

"I don't even know her name," Brooke admitted.

"Roxanne. Roxie. She's two years younger."

"Baby of the family, or are there other hidden siblings you haven't mentioned?"

"Nope, just the two of us. And yeah, Roxie has a little bit of that youngest-child thing going on, but not nearly as much as she should considering my mom's determination to spoil her rotten."

"Spoil *her*, but not you?" Brooke asked.

Alexis gave her employees a pleading look. "Really? We're doing this?"

"If it helps, we could move this out into the reception area," Heather said. "Have you ever laid on the couch?" She backtracked at the sight of Alexis's eyes narrowing. "Not—not that I have, of course, but come *on*, all that buttery leather? Probably feels like heaven to just stretch out on and take a nap. Hypothetically."

Brooke snapped her fingers. "Ooh, and I could see if Jessie has a clipboard . . ."

"Okay fine, you win, I'll talk," Alexis said with her first laugh of the day. "Yes, Roxie was the apple of my mom's eye; I was more of a daddy's girl."

"You're close with your dad?"

"Eh." Alexis wiggled her hand. "As close as anyone can get to him. He and my mom split up when I was sixteen. He's remarried now, but I'm not sure Tawny really knows him, either. He's quiet, reserved. Private."

"Sounds like someone we know . . ." Heather said, exaggeratedly snapping her fingers as though trying to place the familiar description.

Alexis gave her a look. "*Anyway*. Despite our parents being at constant odds—my dad frustrated by Roxie's penchant for shopping, my mom frustrated by my refusal to become a debutante—Roxie and I always got along. Looked out for each other."

Neither Heather nor Brooke said anything, as though knowing there was more to the story but also knowing that Alexis needed to share at her own speed.

She felt a little rush of gratitude for her friends. And they *were* friends, she was realizing. She'd always known that on some level, but the rational part of her brain tried to establish that they were employees first, friends second. Perhaps it wasn't that black and white.

It seemed everywhere she looked these days, lines were blurring. Colleagues became friends, friends became lovers . . .

Or not.

Because Logan hadn't wanted her.

Alexis dragged her hands over her face, wishing she could push away the fog from last night's wine binge. "When I was in grad school, I met this guy. Adam Hogan. We had a bunch of classes together, and I had, like, this *huge* crush on him. And then we got assigned to work on an econ project together, and I started to get the impression that he had a little crush on me, too."

"Who knew econ could be so romantic?" Brooke whispered.

"It was," Alexis said, letting her memory go in directions it hadn't in years. "It was those little tiny moments that made your stomach flip. Like when he'd ask to borrow a pencil, let his fingers brush mine, and then later I'd see that he had a half dozen pencils in his bag. Or the way he'd ask like a million rambling questions before working up to the one he really wanted to ask, which was whether I was going to such and such a party on Friday night. And then the way, when we were done working for the day, he'd make a big deal about wanting to thank me for letting him borrow my class notes the other day, and then he'd ask if I wanted to grab something to eat as though it was a spontaneous suggestion, and I'd find out later he'd been planning it all day."

"Um, this so is the cutest story ever," Brooke said, propping her chin on her fist.

"It was," Alexis said with a sad smile. "Until it wasn't."

Brooke's smile slipped and her eyes went cloudy. "What happened?"

"We dated for a little over year. It was serious, or at least it felt that way. I mean, for me, he was the *one*. Charming, smart, successful, funny. Even more important, he seemed to get me. He never resented the long hours I put in studying, because he did the same. He never minded when I hijacked our date night to go over my latest proposal for the Belles, because he supported me. I sometimes felt like he wanted it for me as much as I wanted it for me."

"He sounds like a good guy," Heather said.

"He was. He is," Alexis amended. "We talked about getting married. And even though it was in the cautious way of two practically minded twenty-three-year-olds that knew anything could happen, I really thought he was the one."

"But he wasn't."

Alexis shook her head. "Not for me. But for someone."

"I really don't like where this is headed," Heather muttered.

Me neither.

Alexis took a deep breath and plowed on. "Taking him home for the first time was sort of huge. My parents on their own . . . semi-awful. My parents together, even worse. I don't know why they tried to make family holidays work after the divorce, but they did, and it was awful for everyone involved. Adam didn't seem to mind though. Said he wanted to know me, all of me, warts and all. Anyway, it was Thanksgiving, and his parents had flown west to visit his little sister in San Francisco. Adam couldn't get that much time off from work, so he stayed in Boston and came home with me for the holiday."

Alexis took a sip of coffee, feeling slightly detached as she recounted a story she'd spent years trying not to think about, much less discuss. It was painful, for sure, but in a way it was also oddly relieving.

Especially after last night's nightmare.

"Adam had met my parents before," she continued. "A couple of times. But Roxie went to college at Notre Dame, and her visits home had never coincided with Adam's schedule."

"Oh, Alexis," Brooke breathed, apparently understanding where the story was going.

"It was like I watched Adam and Roxie fall in love at first sight. As in I *actually* watched it," Alexis said. "I know that sounds ridiculous, but I knew it even as I tried to deny it. It was like the first time my sister and Adam locked eyes, the entire world shifted. Like, the *air* changed. They spent the entire weekend trying not to look at each other, but I knew. On some horrible, instinctive level I knew what was happening."

"I hope you dumped his ass right after that weekend," Heather said.

"I probably would have gotten around to it once the shock wore off, but he beat me to it," Alexis said with a little smile. "We lasted until January before he very quietly told me that it wasn't working out. In his defense, I think he really did try. I think she did, too. They didn't start dating for more than a year after we broke up, and only after they both came to me and asked if it would be all right."

"Of course it's not *all right*," Heather exploded. "It's your sister and your boyfriend."

"By then he wasn't my boyfriend," Alexis said matter-of-factly. "What could I do?"

"Tell them to have some class?" Brooke asked.

"Well, the thing is," Alexis replied slowly, "I love them. And when you care about someone, you want them to be happy."

"Even if it kills you?"

"Even then."

"And they're still together?" Heather asked. "*That's* who your sister is marrying? Your ex?"

"Yes, but . . . they've been together nearly ten years now," Alexis said quietly. "Adam and my relationship was nothing compared to what they have. I see that now."

"Doesn't make it any easier on you," Brooke said, touching her arm.

"No. But it also doesn't mean that I won't go to the wedding."

"Still, why the rush job?" Heather asked.

"Eh." Alexis lifted a shoulder. "That's sort of Roxie for you. She doesn't want to look fat at her own wedding. Plus, she's spontaneous. Fun. Bubbly."

Everything I'm not.

"You sure one of us can't come with you?" Brooke asked sympathetically. "For moral support?"

Alexis shook her head. "I need you guys here. I'm just grateful my sister's spontaneity happened on a weekend where we have two weddings instead of three."

"We'll take care of things on this end," Heather said. "If you promise to take care of you."

"At least she didn't ask you to plan the wedding," Brooke muttered.

"Well, actually . . ."

Heather gave her an aghast look. "Alexis. *No.*"

"Roxie didn't ask," Alexis was quick to explain. "Supposedly they've got someone at the resort to coordinate everything, but—"

"No *but*," Brooke interrupted. "You fly in, grit your teeth and smile through the ceremony, get drunk at the reception, and then fly home."

Alexis almost hurled at the mention of alcohol. *Too soon.*

"I want to help," Alexis insisted. "Uncomfortable as my history with Adam is, this is my little sister's wedding, and I'm a wedding planner, for God's sake. The least I can do is make sure it's unforgettable for her."

Brooke and Heather exchanged a resigned look. "When do you leave?"

"Wednesday," Alexis said, straightening her shoulders and slowly feeling herself slip back into work mode. "That'll give me two full days to make sure everything's exactly right."

Brooke sighed. "Alexis, there's *nothing* right about this."

"Maybe not," Alexis said lightly, much more blasé than she actually felt about the whole mess. "But it's happening, so I might as well get on board."

"What can we do?" Heather asked. "I mean, not about the weddings here—we've got that under control—but for you." She snapped her fingers. "Ooh, I know! What if we found you a hot guy to take with you? You know, like that movie, *The Wedding Date*. Look how it worked out for Debra Messing."

"Perfect," Alexis said dryly. "Because I'm absolutely the sort of person to base my life decisions on Hollywood fairy-tale delusions."

"Maybe you should," Heather argued.

Alexis opened her mouth to say that she didn't believe in that crap. She thought relationships could last, yes. That people could be compatible, definitely. She believed in passion and affection and all that. But that one great, all-consuming Hollywood version of love?

Shrug.

She'd believe it when she saw it.

"What about Logan?" Brooke blurted out.

Alexis couldn't help it. She winced. "No."

"He'd go as your friend," Brooke said gently. "All you have to do is ask."

Alexis snorted. Really? All she had to do was ask? It certainly hadn't seemed that way when she was *hurling her body at his.*

"What's going on with you two?" Heather asked, as ever, blunter than Brooke. "There've been . . . *vibes* lately."

Alexis took another sip of coffee, noting that the headache seemed to be receding slightly. At least *something* was going her way.

It was on the tip of her tongue to shut this conversation down. To issue her go-to "we're fine."

But if Alexis had ever needed friends, it was now, when her heart felt tied up in knots and she couldn't figure out if it was due to her sister, or her ex, or her accountant, whom, after eight years of platonic calm, *she couldn't stop thinking about.*

Alexis groaned and put her elbows on the table, dropping her forehead into her palms. "I made a play for him."

"*What?*" Brooke and Heather asked in unison.

"Yup," she said, not able to look at them. "He turned me down."

"He did not," Heather said, aghast. "That man is smitten with you."

"Nope," Alexis said, dropping her hands and looking at her friends. "Trust me. He isn't."

"When was this?" Brooke asked.

"Last night. I called him after talking to Roxie. Asked him to come over. I know it was dumb, but I just . . . needed someone. And Logan has always been there."

"And he didn't come over?"

"Oh, he came over," Alexis said with a little laugh. "I couldn't have been more clear about what I was looking for, and he shut me down."

"This doesn't make sense," Brooke said with a frown, tapping her fingernails.

"For what it's worth, I'd had a little wine," Alexis admitted. "Or a lot."

"Ah," Heather said triumphantly. "So he was just being a gentleman."

"Maybe," Alexis murmured. "Doesn't make it any less humiliating that I was so easily rejected."

"Oh, sweetie, no," Brooke protested. "It wasn't like that—I just know it. It's just that he cares for you. He wants *all* of you, not just tipsy you. And I'm thinking he'd want you to be sure, too, before you guys went, you know . . . there."

"Really?" Alexis said, pinning her friend with a glare. "So if you took your shirt off and kissed Seth, he'd be capable of saying 'No thanks'?"

"Well—"

"Or you," Alexis interrupted, cutting over to Heather. "Has Josh ever said 'Thanks but no thanks' to sexy times?"

"Yes, actually."

"When?"

"Well, he had mono," Heather admitted. "Which he thought was his cancer relapsing."

"Logan does not have mono," Alexis said through gritted teeth. "Or cancer."

"Have you spoken with him since last night?"

Alexis shook her head. He hadn't shown up this morning for their meeting. She was grateful that he'd spared her that humiliation, at least.

Or maybe he's too disgusted by your behavior.

"Talk to him," Heather urged. "I don't think it's what you thought it was."

"Rejection is rejection," Alexis said, standing and draining her coffee. "And frankly I've had quite enough of it for a lifetime."

Chapter Sixteen

"OKAY, HONESTLY, DUDE? IF you don't stop brooding, I'm going to have to do something drastic."

Logan glared across the pub table at Josh and took a grumpy sip of beer. "Like what?"

Josh glanced at Seth. "Any ideas?"

"Hooker?" Seth asked. "Shots?"

Josh snapped his fingers. "Yes. That's it. Hooker *and* shots."

Logan rolled his eyes.

It was Thursday night. Four nights since his and Alexis's disastrous encounter at her apartment, and he still hadn't seen her.

Hadn't even talked to her.

And his harebrained friends had just informed him that the woman was in *Florida*, for her sister's wedding that she hadn't bothered to mention. And the clowns he'd stupidly agreed to go out to drinks with weren't helping the situation in the least.

"Okay," Logan said, pointing at Josh. "Quiet, for

once. And *you*." He pointed at Seth. "I liked you way better when you were mostly mute."

"Well, we liked you way better when you were the easygoing, likable one," Josh replied. "Oh wait, no. That's always been me."

Logan glared. "You forget that I watched you two clowns have your fair share of troubles with your own ladies. Well, not *you* so much; I didn't know you then," he said, waving at Seth. "But I had to watch all the damage you did to Brooke."

"I didn't damage—actually, you know what?" Seth held up his hands in surrender. "I'm not even going there. You have every right to be having a temper tantrum because your girl is going on a weekend trip to Florida."

"Not my girl," Logan muttered. "And it's not a tantrum."

"Right. So you've called her, then? Texted her?"

Logan shot Seth the bird. He gave Josh the bird, too, for good measure, then signaled the waitress for another round, just for good measure.

"Yes, good plan," Josh cheered sarcastically. "Drink those sorrows away."

Logan glared. "Got a better idea?"

"Yes, either move on or fucking do something about it."

Seth shook his head. "Don't do the first one. The second one, yes."

"The damned woman won't even talk to me. I've tried patience, I've tried jealousy, I've tried manipulation, I've tried more patience and being a gentleman, and I can't ever get within less than arm's reach."

"Except when you kissed her. And then she kissed you."

Logan gave Josh a sharp look, and his friend shrugged. "Heather."

"So she told Heather all about it," Logan said, sitting back in his chair.

"Yes, but while *they* may have had girl talk, we are most certainly not going to, so let's skip to the part where you tell us what the next phase of your plan is."

Logan waited until the waitress set their drinks down before resting both elbows on the table and shoving his thumbs into his eye sockets. "I don't know that there is a play here. I feel like a lovesick swain and I'm positively tired of it."

"I love when he gets British," Josh whispered. He raised his voice back to normal volume. "Hey. Say *bloody wanker.*"

"I myself prefer *bloody hell*," Seth said. "It's very Bond."

Logan dropped his hands and glared at them both.

"Right," Josh said. "Okay, dude, here's what we're going to do . . ."

Logan waited expectantly, and Josh looked at Seth. "Okay, Seth, what are *we* going to do?"

Seth picked up his glass, tilting it from side to side, watching the amber liquid before glancing back up at Logan.

"You still want her."

Logan wanted to say no. For the past couple of days he'd wanted nothing more than to be over an obtuse woman who couldn't decide what she wanted from him.

Instead, he nodded.

"Thought as much," Seth said confidently. "Then you need to go get her."

Logan laughed. "That's your advice? How much do I owe you? The woman ordered me out of her apartment last time we spoke."

"As I understand it, her faculties weren't all in order," Seth said carefully.

"Jesus," Logan said with a laugh. "Their girl talk is certainly thorough, isn't it? As is pillow talk, apparently."

"Seth's right," Josh said. "You keep saying you want her, but from where I'm sitting, you don't seem to want her very much."

Logan sat up straighter, anger spiking down his spine. "Now hold on, you—"

"Bloody wanker?" Josh said hopefully.

"Arse," Logan muttered.

Still, even as he took a sip of beer, his mind was spinning with the possibility.

"Look," Seth said, impatient. "I get what you've been trying to do. Your woman's unbearably complicated, and if you push too hard too fast, you're fucked—I get that. But something's shifted between you two, am I right?"

Logan hesitated, then nodded. "Yes. We seem to alternate between our usual ease and something . . . *not* easy."

"That's what you want," Josh said. "You need her

to start seeing you differently, and that's not going to happen until you start acting differently."

"You mean, chase her down on her holiday to Florida," Logan said skeptically.

After she yelled at me to get out of her flat.

After she *cried*.

"No, you're right," Josh said, taking a sip of his beer. "*Much* better to sit scowling in a dark bar with us. That should bring her to heel."

"You know what'd be fun?" Logan said. "If you made that women-as-dogs reference in Heather's presence and then let us watch whilst she maims you."

Josh winced. "Right. I suppose I didn't phrase it quite right, but Logan, man, Seth's right. You can't really blame her for treating you like her accountant when that's how you act."

"As you've pointed out, I'm British. Not exactly the cavemen of the modernized world."

"Bullshit," Seth said quietly, leaning forward.

Josh nodded. "I'd have to agree. I'd bet serious money that caveman is a hell of a lot more your style than the passive, patient game you've been playing for far too long."

They were right. More right than he'd let himself admit in a long time. Waiting for Alexis had been pure torture. He wanted nothing more than to throw her over his shoulder and haul her to his apartment, bedding her until she was *thoroughly*, forever his.

"Hold on," Josh said, pointing a finger at him. "I know that look, and I support it, but you're going to want an in-between step. You've been chill, nice

Logan for far too long. If you show Caveman Logan now, she'll freak."

"Fuckin' A, you know you're contradicting yourself?" Logan said in exasperation.

"You need an in-between step," Josh repeated patiently. "Look, man. There's just . . . there are things you don't know about Alexis. Things none of us knew about her past."

Logan snapped to attention. It was exactly as he'd expected that night she'd thrown herself at him and then promptly broken down. "What am I missing?"

Neither man said a word.

"Fine," Logan ground out. "Since you two both landed women better than yourselves, I'll bite. What's the grand plan?"

His friends exchanged a look, as though mentally flipping for who was going to drop the bomb.

Seth apparently lost. "You're going to Florida."

Chapter Seventeen

IT WAS A BEAUTIFUL, sunny day in Florida at the utterly gorgeous Ritz-Carlton.

"How *dare* you call my family broken, you over-processed tart. At least I have a family. You've got nothing but silicon and another woman's husband."

"*Ex*-husband, you shriveled-up, ice-for-tits—"

Annnnnnnd then there was this.

"Okay, wow," Alexis said, maneuvering between her mom and stepmom. "How about we bring it down about five hundred notches, hmm?"

"I *told* you not to let her come," Cecily Morgan hissed at Alexis.

"It wasn't up to me," Alexis said smoothly. "It's Roxie's wedding. Roxie wanted Dad here, and where Dad goes, Tawny comes."

"And yes, I *certainly* do," the other woman said, purring like a cat for Cecily's benefit.

"Okay, and you," Alexis said, turning to Tawny. "Why is it that you go from perfectly nice to a little vicious every time you're around my mother?"

Tawny laughed, revealing perfect white teeth, stark against her fake-tan skin. "Oh, honey. When you get married, you'll understand."

"Like you'd know," Cecily sniped. "I was married to Jack for twenty years and bore his babies."

"Yeah? Where's the ring?" Tawny lifted her own three-carat monster to prove her point.

Alexis held up both hands before they could go at each other again. "Enough. For *real*, enough. I'm not going to ask you two to get along, because, impossible, but I'm going to demand that you stay out of each other's way for the duration of our time in Florida. Especially when Roxie's around."

"Yes, where is Roxie?" Cecily frowned, glancing at her watch. "She was supposed to meet me for lunch."

"Puking up her guts with morning sickness," Alexis said. "You and I will do lunch."

"Morning sickness? But it's not morning," Tawny said in confusion.

"Morning sickness is just a phrase; the nausea can happen at all hours," Cecily said, speaking slowly and over-enunciating as though she were addressing a child. "*Clearly* you've never borne children."

Tawny ran a hand over a figure that was darn impressive for a forty-eight-year-old. "*Clearly*."

"Yeah, okay," Alexis sighed, pulling out her phone and making the call.

"Dad?" she said the second he picked up. "Come collect Tawny."

"Can't, sweetheart. About to tee off."

"Yeah, okay, *that's* more important," Alexis said.

"I'll just leave the dead bodies of your ex-wife and current wife in your suite, then?"

Jack Morgan sighed. "Tell Tawny to take a spa day. On me."

She rolled her eyes. Tawny had quit her job the day she met Alexis's father. Alexis was pretty sure most everything expensed in Tawny's life was *on Jack*.

"Fine." She hung up with her father without saying good-bye. "Tawny, take a spa day. *All* day. Dad's orders."

"I remember when Jack and I used to vacation together, he used to want to actually spend time with me," Cecily said pointedly, examining her fingernails.

Actually, that wasn't even *remotely* true, but loyalty to her blood relation kept Alexis from saying so.

Alexis plastered on the megawatt smile she reserved for her most problematic brides and turned to her mother. "Mom, lunch? I could use a glass of wine."

"Yes, you could," her mother said, giving her a once-over. "You've been so stressed all week."

"I've only been here two days."

"Yes, dear, but you seem to fit more hours into the day than the rest of us, and it's getting exhausting to watch," Tawny chimed in. "Your mother's right. You could use a drink. And a man."

"Yes," her mother nodded. "Definitely a man. Honestly, sweetheart, I can't believe you didn't think to bring a date. It would have made things so much less awkward for Adam and Roxie."

Alexis shoved aside the pang of hurt, decided to cling to annoyance instead.

"Really," Alexis said, flicking her index finger between the two of them. "This is happening? You two decide now to get along, to gang up on me?"

"No, not gang up, sweetie. Help. Have you even done your hair this morning? It's always in that angry little knot at the back of your neck."

Tawny lifted a hand to tap the "angry little knot." "Cecily's right. It's vacation. You should let your hair down, literally."

"It's not vacation; it's my sister's wedding, which I'm planning."

"Did Roxie ask you to plan it?" her mother asked knowingly.

Alexis kept her mouth shut, refusing to engage.

The truth was, other than a hug and a cup of tea the day she'd arrived, she'd hardly seen her sister, and she hadn't seen Adam at all.

He'd been busy entertaining the male portion of the guests with golf and snorkeling and whatever else, while Alexis had been running around selecting flower arrangements, color schemes, and trying to find a competent seamstress to alter the wedding dress that Roxie had sheepishly admitted was too tight around the middle.

As for her sister, she was indeed suffering from morning sickness at all times of the day, which meant Alexis was mostly on her own.

She liked it that way, she *did*; it was just, well . . . she really did want that glass of wine.

Just as Alexis was preparing to physically shove Tawny in the direction of the spa and her mother in the direction of the chardonnay, she caught both women staring over her shoulder in a mixture of curiosity and admiration.

Probably one of the bronzed pool boys.

Alexis turned, tempted to tell the poor kid to run for his life before the cougars got to him.

She froze.

There *was* a guy, but it was no boy. It was a *man*. All man.

And he was striding toward them, but not toward her mother and Tawny.

Toward *her*.

Alexis's lips parted, but no sound came out as Logan came to stand in front of them.

He was here, and she felt . . . oh, how she *felt*. Her heart felt both heavy and light, her body both longing to run to him and away from him. A mixture of deep embarrassment upon remembering their last encounter, and an even more overpowering sense of lust and want.

Great. Just when Alexis had finally finished convincing herself that the outcome of Sunday night had been for the best—that she would have deeply regretted a one-night stand with Logan, no matter how drunk and desperately sad she'd been—here he was. He'd come for her. She'd thrown herself at him, then swiped at him, but he was here anyway.

For her.

But why?

"Hi, sweetheart," he said in that delicious accent before bending and kissing her cheek. He'd kissed her cheek a million times before, but this was different.

Not only because he was wearing a white linen shirt

and dark navy shorts, but because his lips hit closer to her ear, lingering longer than they usually did.

It was the kiss of the familiar.

Of a lover.

And *sweetheart*? That was new. She got the occasional *darling*, but he called Heather and Brooke darling sometimes, too. This felt different. Personal.

It also felt nice.

"Hi," she breathed, because he smelled good and felt even better.

"Sorry I'm late," he said, turning his attention to the other two women. "I was supposed to fly out last night, but work got in the way, and then this morning my first flight got delayed. Anyway, Mrs. Morgan, it's so nice to see you again," Logan said, extending a warm smile to Alexis's shell-shocked mother.

"I'm Alexis's stepmother," Tawny said, honest to God playing with a strand of hair. "And you are?"

"I'm Logan Harris." Logan's brown eyes snapped back to Alexis as he extended a hand to Tawny, giving her the slightest wink. "Alexis's boyfriend."

Chapter Eighteen

I'M LOGAN HARRIS. ALEXIS'S boyfriend.

Alexis stared at him after he dropped the bomb.

As did her mom and stepmom.

There was a beat of silence as the eyes of both Alexis's mom and stepmom widened in unison and swiveled toward Alexis, like something out of a movie.

"Logan, a word?" Alexis managed.

His smile grew even wider as he continued to hold her gaze. He knew that tone. That was the tone she reserved for moments where she was teetering on the very brink of sanity. "Of course, dear. We can talk when you show me to our room."

He saw her eyes go wide at that, but he reached forward, snagging her hand and pulling her forward before she could undo his handy lie.

"What the hell are you doing?" she whispered angrily as he pulled her toward the cart where the bellhop waited with his luggage, leaving behind a speechless Cecily and Tawny.

"Not now, sweetheart," he said, bending to nuzzle her ear.

"Stop that." She started to twist away, but his arm wound around her waist, the feel of her slim curves sending an instant shot of lust through him.

"Let's just get to the room," he said. "Then I'll explain."

"You'll need to get your own room. Honestly, Logan, this is . . . I don't even know what this is."

"If you want to get pissed, do it at Seth—this was his idea."

"Seth told you to do this?"

"Well, him and Josh. But I wouldn't be surprised if your girls were the ones to plant the seed in their tiny little brains." Although to be fair, the guys had told him only to go to Florida. They hadn't told him to pretend to be Alexis's boyfriend, but hell, it had just sort of slipped out upon seeing her, and he was going with it. If nothing else, it would explain his presence to her nearest and dearest.

And, if it went the way he intended, it would show her what a great boyfriend he would make for real. How great they would be together.

"This is unbelievable," she said, smoothing a hand over her hair, which was pulled back in its usual Alexis knot.

Apparently loose, sexy Alexis wasn't planning to make an appearance this trip.

We'll just see about that.

Logan handed money to the bellhop. "If you could please take this stuff to . . . ?"

He paused and gave Alexis an expectant look. Her

eyes narrowed before rolling. "Fourteen twelve," she said through gritted teeth.

"Fourteen twelve," Logan repeated cheerily.

"But the *second* we get this sorted out, you're getting a bed of your own—"

"Interesting," he interrupted, taking a step closer as the bellhop wheeled the cart away.

"What?"

Her eyes were still wide and dazed.

He dropped his gaze to her mouth. "Interesting that you said *bed* instead of *room*."

"I did not."

Logan smiled. "You did. Almost like you were thinking about bed."

"Well, I wouldn't be, would I? Since you have zero interest in that."

Logan's smile dropped. It was as he'd feared. Sober Alexis had looked back at that disastrous night in her flat and gotten it all wrong.

"You have no idea what I'm thinking, Alexis," he said, letting his gaze roam over her.

She stared at him. "Who are you? What is even happening right now?"

He sighed, taking a bit of pity on her. "Walk with me."

Alexis's mother and Tawny were still staring after them, whispering in what he was willing to bet was the first hushed conversation those two had ever had that didn't involve death threats.

He gave the older women a wink, and Alexis made a disgusted noise. "Stop—you'll only encourage them. Honestly, what has gotten into you?"

Logan grinned, realizing he hadn't had this much fun in years. It had obviously been too damned long since he'd let himself act spontaneously—since he'd done what he wanted.

The countdown was on. He had only a couple weeks before he'd promised his father a decision.

Only a couple weeks to coax this woman out of her shell.

He put a hand on her back as he led her through the open archway toward the beach, her skin warm through the thin fabric of her sundress.

Logan made an appreciative noise as they walked through the manicured gardens, taking in the enormous infinity pool to their left, the open-air restaurant to their right. "Not a bad place to get married. Where are you thinking for the ceremony?"

Alexis paused, then seemingly unable to help herself from talking about weddings, extended her arms to the beach. "On the sand. A little messy, but what's the point of a beach wedding without the gently lapping waves and the sun setting behind you? There'll still be noise from the pool, of course, but I think we'll be far enough away, and by the time we pipe in the music, which I'm still deciding on—"

She broke off and turned to glare at him. "You did that on purpose. Trying to distract me from the fact that you're totally invading my privacy."

"Guilty," he said, turning to face her. "I know talking about weddings relaxes you, although not this wedding maybe as much as others. You seem . . . tense."

"Probably because my accountant, who saw me naked last I saw him, then walked away, shows up at my hotel and informs me we'll be sharing a room and that he'll be posing as my boyfriend. Really, Logan, it's terribly high-handed of you."

He smiled a little and stepped closer. "You know that you sound British sometimes, right? Not the accent, but the choice of phrasing. Am I rubbing off on you?"

Her eyes narrowed. "You're changing the subject."

Good Lord, this woman was hard to charm.

"All right, here's the thing," he said. "I only saw you half-naked last time."

She punched his shoulder. "Logan—"

"Alexis," he said mildly. "Shut up. You like to be in control of every situation, and I get that. I respect that. But I'm also damn sick of being one of the players for you to move around. I've let myself up until this point, and that's on me, but it ends now."

She rubbed her forehead tiredly. "Okay, oddly enough, I think I understand all that, but my sister's destination wedding is *really* not the time to change it up."

He stepped closer and hooked a finger beneath her chin, lifting her face to his. "It's the perfect time. New scenery for a new phase."

She sighed. "Look, I'm sorry if that night at my place gave you the wrong idea. I was—I wasn't myself. But that was clearly a lapse in judgment, and I promise, from now on I'm going to be much more professional. Everything as it was before. I'm not ready for this."

"I'm not asking for anything," he said quietly. "Other than to be your friend. Just like you wanted me to be."

She studied his face. "And the fake boyfriend routine?"

Logan's parents had called three times this week alone, trying to see where his head was at. He felt the clock ticking on this decision—London versus New York—even as he insisted they back off. He'd told them he needed more time, but he needed something from Alexis. Anything. He gave her his best not-my-fault smile. "Like I said. Seth's idea."

"Logan."

"Hush," he murmured, moving closer, letting his hands span her waist and feeling a surge of triumph when she didn't stiffen or move away. "I don't know the deal with your sister's wedding; I don't need you to tell me until you're ready. But don't forget that I know you, and I know that something's been going on with you lately. Something having to do with your sister, with all of this. I know it's to blame for the debacle of the other evening."

Her tongue snuck out, touched the corner of her mouth nervously. "You're not wrong."

"I know." He smiled. "And I'm not going to say that having a date to this wedding is going to solve everything, but it's not going to hurt either, is it?"

Her eyes dropped to the top button of his shirt. "I'm not ashamed of being single. I shouldn't have to lie to my family."

"This isn't about you being ashamed of being single," he said, his fingers pressing into her waist and easing her even closer. "This is about you letting someone else make your life a little bit easier."

"My life is fine."

Logan tilted his head back and prayed for patience. This woman . . .

He took a deep breath and looked back at her. "You deserve better than *fine*, Alexis."

She lifted an eyebrow. "And you think you're the key to that?"

"I think you should give us the chance to find out."

"Logan—"

"Just let me be here for you. As your friend. I won't make a move, I'll sleep in the bathtub, and I won't kiss you until you ask me to."

"Until I ask you to? You seem pretty confident that it's an inevitability. And don't hold your breath, not after last time."

He gave her a cocky grin and slowly slid his hands from around her waist before holding one out to her. "Show me our room?"

She rolled her eyes. "I'm so going to regret this."

But then she put her hand in his, let him lead her back into the hotel.

Logan smiled in quiet triumph. The seduction of Alexis Morgan had begun, and she didn't have a clue.

Chapter Nineteen

ALEXIS'S FOOTSTEPS SLOWED AS she approached the table the hostess had indicated.

There were few things more aggravating than lunch with her mother, but lunch with her mother *and* Tawny definitely qualified.

For a moment, she considered retreating to her room, but that would only leave her alone with thoughts of Logan and the fact that he was here. Plus, there was no sign of bloodshed at the table, and there was wine, so . . .

"Am I going to need to ask the server for a fire extinguisher?" Alexis asked as she pulled out the chair next to her mother and set the pristine white napkin over her lap. The hotel restaurant was gorgeous. Fresh flowers on every table, perfectly polished crystal, a view of the ocean.

Alexis took a sip of her water, wondering if maybe she'd been wrong to chalk this weekend up to an obligation. Maybe she could enjoy herself. Relax, consume too many calories, maybe have a piña colada by the pool, enjoy her family . . .

"Sorry, what was that, Alexis darling? I was just counting your mother's wrinkles and got distracted because there are just so many—"

"Did you hear that, Alexis? Tawny wants us to believe she can count above five."

"Five? Try fifty. I've seen shar-peis with fewer creases on their face."

Alexis's mother sniffed. "You'd have a few frown lines, too, if your husband had left you for a fake-tanned, fake-boobed space cadet."

"You know, I'm sort of thinking you two actually enjoy this whole bickering thing," Alexis said, glancing around for their server.

"*Hardly*," Cecily said.

"Huh," Alexis said, catching the server's eye and pointing to her mom's wineglass, and then to herself. Translation: *Me. Wine. Now.* "So Tawny invited herself to lunch, then?"

The older women exchanged a glance. "We mutually agreed to tolerate each other so that we might unite on an important cause."

"Let me guess," Alexis said, folding her hands on the table and leaning forward. "I'm the cause?"

"You and that delicious hunk of Prince William," Tawny said, wiggling her drawn-on eyebrows.

"Prince William must be half your age," Alexis's mother said disdainfully.

"Then he's a quarter yours," Tawny shot back.

Alexis picked up her menu. "I'm not going to discuss Logan."

"I always knew it was only a matter of time until you two hooked up," Cecily mused as she swirled her wineglass. "I just knew it."

Alexis rolled her eyes and barely resisted the urge to storm off to her room and slam the door. That was a mother for you. Able to make you revert back to your rebellious teenage self with little more than a smirk.

"You knew nothing of the sort," Alexis said as she tried to focus her attention on salad choices and not the fact that just an elevator ride away, there was Logan Harris and a king bed and *oh so much potential*.

"I did too know," her mother said stubbornly. "It was all in the way he looked at you. Your father used to look at me that way."

Tawny snorted, and Alexis felt disloyal to even have the thought, but she was inclined to agree with her stepmom. She couldn't really imagine her father staring adoringly at any woman.

Not that Logan stared at Alexis adoringly.

Except . . .

Had he?

For years, Alexis had been stubbornly ignoring the Belles' insistence that Logan carried some sort of torch for her, but it was increasingly clear that she'd most definitely been wrong about that.

Or willfully oblivious.

He may have rejected her drunken advances last weekend, but the version of Logan she'd seen just moments before—the one that had followed her to Florida—that was a man who knew what he wanted.

He was a man who wanted her.

But for how long? And for what?

A weekend fling? A month-long fling?

"You stared at him, too, you know," her mother said.

Alexis lifted her gaze from the menu and narrowed her eyes on her mom. "Meaning?"

"Meaning that I think the reason you've never been in a serious relationship is because your heart was all tangled up with your accountant."

Tawny's nose wrinkled. "Accountant? I was hoping for a Buckingham Palace guard. With the little red outfit."

Both Alexis and Cecily ignored her.

"I haven't been in a serious relationship," Alexis said calmly, "because the last time I was in one, the first time, it ended with my boyfriend falling in love with my sister."

There was a moment of stunned silence at the table. Hell, Alexis herself was stunned. She rarely let herself have those thoughts, much less speak them aloud. And she certainly knew better than to speak them aloud at her sister's wedding weekend.

It was Tawny who reached across the table, resting her sunspotted hand on Alexis's. "This must be hard for you, sweetie. I didn't realize you still had feelings for Adam."

Alexis closed her eyes and blew out a breath. "I don't. It's just that I don't get why nobody seems to understand why I'm not in a relationship. Why I choose to be cautious."

"We understand," her mother said, and not to be outdone by the more affectionate Tawny, patted

Alexis's shoulder awkwardly. "It's just that we're all looking forward to you moving on."

"Yes, because you did such a good job of that yourself," Tawny said, with a pointed look at Cecily.

Alexis's mother's jaw dropped as she stared across the table. "Surely you're not implying I'm still hung up on my wastrel of an ex-husband?"

"I don't think you have feelings for him," Tawny said calmly, taking a sip of wine. "I think your pride can't handle the fact that he has feelings for someone else."

Oh boy.

Alexis looked around frantically. How long did it take to come back with one glass of wine? She was *dying* over here.

Desperate, she took a swallow of her mother's wine, even as Tawny's words sank in.

I think your pride can't handle the fact that he has feelings for someone else.

Granted, Tawny had been talking to Cecily, but she might as well have been talking to Alexis. It summed up Alexis's turmoil perfectly. Alexis didn't want Adam. She didn't even know Adam anymore. But she was still having a hell of a time with him choosing someone else. Just like her mother refused to accept that Jack had chosen Tawny over her.

Holy crap, Alexis thought, slumping back in her chair in dismayed shock.

There were few more startling come-to-Jesus moments than the realization that you were turning into your mother.

For years, Alexis had been exasperated by her mother's refusal to move on and be *happy*. Cecily and

Jack Morgan were never going to be happy together, but Cecily seemed determined not to be happy without him, either. Time and again, Alexis's mother chose to live in the past—had chosen unhappiness over the chance at joy.

Just like Alexis had been doing.

She took another sip of wine. Then another, although both were small sips. She didn't need a repeat of last Sunday's sloppiness or Monday's hangover. She did, however, need courage.

Alexis may not have been as vocal in her bitterness as her mother, but she'd let her heartache over Adam and Roxie dictate her life every bit as much as her mom had.

It ends here, she promised herself. *It ends this weekend.*

It ends with Logan.

Chapter Twenty

ALEXIS HAD DECIDED THAT Operation Get Over It started tonight.

Only, it was going to be a teeny, *tiny* bit more difficult than she anticipated.

Alexis had seen Adam Hogan a handful of times since he'd fallen in love with her sister. Mostly at Christmas or Thanksgiving dinners where they'd sit at opposite ends of the table avoiding eye contact until Alexis made an excuse to leave at the earliest possible moment.

It had gotten easier over the years. Not easy. Not by a long shot, but eventually her brain had come to accept that he was a part of her family, if not exactly in the way she'd once envisioned.

But seeing him for the first time on his wedding weekend—that was a whole separate ball game, and one she'd been dreading all week. In some ways, she supposed she should be grateful to Roxie and Adam for their shotgun wedding. This way she could rip off the Band-Aid instead of suffering through a long, drawn-out engagement.

But quick and sharp or slow and dull, pain was pain, and everything in her rebelled at willingly walking into a situation that would hurt.

They were nearly to the private event room where the rehearsal dinner was taking place when Alexis skidded to a halt.

Logan stopped with her and glanced down. "You okay?"

She put a hand to her throat. "I don't know if I can do this."

He shifted so that he was in front of her, his hands finding her upper arms—bare, courtesy of the strapless blue cocktail dress—and rubbing soothingly. "Of course you can do this."

She swallowed. "Okay, I'll rephrase. I don't *want* to do this."

All of her girl-power confidence from lunch was rapidly ditching her.

He laughed, warm and low. "This is what I like about you. Honest to a fault."

She gave him a look. "That's what you like about me? My faults?"

His eyes skimmed over her and turned speculative. "There may be a couple other things."

Alexis felt herself go warm, and she lifted a finger. "Don't. You said you were here as my friend."

"I am," he said, rubbing her arms again.

Alexis took a deep breath. "Okay, let's do this."

"Yes, let's. But first things first . . ." He gestured a finger over his smile. "Lipstick on your teeth."

Her hand flew to her mouth. "Seriously?"

"If it makes you feel better, I think it's the first

time in all the years I've known you that I've ever seen that."

"I tried this new stupid lipstick," she muttered. "I should have known better." She swiped at her teeth and gave Logan a wide-toothed grin. "Better?"

He nodded. "For what it's worth, I like the new look."

"You have to say that because you know exactly how long it took me to make this all happen," she said, waving her palm over her body to indicate the hour and a half's worth of prep time.

"Worth every minute," he said.

"A gentleman to the end," she said with a small smile. Before she could think better of it, she reached out and ran a finger over the lapel of his suit jacket. "Although it's a little unfair to know that you ended up looking like this in about five minutes."

His eyebrows lifted. "Is there a compliment in there somewhere?"

She pursed her lips. "No. I'm still not sure I'm not mad at you for this stunt."

But there was no denying that Logan Harris looked damn good. She'd seen him in a suit hundreds of times—thousands of times. But tonight she was seeing him differently.

Instead of the buttoned-up pin-striped suit with a conservative tie in its tidy Windsor knot, he'd opted to skip that in favor of a crisp white shirt undone at the top button as a nod to the humid Florida evening, a charcoal suit jacket draped over his shoulders.

Adding to the fact that they'd gotten ready alongside each other, which had been both strangely comfortable and acutely intimate.

She'd seen Work Logan, she'd seen Casual Logan, she'd even seen Dinner Party Logan, but Vacation Logan was different.

Vacation Logan was . . . kind of hot.

His smirk showed that he knew it, too, and for the life of her she couldn't figure out if this newfound cocky thing he had going on was annoying or sexy.

She was very much afraid it was the latter. Was afraid that his certainty of her asking him to kiss her at some point over the course of this godforsaken weekend was absolutely justified.

"So, we doing this?" he asked, nodding toward the party.

She took a deep breath, feeling a good deal more centered than she had a few moments before, and nodded.

"Anything I should know? Anyone I need to beat up?" he asked, putting a hand on her back as they approached the party.

For a moment, she debated giving him the *Reader's Digest* version of her history with the bride and groom, but she couldn't bear the thought of Logan feeling sorry for her. There'd be enough of that going on tonight as it was. She needed one person in that room who knew her as the strong, independent career woman, not the discarded ex-girlfriend of the groom.

"It's enough that you're here," she said in reply to his question.

And then she stepped into the room, and none of her nightmares came true. No awkward silence descended, nobody stopped and stared, there were no whispers, at least that she could hear.

Then she registered the sensation of Logan's hand hot against her back and realized that even if those things had happened, she wouldn't have been alone.

"Lexie! Honey, you're late!"

Alexis turned toward her father and smiled, giving him a hug and a peck on the cheek. "Hi, Dad."

But her father's attention was already on Logan, doing the whole stare-down thing typical of dads of daughters everywhere.

"Dad, you remember Logan Harris," Alexis said simply by way of introduction.

"Yes, of course," he said, shaking Logan's hand. "Tawny said you two are a thing now. When did that happen?"

"Great question," she muttered under her breath.

"Just sort of one of those things that sneaks up on you," Logan interjected smoothly. "How are you, Mr. Morgan?"

"Jack, please. And I'm good, I'm good," her dad said, taking a sip of whisky. "Keep thinking I'll retire one of these days; can't quite seem to pull the trigger though. You're an accountant, if I'm remembering correctly."

"Dad, we talked about this," she said gently. "No work talk at Roxie's wedding."

"Easy for you to say," her dad grumbled. "This *is* your work."

"I didn't do much for tonight's dinner," she said. "The hotel's wedding planner had it under control."

Logan gave her a look, and she shrugged. "Okay, I *may* have suggested the shrimp spring rolls over the crab dumplings, and double-checked the playlist, and you wouldn't believe the crappy gin they were trying to pass off as top-shelf—"

"On that note, how about we get you a drink?" Logan interrupted. "You can make sure the ice cubes are to specification."

"I *do* like square ice cubes," she said, more to herself than anyone else as Logan said bye to her father and guided her to the bar.

"I know, sweetheart," Logan replied, a smile in his voice.

"You don't have to call me that when nobody's around," she grumbled.

He ignored her as they stepped up to the bar. "Vodka soda for me, and for the lady . . . sweetie, what was it that you were saying about the gin?"

She resisted the urge to kick his shin. "White wine, please."

"Are you sure it's up to snuff?" he asked, his eyes wide in mock panic.

"Of course it is," she said, accepting the glass. "I selected it."

She turned and gave the open-air space a critical once-over, relaxing slightly when she saw that the resort staff had done an exceptional job. The main part was covered, but on nice nights like the one they were having, it opened onto a terrace where long rows of tables had been set up parallel to the water, each covered in large white bouquets.

Roxie had said she didn't care about colors, so Alexis had chosen for her, opting for various shades of white with fresh spring green coming out in the greenery and the accents. It was an easy color scheme to implement on short notice and managed to be elegant without being fussy.

Her mother, of course, had hated it, but then her mother tended to dislike anything that wasn't coral.

Logan tipped the bartender and they moved through the crowd, Alexis stopping occasionally to greet friends of her parents, cousins she hadn't seen in years, and although it took a bit of getting used to, by the fourth introduction or so, she realized she didn't even hesitate before introducing Logan as her date.

Much as she wanted to strangle her friends and Logan for hatching this plan without her consent, she had to admit that now that it was in motion, she was grateful.

She would have been fine on her own, but honestly? It was nice to be better than fine. It was nice to feel part of a pair. It was nice—

Alexis's thoughts scattered as a break in the crowd revealed the guests of honor, whom Alexis had been both looking for and avoiding all night.

Roxie, of course, looked utterly stunning, as she always did, in a white dress that hit her knees in a flirty, asymmetrical hemline. Her long blond hair was pulled into a low side ponytail, falling in lush waves over one shoulder, the pale pink lipstick perfectly matching her subtle baby-pink blush. Roxie had forgone her usual smoky-eye look in favor of a light, shimmery shadow that made her brilliant blue eyes sparkle.

No sign of a baby bump yet, but Alexis thought she seemed just a little bit softer somehow. Beautiful, like some sort of heaven-kissed angel.

A very happy angel, Alexis noted, taking in the brightness in her sister's gaze, the lightness of her laugh.

But then, of course, Roxanne had every reason to be light and bright. She had a man she loved and the baby she'd always wanted on the way.

Alexis took a sip of wine, registering that it tasted bitter, likely courtesy of the jealousy she felt suddenly threatening to overtake her.

Finally, *finally*, Alexis forced her gaze away from Roxanne and on to him.

Adam looked . . . like Adam.

He'd aged well, as Alexis had always figured he would. His suit was well fitted to his lank frame, and at thirty-three, there was just the slightest hint of gray mingling in with the dark brown hair at his temples, his blue eyes darker than Roxie's but no less happy as he stood protectively close to his girlfriend.

No, *fiancée*.

Roxie and Adam were getting married.

Another sip of wine. Still bitter.

"You okay?" Logan asked.

She jolted a little, having forgotten he was there, but looking up, she saw that he was as protectively close to her as Adam was to Roxie, as though knowing somehow that she needed him now more than ever.

"Yeah. I'm good," she replied.

But then Adam shifted, as though sensing her gaze, and he turned toward her, his blue eyes finding hers.

Alexis sucked in a breath, and Logan gave her a sharp look. Before she could explain, Adam had whispered something in Roxie's ear.

Her sister turned toward them, her face breaking in a wide smile. "There you are!"

She moved toward Alexis, Adam following behind.

Alexis registered her sister's trademark grapefruit perfume a half second before she was wrapped in a warm hug. "I've been looking everywhere for you! For some reason I wasn't thinking it would be this crowded."

"That's the thing with destination weddings," Alexis said. "When everyone's an out-of-town guest, they all get invitations to the rehearsal dinner, which makes it about as big as the wedding itself."

Roxie grinned. "Look at you being all sharp and smart and knowledgeable. One would almost think you do this for a living or something. It's so fun seeing you in your element. Is this what you're like in New York?"

"Definitely," Logan answered for her.

A good thing, too, because Adam had joined their foursome, and Alexis was suddenly finding it a little hard to breathe. She channeled all of her kick-ass wedding-planner professionalism to keep her face neutral and composed.

"You must be Logan," Roxie said, extending a hand. "My mom's been gushing about you all day."

"And she does mean *all* day," Adam chimed in before he shook Logan's hand.

Alexis took a sip of wine and tried to soak in the weirdness of this whole scene.

"I appreciate you guys letting me tag along with Alexis here."

Alexis gave a quiet snort, and Logan pressed a warning hand to her back.

"Oh, we're so glad you could make it," Roxie gushed. "I knew Alexis must be hiding some extra delicious secret."

"You know our girl," Logan said easily. "Secretive."

Out of the corner of her eye, Alexis watched Adam as Logan spoke, looking for something—anything—to register at Logan's possessive *our girl*.

But there was nothing. It was both a relief and a pang.

Clearly she'd been the only one wondering *what if* for the better part of a decade.

But no more, remember?

"Anything from the bar?" Adam asked, holding up his empty glass. "I'm due for another."

"I'm all set," Roxie said on a sigh. She glanced at Adam as her fingers touched her stomach just briefly. Alexis watched as the two of them exchanged a private smile, and it was . . . sweet.

So far, so good. No raging jealousy.

"Oh, there's Aunt Carrie!" Roxie said, lifting a hand in the direction of the formidable woman eating a passed appetizer and giving an enthusiastic wave. "We should go say hello!"

"Been there, done that," Alexis said with a levity she didn't really feel. "She informed me that my dress had too many purple undertones to suit my 'interesting complexion.'"

Roxie laughed. "Please. You look gorgeous. I love your hair down, and that lipstick looks amazing on you. Besides, don't worry. My stomach is churning again, which means she'll have plenty to talk about with interesting complexion when mine turns green."

Roxie gave Alexis another big hug and then rested a hand on Logan's arm. "So nice to meet you, Logan. I've been hearing good things about you for years, but she's failed to mention how good-looking you are."

"Hmm," Logan said, glancing down at Alexis. "I'm sure she has."

"Go," Alexis said jokingly to her sister. "Trust me—this one does not need his ego fed these days."

Roxie moved away with a laugh, and Alexis relaxed slightly when she saw Adam approach their little group and, upon seeing Roxanne was headed in another direction, course correct and trail his fiancée.

She needed air.

"She's lovely," Logan said, taking a sip of his cocktail as he followed Alexis toward the open terrace.

"She is," Alexis said, continuing to walk as fast as her heels would allow until she got to the hedge that separated the terrace from the beach. Daylight was starting to fade, giving the ocean a sort of dark and sultry flow. Alexis inhaled a deep breath, welcoming the vaguely salty, fresh air as it infiltrated her lungs.

"How'd they meet?" Logan asked.

She realized he was looking at her rather than the view.

"Through me," she said, taking a sip of her wine without glancing at him.

"You set them up?"

Alexis gave a humorless laugh, although the bitterness wasn't as fierce as she was braced for. "Not exactly."

He didn't press, but she knew *he* knew there was more to the story. Logan didn't say another word as they stayed watching the sunset, shoulder to shoulder, the din of the party behind them.

Alexis stayed lost in her thoughts for several minutes, trying to sort through her feelings, when she glanced down and saw that her glass was empty.

"Another?" Logan asked.

Alexis opened her mouth. *Yes, please* was what she meant to say.

It wasn't what came out.

"Adam and I used to date," was what she said instead.

Logan inhaled long and slow through his nose as though sorting through this in his head before he nodded. Then he took her glass out of her hand, setting both her glass and his on a nearby tray.

He took her hand and started pulling her forward.

"What are you doing?" she asked. "Did you hear what I said?"

"I did," he said in a disinterested tone.

"Are you going to say anything? Ask anything?"

He turned and looked down at her before gently pushing a strand of hair behind her ear. "Yes. I'd like to know if you'd walk on the beach with me."

Chapter Twenty-One

NOPE, NO WAY," ALEXIS said, tugging her hand free as they reached the bottom step away from the terrace.

She pointed down at her sexy silver sandals. "These are Jimmy Choos. They don't do sand."

Logan bent to remove his own socks and shoes before rolling his suit pants up to his knees and grinned at the thought of his tailor having a heart attack at the sight.

He tucked his shoes behind a log and held out his hand to her once more.

Alexis stared at him, entirely nonplussed. "Obviously you're unaware of what Jimmy Choos cost."

"Come on now, darling," he said, wiggling his fingers. "I'll carry your precious shoes."

She bit her lip, and he lifted his eyebrow in challenge. "If you'd like, I can take them off for you."

"Damn," she muttered quietly. "Brooke's right—that is a sexy move."

"Sorry?"

"Nothing. Girl talk. Seth once removed Brooke's shoes early in their courtship. She said it was the best move she'd ever seen on a guy."

Logan laughed. "Oh man. I can't wait to see the look on his face when I mention that little tidbit of information."

"Don't you dare."

Logan winked and reached his hand toward her calf. "Shall I?"

"No," she said quickly, a little nervously. "I've got it."

She made quick work of the small buckles at both ankles and he hooked the fingers of one hand into the ankle straps, extending the other hand toward her.

"You've been doing this a lot lately, you know," she said, resting her palm on his as her narrow feet sank into the sand beside his.

"Doing what a lot lately?"

"Extending your hand to me."

"So I have. One might also say you've been *taking* that hand a lot lately."

"One might say that," she said coyly.

Once they started walking, though, she gently tugged her hand free. He wanted to protest, but he understood. Walking on the beach lit at twilight was romantic enough without adding hand-holding to it.

One step at a time.

They walked for several minutes in quiet, content in their silence. The beach had plenty of people, but it didn't feel crowded, most of them out for the same thing he and Alexis were. Quiet.

Intimacy.

"How long before you think they'll miss you?" he asked, glancing down at her.

She blew out a long breath as she lifted a hand and pushed some wayward strands of hair out of her face. "Ten minutes ago."

"For family duty, or wedding-planner duty?"

"The first," she said quietly. "The resort's assigned wedding planner is plenty competent enough to oversee a seated rehearsal dinner."

"But you want to be there for your sister?"

Alexis shrugged. "She doesn't need me. My mom's always been the quintessential helicopter mom. And Roxie's never been as close to Dad as me, but she's still his little princess. They've got her needs covered."

"And Adam," he said gently.

"Right," Alexis said. "And Adam."

He listened carefully to her tone then, trying to identify how much of what was going on here was bitterness, how much was embarrassment, and most damning of all, how much was pain.

A little bit of everything, if he had to guess.

"You can ask about it, if you want to," she said, glancing up at him.

"Have I ever told you about Kara?" he asked, not looking at her.

She shook her head. "I don't think so."

"Ex-girlfriend," he said, slowing to a stop as he turned to face the water.

Alexis came to stand beside him, the sand damp underfoot.

"I thought I was going to marry that girl," he said,

more to himself than to her. "I used to think about the chubby, fat babies we'd have. The chubby dog."

"Why was everyone chubby?" she asked. "What were you feeding them?"

Logan tilted his head back and laughed. It was such an Alexis thing to say—so very practical and no-nonsense—and yet he found it was precisely those sort of comments that made him fall all the deeper.

"I met her when we were fifteen. She was my everything, and when our academic goals had me moving to New York for university and her staying in London, it never even occurred to me that we wouldn't make it."

Alexis smiled. "You're a romantic."

"I suppose. Or a fool."

"No," she said firmly. "A romantic."

"Aren't those the same thing in your book?" he said, looking down at her.

She met his eyes. "Is that what you think of me? That I don't believe in romance?"

"Oh, I think you believe in it. For other people."

She lifted her shoulders and looked back out at the water. "So what happened to your Kara and all your chubby dreams?"

He smiled. "What you expect. We started out emailing every hour, talking every day. I'd phone her right before I knew she'd be going to bed, and talk her to sleep, then go about the rest of my afternoon and evening. Then it was emailing every day, talking every week. Then . . . I don't know—less than that, I suppose. I guess I noticed, but I don't know that I cared. I just thought it was the nature of busy university schedules and that everything would be back to normal during holiday and summer. And then after graduation . . ."

"The fat babies and dog," she supplied.

"Yes, and for what it's worth we also had a cat, but the cat was never fat," he mused.

Alexis laughed.

"She broke up with me," he said. "Quietly, over the phone, about a year after I moved to New York. She met someone else, a bloke that lived in the dormitory across the way."

"I'm sorry," she said quietly.

He put his hands in his pockets and shrugged. "It was a long time ago. But it hurt. I know that's not a guy thing to say, but it took me a while. The thought that someone I loved would choose to love another instead of me . . . that took a while. When I found out she and the wanker were getting married, and that she would have the fat babies and the fat dog with him and not me, that hurt, too. Even though it was years later and I'd moved on. What I'm saying is that it's okay to hurt, Alexis. It doesn't make you weak or pitiful. Sometimes you can just hurt."

She nodded, and for several moments she said nothing, but then she took a deep breath and started to speak, the way he knew she would.

"My story's a lot like yours, but I suspect you already know that," she said, standing perfectly still, eyes locked on the waves.

"Tell me anyway."

"Adam and I met at Harvard Business School. He was . . . well, like you said, he was my everything.

I think it was the first time in my life that anything had really mattered to me as much as school and my professional dreams."

She licked her lips, tucked another strand of hair behind her ear even though they refused to stay. "I didn't date much in high school, and when I did, I figured there must be something wrong with me, because I never developed that gushing, all-consuming infatuation that my girlfriends had. But then I met Adam, and I *got* it, you know? I got what the whole love thing was all about. I understood what it meant to be consumed with another person."

Logan gritted his teeth and tried to remember that they were talking about a long-ago boyfriend from a decade earlier.

"We talked about marriage. Not in the imminent sense, but I think we both thought it was an inevitability. We were so good together, you know? We knew that we both wanted a career and a family—"

"Were your pretend babies chubby, too?"

She laughed. "I suppose so. To be honest I didn't visualize that part quite as much as the Belles, I suppose because I thought I had all the time in the world. Adam and I would date, then get engaged, then get married, then be married, then build our empires, then have the babies . . ."

"You're a bit terrifying. You know that?" he said.

She smiled, but it was small. Forced.

"I took him home for Thanksgiving. It was the first time he'd be meeting both my parents at the same time, since they insisted we all spend holidays together, even after the divorce. And it felt very . . . I don't know, grown-up. *Real*. And the part that bugs me more than anything is that I wore the fancy black dress and the heels, got my hair blown out and my makeup professionally done—not because my mother expected it, as was normally the case, but because I wanted to. Because I wanted to look pretty for Adam. I thought it would be our next important step forward."

Ah, sweetheart, he thought, already not liking what he was hearing.

"You can probably get where this is going," she said with another smile that wasn't a smile. "Roxie was home that same weekend, and even though I knew she'd always been beautiful, always been charming, always been perfect, I didn't think . . . I just never saw it coming."

Logan's teeth clenched. "Behind your back?"

"No," she said quickly. "No, nothing like that. They're better people than that. But sometimes I wonder if *that* would have hurt less. If walking in on them kissing or screwing while I was still with Adam might have hurt less than seeing the moment they fell in love."

"They've been together all this time?"

She nodded. "Yep. Nearly ten years. And if you're wondering why they haven't gotten married until now, if it's had something to do with me . . . I don't know. I think so."

"Is your family the hash-it-out type, or the sweep-it-under-the-carpet type?" he asked, looking down at her bent head as she intently watched her toes curl and uncurl in the sand.

"Somewhere in between. My dad tried not to get

involved, my mom was scandalized but also elated that at least *one* of her daughters had landed a guy like Adam for the long haul, and Roxie and I . . . I don't know. We talked about it back then. Adam and I had been broken up for about a year by then, before she came to me. She asked my permission; I gave her my blessing. Adam, too, and then we've all just sort of . . . moved on. Done the best we can to avoid the awkward."

"But you haven't moved on," he said quietly.

He thought at first she wouldn't respond, and when she did, she spoke quietly. "I thought I hadn't. Up until tonight, I thought the wound was still raw. No, it *was* raw."

"But?" he asked, turning to face her.

"But . . ." She glanced back out at the water again. "Looking at Adam isn't easy, seeing him with Roxie the night before their wedding isn't easy, but in some ways I'm relieved that it's happening. Like maybe this is the closure I've needed. I've never really let myself think about what would happen if Adam came back to me, but seeing him tonight I realized that I wouldn't know what to do if he did."

"You're not in love with Adam, Alexis," he said quietly.

"I know," she whispered, turning toward him and lifting her face. "But I'm not ready to be in love with anyone else, either."

He smiled, even though her words dug at his soul a little bit. "Nobody's asking you to be."

Her brown eyes drifted over his face, and when she smiled again, he saw that it was genuine—that she was relieved to know that he wasn't going to insist that she love him.

Don't rest too easy just yet. I have plans for you.

He had the pieces of the puzzle now. He understood that she wasn't some fragile girl on the verge of heartbreak but a confused woman who knew she needed *something* but didn't know what.

Lucky for her, he *did* know what she needed.

"So what now?" she asked quietly.

"Now," he said, extending his elbow, waiting until she took it before turning them back the way they came. "We go back, drink some wine, and eat the food the servers are probably terrified to put in front of you lest you don't like your garnish. We'll laugh at the way your father's wife will ogle my fine arse. Then we'll go back upstairs, flip to see who gets the bed and who gets the tub as a bed."

"You get the tub," she said stubbornly.

"Is that so?" He dangled her Jimmy Choos out over the water.

She laughed and grabbed at his arm. "Don't you dare."

"I can get my own room if you'd like," he said, watching her face. "I realize I'm crossing a line, and I don't want to make you uncomfortable."

She gave a laugh. "Didn't we prove last week that it's the other way around? You're the one who needs to watch yourself around me."

There it was.

Logan stepped forward, slipped his free hand behind her neck and waited until she reluctantly met his eyes.

"About that night," he said softly.

She groaned. "Do we have to?"

"I was trying to do the right thing," he said softly. "I did do the right thing. You'd have hated one of us in the morning. You know you would have."

"I know," she said quietly. "And I know I'm supposed to thank you for being a gentleman, but the thing is . . ."

"Yes?" he pressed when she broke off. "Be brave, Alexis. What is the thing?"

"It hurt," she whispered. "It hurt that you didn't want me enough."

Or was it that I wanted you too much, he wanted to retort. *Was it that one night wasn't worth risking a whole forever's worth of nights?*

"Let me show you otherwise," he said, letting his thumb brush her cheek.

"I can't," she whispered.

Logan shoved aside his disappointment

"Tell you what," he said softly. "Tonight, I get my own room. Give you some time to think."

"About what?"

He leaned his mouth down until it hovered just a heartbeat from hers. "About how good we could be."

She leaned in slightly, and he leaned back, though it nearly killed him to do so.

"Think about it, Alexis."

"And then what?"

"And then tomorrow night, you'll decide. Do you want me to sleep in my own room?" His thumb slid down and drifted across her lips. "Or yours?"

Chapter Twenty-Two

THIS ONE. DEFINITELY THIS one," Logan said with an appreciative moan, warbling around a bite of Bavarian cream–filled chocolate cake.

"You said that about the last five," Alexis said as she snuck another bite of decadently rich cake off their shared plate.

"How many options do we have?" he asked.

Alexis glanced down at the beautifully printed tasting card. "Seven. We still have carrot cake with mascarpone frosting and key lime with coconut cream frosting."

Logan scooped up another bite of chocolate cake. "All this time, how did I never know your job was this amazing? I'm thinking of dropping the silent-partner bit, tagging along to all your tastings. I'm quite good at it, you see."

She smiled. "I do see. But here's where I break your heart and tell you that while wedding planners often coordinate cake tastings, we don't usually taste the cakes ourselves."

"But sometimes?" he asked hopefully.

Alexis rolled her eyes. "Sure, I guess. If the bride's the indecisive type that wants a second opinion."

"Excellent," he said, waving his fork at her. "I'd like to meet these brides."

Alexis smiled as she allowed herself another bite of cake. Generally speaking, she wasn't prone to having a sweet tooth, but the pastry chef at the Naples Ritz-Carlton most definitely knew his or her way around chocolate cake.

"Isn't it a little last-minute to be doing this?" Logan asked.

"It was supposed to happen on Thursday," she said, licking her fork. "But Roxie wasn't feeling well."

Roxanne had called Alexis at seven a.m. this morning from the foot of the hotel toilet with yet another round of morning sickness. The eight o'clock rescheduled tasting was a no go.

Alexis had been about to suggest to her sister that they default to a safe vanilla with raspberry filling when Logan returned from the hotel gym and suggested that they do the cake tasting.

And it had sounded . . . well, hell, it had sounded *fun*.

"Okay, I have a question," Alexis said as she reached forward and pulled the carrot cake from the lineup of remaining plates. She liked the way they'd done things around here. There was no hovering by hotel staff, rushing them to choose. Instead, a sharply dressed woman named Summer had presented the seven options along with the tasting card and her phone number, telling them to take their time and call her when they'd selected their favorite.

The complimentary champagne didn't hurt, either.

"Hit me," Logan said, his fork already poised to dig into the carrot cake the second she removed the plastic wrap.

"Logan. Does the silent-partner bit of our arrangement ever bother you?"

He glanced up in surprise. "You talking specifically about the *silent* part of our arrangement, or the fact that I own half the company?"

"The silent part," she clarified. "If you tell me you question owning half the company, you may as well pulverize my heart."

He flicked a finger over her nose. "Well, aren't we hyperbolic this morning? The answer is no, I don't mind in the least that my role in the Belles is just between us. But . . . neither would I mind if that information was made public."

"It would certainly make dinner parties easier," she said. "I'm always thinking that one of us might slip and mention it, and while I wouldn't mind the others knowing, I do worry they'd be upset they didn't know earlier."

"Well," he said, taking a bite of the carrot cake, "I've got a bit of good news, then. They know."

Her mouth dropped open. "What?"

"They know," he said, waving his fork. "I told Josh on account of the NumberSync arrangement, he told Heather, and so on."

"Huh," she said after a long pause. "How do you feel about that?"

Logan adjusted his glasses. "Don't mind one bit."

She studied him. "Really? But it was your idea to keep it quiet."

"Yes," he said slowly. "But that was a good many years ago. Things change."

They certainly do, she thought, as she fiddled with her watch.

Take, for example, the fact that she and Logan might very well be spending the night together tonight.

Alexis was surprised to realize just how much she didn't want the weight of that decision to be on her shoulders. Normally she loved control. Needed it. But with this, she was too afraid of making the wrong decision.

On one hand, she thought perhaps they needed to do this to move on.

On the other hand . . . it could ruin everything.

No big deal.

Oddly enough, it wasn't the thought of sex with Logan that had her on edge.

It was moments like last night, when he'd held her hand. Stayed up way too late watching a movie with her before going to his own room.

Moments like now, when they sat side by side, the conversation easy, the mood light.

It planted the seed that the sex could be something more.

Alexis was a little alarmed by how much she wanted to pursue that.

"I know that look," Logan said, giving her the side eye. "Have a bite of carrot cake. It heals all manners of tricky problems."

"I don't like carrot cake," she said. "Vegetables do not belong in cake."

"So why are we tasting it?"

"Because it's not my wedding, it's Roxie's, and Roxie likes carrot cake, so if this one's good, it should be in the running."

"Unless the cake is made of saltines and ginger ale, I doubt your sister is going to be enjoying much of it regardless. As far as whether it's good," he said, taking another huge bite, "I can't decide."

She smiled. "Yes, the way you're wolfing it down suggests that it's complete rubbish."

"There you go again with the Britishisms."

Alexis sipped her champagne. "Can we go back to the whole silent-business-partner thing for a minute?"

"I figured we would."

She studied him. He was wearing shorts and a blue polo shirt that managed to look both country-club and resort casual, especially with his hair still a little damp from the shower.

"Have you ever wanted to get out of our arrangement?" she asked. "I could afford to buy back your half. Own the Belles outright."

He gave a small smile as he shoved the carrot cake aside. "I figured this conversation might be coming someday."

"Would you sell?" she asked.

He blew out a breath. "Is that what you'd want?"

Alexis looked down at her glass, slowly rocking the remaining bubbles back and forth in the flute. The truth was, thirty-three-year-old Alexis didn't think about owning her business outright nearly as much as her twenty-three-year-old self might have imagined.

On one hand, the career woman in her loved that

idea. On the other hand, the thought of the Belles without Logan didn't feel like the Belles at all.

Sure, it was her company, her brainchild, her baby. Logan's contributions had been solely financial over the years, and yet . . . that wasn't quite accurate.

There was plenty to be said for his role as sounding board. He'd been there since the very beginning. Believed in her when nobody else had, let her talk through the bad ideas, then nudged her back toward the good ones.

Alexis was the face of the Wedding Belles—she was its heart—but Logan Harris was its skeleton. The sturdy, constant frame that enabled it to exist.

"You're my partner," she said, holding his gaze. "I like it that way."

"Is that your way of saying you've made a decision about tonight? You'll need to give me some warning. I need to prepare myself for being a soiled dove if I let you have your way."

Alexis giggled. An honest-to-God giggle. Who was this light, charming version of Logan? And who was she when she was with him?

"You really should decide to invite me over though," he said a bit huskily. "I've been tortured these past few days, you see. Tortured by the memory of you in those delectable pajamas. Tortured by the memory of how perfect your skin felt beneath my palm."

Alexis choked on her champagne.

"Sorry," he said with an unapologetic grin. "Was I not supposed to mention that?"

"You were not," she said, her voice husky, both

from the champagne burning her esophagus and something that felt suspiciously like arousal.

"Okay, so we've established that I'm the best silent partner of all time, you don't like carrot cake, and that your pajamas are far too tiny. What's next? Shall we talk about your knickers?"

Knickers, she thought with a smile. Honestly.

"Key lime," she said, pulling the last plate forward.

"So fruit is acceptable in cake, but not vegetables?" he asked skeptically.

"Precisely," she said, taking a bite and then moaning a little. "Oh my God. That one. It has to be that one."

He said nothing, and she glanced over to find him watching her with dark eyes.

"What?" she asked.

He shook his head and jabbed his fork at the plate. "Nothing. Just feeling a bit . . . frustrated."

You and me both. Alexis let herself wonder what it would be like to let her mouth melt against Logan's, to let the kiss evolve into the removal of clothes and the feel of skin on skin, hands everywhere, mouths everywhere . . .

Alexis touched her fingers to the side of her neck, finding it slightly damp. When had it gotten so warm in here?

Logan was digging his fork into the cake, but instead of lifting it to his mouth he held it out to her, eyebrows raised in challenge. "You seem to like this one."

I like you.

Alexis hesitated only briefly before closing her lips over the fork, tasting the way the tart lime mingled with the sweet coconut. And it was delicious—it really was. But not nearly as delicious as the way Logan was looking at her, watching her tongue as it dabbed frosting off the corner of her mouth.

Nor was it as delicious as the way he made her feel.

Her gaze dropped to his mouth, and she remembered his words from yesterday: *think about how good we could be.*

She'd been thinking about it, all right. Thinking about putting a hand behind his head, tangling her fingers in his hair, and kissing him until they had no choice but to go upstairs to her room . . .

But then *her* head kept getting in the way. Along with her stupid, logical brain that told her this was a very, very bad idea.

Something told her she was about one Logan gaze away from telling her brain to stuff it.

"So how are we coming along?" Summer chirped, striding back into the room, her bright aqua stilettos announcing her presence. "Narrow it down?"

Alexis's eyes closed briefly in frustration, but Logan looked unfazed as he smiled at the other woman. "Yes, we're thinking half chocolate, half key lime."

"Can do," Summer said, tapping it into her iPad. "Seventy-five of each, right? I think it's so smart that you opted for cupcakes. Not only can we make those same day, but they're so much more fun to eat, don't you think?"

"I do," Logan said as he stood and drained his champagne.

He held out a hand to Alexis, and she rolled her eyes, because this was becoming a thing with him, the hand-holding.

She ignored the hand and he blew her a little kiss in response.

Summer was beaming. "You two make a gorgeous couple."

"We get that a lot," Logan said, before Alexis could respond.

"What are you doing with the rest of the day? The ceremony's not until seven, and if I remember correctly, hair appointments start at four?"

It was a little unnerving hearing someone other than herself rattle off wedding details.

"What time are they setting up for the beach ceremony?" Alexis asked. "I can head down there, make sure the chairs and arch are exactly—"

"They've got it under control," Logan said, gently taking her arm and leading her toward the door.

"No, but I can—"

"We really do have it under control," Summer said, a little tightness in her smile. "I've been here four years, and my associate's been here for eight. We've got a few of these under our belt."

Alexis gave an apologetic smile. "I'm meddling, aren't I?"

"The term you're looking for is *control freak*," Logan said, sparing Summer from having to answer. "Now quit your interference so we can get a good spot."

"A good spot where?" she asked in confusion as he led her out of the cake-tasting room.

He gave her a once-over. "Tell me you brought a bathing suit."

"It's Florida. Yes, I brought a bathing suit."

"Tell me it's a bikini."

Her eyes narrowed. "It is."

"Tell me it's tiny."

"Logan."

"That's all right," he said, tugging her toward the elevators. "I'll just see for myself in a minute."

Chapter Twenty-Three

S ERIOUSLY, ALEXIS, WE'RE FINE," Heather's voice chirped on the other end of the phone. "The bride's getting her hair done, sipping a Bloody Mary, and eating a bacon breakfast sandwich from Starbucks. She couldn't be happier or less stressed."

"A Bloody Mary? She better not be wearing her dress!" Alexis said, as she stood in front of the mirror and held her cell phone with one hand, reaching up to adjust the strap of her bikini top with the other. Damn, she shouldn't have eaten all that cake and champagne before prancing around half naked in front of Logan. She felt super bloated.

Since when did Alexis care what she looked like in front of Logan?

"Oh shoot, you're right," Heather said. "And I probably shouldn't have had her put the dress on *before* feeding her pomegranate seeds and a grape Popsicle."

Alexis sighed and dropped her hand. "Am I being a control freak?"

"A little, but I sort of expected it."

"Yeah, you're not the first person to tell me that today," Alexis said as she pulled her Kindle off the nightstand and dropped it into her beach bag.

"Logan?"

"And the resort wedding planner. And I'm sure my mom is saying it, but I haven't really had to spend time with her yet, so I'm pretending she's not here."

"But you're having fun, right? Tell me you're having fun."

"You know, I kind of am," Alexis replied slowly.

"You sound surprised. Honey, a beach vacation in Florida is supposed to be fun."

"I know, it's just . . . the circumstances for coming down here aren't exactly ideal."

"Right, what with the whole my-pregnant-sister's-marrying-my-ex thing, you mean?"

"Yeah. That."

Although interestingly, hearing Heather say the words aloud didn't nip at her emotions quite as much as they had even yesterday, and she had a good sense of why.

Logan.

"And how's our boy from the other side of the pond faring?" Heather asked casually.

"Oh, you mean how is the accountant you sent down here to rescue the damsel in distress doing?"

"Does he sunburn?" Heather mused. "I want to say yeah, but I could also see him being one of those annoyingly easy-to-bronze types."

"Don't change the subject. He shows up pretending

to be my boyfriend? Really? What is this, a Nora Ephron movie?"

"It was the group's idea. You know how he gets. Very out of hand."

"Who?" Alexis demanded. "Specifically."

"Can't remember. Like I said, group decision. As in, there *may* have been a group message going around, and it may have come up that it would be great if you didn't have to be single while you were down there."

"But I am single," Alexis ground out. "And I'm fine with that."

"I know, but come on—isn't it a little fun to pretend?"

"I guess it isn't completely miserable," Alexis responded carefully. "Especially if he hangs up his towels in the morning"

There was a moment of silence.

"Wait," Heather said slowly. "He's staying in your room?"

Alexis paused in the process of dropping her sunscreen into her bag. "No. I don't know. Maybe tonight."

"Definitely not part of the group plan," Heather said with a laugh. "But apparently it was part of *Logan's* plan. That sly dog."

"Sly indeed," Alexis said. She went to the window and looked down at the pool. She scanned for Logan, but she was too high up, the pool too crowded. She'd sent him down without her, saying she needed to work.

Mostly she needed to get her head on straight.

"But you're considering it? Letting him stay over tonight?" Heather said.

"Honestly?" Alexis muttered. "I'm not really sure I've been *letting* Logan do anything the past couple days. Has he seemed . . . different to you?"

"How so?"

"I don't know. Cocky. Deliberate. A little cunning."

"I don't know. Logan's always seemed a little that way to me."

Alexis wrinkled her nose. "Really?"

"Sure. You know, like, first glance, shy and bookish, second glance, sneaky sex god."

"Huh," Alexis said slowly.

Heather sighed. "You're hopeless. Okay, I've got to run, but just tell me one thing: Has he kissed you yet?"

"No."

"You sound glum."

"I'm . . . confused," Alexis said. "One minute he's making it very clear that he wants me, the next he's stepping back."

"He knows you well," Heather said. "He knows it has to be your decision. He's just doing what he can to make sure you make the right one."

"Which is?"

"Let's just say when you do sleep with him, promise to tell me how it is?"

"Heather!"

"Oh, would you look at that—bride's gone and gotten red dye number three all over her dress. Gotta run!"

"Heather!"

"Love you. Bye."

Alexis took a deep breath after Heather had clicked off, knowing that she was just playfully pushing her buttons, but the thing was . . . Alexis didn't used to have buttons to push. At least not ones that anyone knew how to find.

Now she was feeling all . . . confused.

She had free time, sunshine, an ocean view, and she couldn't seem to remember why she was upset about Adam and Roxie's wedding in the first place.

And she knew exactly whose fault it was.

Slipping into her beaded flip-flops, Alexis threw on her cover-up, pulled her hair into a haphazard knot, and stormed out of her room and toward the swimming pool, fully prepared to tell Logan to stop meddling with her tidy little life.

His text had indicated he'd grabbed them two chairs just to the right of the pool bar, but when she got down there, she figured he must have moved. There was an elderly couple reading the newspaper under a giant umbrella, a dad with his little girl who was eating a jelly sandwich, most of which was on her face, a group of giggling twentysomething girls, an insanely good-looking gay couple rubbing lotion on each other, a rather large man eating a cheeseburger, but no sign of Logan.

She started to pull out her cell to text him when the group of cute girls shifted slightly, revealing what they were flocking around.

Who they were flocking around.

Logan.

What the—

Alexis took a step forward, only to skid to a halt again once she took in why they were flocking around him.

Holy crap.

In all her fantasies—and there may have been a few, against her better judgment—Logan Harris hadn't looked like this.

To think for eight years she'd been drinking coffee every Monday and Thursday with Clark Kent when she should have been sharing a hotel room with Superman.

Alexis was pretty regimented with her fitness schedule. Yoga on weekdays, cardio on weekends. But Logan apparently was in a whole different ball game, because he had abs, biceps, the whole deal.

And his little flock of admirers had definitely noticed.

He said something likely adorably British that sent the girls into a flurry of giggles.

Alexis moved forward, and even though he was wearing aviator glasses shielding his eyes, she knew the second he saw her. She knew because she felt it. Felt the heat rise from her toes to her scalp, and not from the sun.

He smiled then, and a couple of the more observant girls turned to see who he was looking at, disappointment unmistakable on their faces.

Yeah, that's right, ladies. He's with me.

Wasn't he?

Sort of.

"Hello, Alexis," he said casually, once she was within speaking distance.

"Oh my God," one of them whispered. "That accent."

"Hi," she said, feeling a little nervous.

"Sorry, darling," Logan said to one of the bolder girls, a blond coed with huge tanned boobs. "That seat's saved for my friend here."

"Friend?" the girl asked hopefully. Teasingly.

For God's sake, take a hint.

"Run along now, love," he said, adding a wink to soften the dismissal.

They sighed, giving Alexis one last glare and Logan a chorus of high-pitched, breathy *"Bye, Logans!"* before they sauntered their tight college-aged butts to the bar.

"Well. Someone's popular," she said, her tone a little snippy as she dropped her bag to the pavement.

"Someone's jealous," he countered.

She started to take off her cover-up but then bit her lip and glared at him. "Okay, seriously, I have to ask. What is with all of this?"

She waved her hand over his body.

He glanced down. "I take care of myself."

"No, *I* take care of myself. You look like you're from Krypton."

He laughed. "If it makes you feel any better, I have to wear the glasses whether I'm wearing the suit or the cape. My eyesight's for shit no matter what."

"So those are prescription?" she asked, glancing at his aviators. "Are you nearsighted or farsighted? I always forget."

He laughed and lay back in his chair, long legs stretched in front of him, tanned, toned, with just the right amount of body hair. "Just when I think you're about to start thinking of me differently, you want to know about my vision. Sit down, Ms. Morgan, before you piss me off."

She did, but she didn't remove her cover-up, and he looked over at her, pulling down the tops of his glasses so he could stare at her still mostly clothed body. "Seriously? You're going to be that woman."

Ugh. Fine.

Faking confidence she didn't feel, Alexis reached for the hem of the cover-up, quickly yanking it up and off before she could rethink it.

His smile was slow and teasing. "So it *is* a small bikini."

"It's a bikini," she snapped as she grabbed her suntan lotion out of her bag. "Of course it's small."

She'd just popped the top of the lotion when he snatched it out of her hand.

"Hey!"

"SPF seventy," he said with a smile. "I should have guessed."

She reached for it again, but he held it away, sitting upright and patting the spot between his spread thighs. "You need someone to do your back."

"I can do it."

"Not as well as I can do it."

"Logan—"

"Are you scared, Alexis? Scared of my hands on you? Worried you'll invite me to your room tonight?"

His tone was joking, but somehow Alexis knew those eyes had just gotten several shades darker, even behind their protective aviators wall.

"Of course not."

He patted the spot again, wiggled the SPF in a taunt. "All right then. Prove it."

Chapter Twenty-Four

THE SECOND ALEXIS'S TIGHT butt hit the chaise lounge in front of him, Logan wondered if he'd made a mistake.

Not with the *what* so much as the *where*.

Nothing but a little string tied in a tiny bow kept Alexis from being topless and within easy reach, and a crowded pool was not where he wanted to be right now.

"You smell like lemonade," he said, trying to distract himself as he squirted some of her sunscreen into his palm and began to warm it between his hands.

She turned her head, showing him her incredulous profile. "Lemonade?"

He laughed at the irritation in her tone. "It's a good thing. Who doesn't like lemonade?"

"Yeah, see if you can find me a woman who appreciates being compared to a tart flavor that usually makes people purse their lips in repulsion," she said sarcastically.

"I didn't say you smelled like lemons; I said you

smelled like lemonade. Which has sugar in it. Also, why are we having this conversation?"

"You started it," she muttered, turning her head back around.

He smiled a little at the tension in her shoulders. She sat ramrod straight, and he knew instinctively she was nervous. Nervous about him touching her. Nervous, perhaps, about her reaction to him touching her.

Although the last bit might have been wishful thinking on his part.

The second Logan put his palms on her, he didn't just think he'd made a major misstep. He knew.

Her skin was smooth and warm from the Florida sunshine, the shape of her lean and toned. No way would touching her back be enough. He wanted all of it—all of her.

And he'd put the damn ball in her court.

Stifling a groan and hoping his stirring cock didn't turn into a full-blown hard-on, Logan moved his hands from the tops of her shoulders to the center of her neck, his thumbs swiping down along her spine as he explored her shape.

Alexis's head fell forward, and he brushed a strand of hair away that had fallen out of her bun.

"Okay?" he asked, his voice a good deal more raspy than it had been just minutes before.

She nodded once.

Logan's hands continued their exploration, taking his time as he smoothed the lotion over her skin. They both stilled when his fingers brushed the string of her bikini top, and he wondered if she was imagining what he was imagining. He closed his eyes, his fingers demanding the slow tug of one of the dangling ends until the knot released, until the top loosed so that he could slide his hands around to her front . . .

Alexis's breathing quickened and Logan gave a pained smile, realizing that she was doing exactly as he was: fantasizing about the two of them together.

Torturing them both, he trailed his fingers along the top of the string, showing her the promise of what would happen if they were alone.

Growing bolder, he slid his hands around toward the sides of her body.

His palms were all business, keeping up the pretense of rubbing in the lotion, but his fingers were all play as they flirted with the soft skin of her sides, skating over the outer edge of her ribs.

Her breathing hitched, and Logan grew ever bolder, his fingers sliding upward until the pads of them just barely skimmed the outside of her breasts.

He couldn't help it. He groaned. A barely there, under-the-breath groan, but it was real and raw and he wanted her to hear it, wanted her to hear him wanting her on this primal, essential level.

He wanted this woman. Years of fantasizing about what it would be like to feel her, and here he was so close and yet so damned far.

"Excuse me, is somebody using this chair?"

Both he and Alexis jumped, and he turned his head to see a middle-aged bald guy with a hot pink frozen drink in his hand pointing to Alexis's vacated chaise lounge.

"Oh yeah, that's mine," Alexis said, scooting further away from Logan.

"Ah, sorry. Looked like you two were sharing," the

man said with a friendly wink before he wandered away to find an available chair.

Shit. Exactly what Alexis didn't need: a reminder that they'd come rather close to putting on a public show.

Alexis all but plastered herself against her own chair, and as he expected, her cheeks were flushed pink, although he didn't know how much was embarrassment and how much was arousal.

She reached forward and snatched up the sunscreen bottle from the table between them, refusing to meet his eyes as she squirted some into her hands and smoothed it over her lower back, which he hadn't gotten to, what with all but feeling her up.

"Alexis—"

She shook her head to interrupt him. "What was your plan there, hotshot?"

He didn't reply, pushed his glasses on top of his head and waited patiently until she huffed out a breath and met his gaze.

"Don't know that I had one," he said slowly. "I was acting on instinct."

"It was—"

"You liked it," he said. "Don't try to take away what just happened."

"I don't even know what just happened."

"Game playing isn't usually your style, Ms. Morgan."

"Neither is public groping," she said.

Logan smiled at the uncharacteristic snippiness of her tone, knowing she was unbalanced. Exactly as he needed her to be.

He reached up, flicked a finger so that his glasses slid back down on his nose, ignoring her.

Lord, but she was difficult.

Out of the corner of his eye, he watched as she put sunscreen on her lower body. His teeth ground as her hands moved up over her inner thighs, exactly where he wanted *his* hands. His mouth.

Was she trying to kill him?

She blew out a breath as she snapped the lotion closed and sat back against the chair, her fingers tapping against the towel.

He wasn't the only one who was on edge.

He didn't even bother to hide his grin as he lay back in his own chair, face tilted up toward the sun.

"You seem agitated," he said.

"I'm not."

"Okay."

She crossed her arms. Uncrossed them, then sat up once more. "Maybe I need a drink."

"I'll get it," he said, swinging his legs around the side of the chair before she could. "White wine?"

She bit her lip thoughtfully. "How about a margarita?"

"Coming right up," he said, looking down. "But Alexis?"

"Yeah?" She glanced up at him.

"A drink won't fix what's got you all riled up."

"And I suppose you have a solution," she said, pushing her sunglasses further up her nose.

Logan reached down, toyed with the string tied around her neck, letting his fingers linger at the nape momentarily. "Maybe I do."

Chapter Twenty-Five

"Lexie, honey, your nose is sunburned! How'd you let that happen?"

"Her name's Alexis, Mom. And she looks beautiful."

Alexis glanced up from where she was helping to zip Tawny's dress and smiled gratefully at her sister, although she wanted to tell Roxie not to bother. Her sunburned nose was just the hundredth thing her mother had found to complain about since the women had met up to primp for the wedding.

"Oh honey, don't be shy. Just push the back fat in there," Tawny said jovially, taking a sip of her white wine. "Spanx can only do so much."

Alexis couldn't help the small smile, because while it wasn't the first time she'd tried to help an older woman into a too-tight dress, and she was certainly no stranger to the role of Spanx in today's wedding market, it was different being a part of the wedding party.

Roxie had pulled her aside after dinner last night and made Alexis promise that her primary role in the hours and minutes before the ceremony would be as sister and not wedding planner. And though Alexis had to admit it was taking all of her self-control not to dash down to the beach and double-check that everything was perfect, she also had to admit it was sort of nice to kick back and sip champagne in the enormous bridal suite her father had reserved for the day.

Even her mother's constant jabs couldn't get her down. In fact, she was even starting to find them sort of entertaining, in an eye-roll sort of way. For years, Alexis had thought she was the bane of her mother's existence and had avoided her as much as possible. But seeing Cecily now through the eyes of an adult, she realized that her mother was pretty indiscriminate when it came to her criticisms.

With the exception perhaps of Roxie, nothing pleased Cecily Morgan. Her bed was too soft, her pillows too hard. Her oceanfront suite was noisy, her bathroom too steamy, the provided bottled water not her favorite brand. And so on.

Disloyal as it was to think so, Alexis couldn't help but think that maybe there was a reason her dad had found happiness with Tawny. The older woman was a piece of work, liking her wine a bit too much, her clothes consistently a size too small, but Tawny also seemed to love life, liked to laugh too loud, and with the exception of Alexis's mother, she seemed to get along with pretty much everyone.

Finally Alexis managed to get the zipper up, although she was slightly sweaty and out of breath by the time she accomplished the feat.

"There!" Tawny said happily, patting her mostly flat stomach. "A size four!"

Alexis's mother rolled her eyes. "I'm a size two."

"Yes, dear, but you look like a cadaver," Tawny muttered as she pulled a bottle of pinot grigio out of an ice bucket and refilled her glass.

Cecily turned furious eyes on Alexis. "Isn't part of your job supposed to be keeping the peace?"

Alexis shrugged. "You told me to stop being a control freak."

"Besides, Mama, if it were Alexis's job to keep the peace, she'd be escorting you out," Roxie said gently, kissing her mother's cheek to soften the criticism.

Cecily stiffened. "I just want my beautiful baby's day to be perfect."

"It is perfect," Roxie said, smiling at the small group of women. "Because I have all of you."

Although Roxie had invited a good number of friends, everyone from sorority sisters to her country-club cronies, she'd insisted that it be family only before the wedding.

Alexis thought it was sweet that she'd included Tawny in the family gathering, even if her mother had looked like she wanted to murder someone—probably Tawny.

"You look beautiful," Tawny said, patting Roxie's shoulder affectionately. "That dress is perfect."

"You think so?" Roxie asked nervously, glancing down. "It seems so plain, but a beach wedding isn't really the place for a ball gown. Plus, my figure's not exactly what it once was."

Roxie may not have been quite as slim as her nonpregnant self, but she was no less beautiful. She'd opted for a cocktail-length dress in pure snowy white.

The one-shoulder cut was the perfect choice to show off her toned upper body, and the shimmering embroidery on the bodice kept it from being too plain.

As for the bride herself, she looked every bit as radiant as she should. Roxie had opted to leave her hair down in loose waves, her makeup fresh and glowing with a swipe of coral gloss to complete the look.

"You're perfect," Cecily said, dabbing at her eyes. "And nobody say another word that will make me cry."

"You should have used waterproof mascara," Tawny said sympathetically. "You want to borrow mine?"

Cecily opened her mouth, likely to say something catty, but Alexis cleared her throat.

"No, thank you," Cecily managed through clenched teeth. "I'll be fine."

"Okay, but—"

"Ladies," Roxie interrupted before the two older women launched into fight number 402 of the day. "Can I get a moment to talk to Alexis alone?"

Cecily looked at her phone. "Oh, but the ceremony starts in twenty minutes. We have to get you down there—"

Alexis wrapped her arm around her mother's shoulders and led her toward the door of the suite. Tawny followed after, blowing a tipsy kiss at Roxie.

"I'll make sure she's down there on time," Alexis said as she gently eased her mother out the door.

"But—"

Alexis held up a finger. "No *but*s. I've done this before, remember? On-time weddings are sort of my specialty."

"Okay," her mother said. "But don't upset her."

"I'll try not to pull her hair," Alexis murmured.

"Okay, and no talking about—"

Alexis shut the door in her mother's face and felt only the tiniest bit bad about it.

She turned back to her sister. "You okay?"

To her dismay, her sister's eyes were filled with tears.

"Roxie." Alexis moved toward her sister, already reaching for the box of tissues she insisted be kept stocked in bulk in the bridal suite for exactly these types of occasions. "Don't you dare cry," Alexis said, handing her sister a tissue. "Then Tawny will be back up here shoving waterproof mascara at you, as though we hadn't already thought of that, and Mom will feel threatened and then the whole day will dissolve into a size two–versus–size four fight club."

Roxie let out a watery laugh as she flicked her eyes upward and blinked rapidly. "I will not cry, I will not cry."

Alexis waited patiently for the threatening tears to go away before speaking.

"Talk to me," she said quietly. "Preceremony jitters, or something more? Do you need me to get Adam?"

Roxie glanced down at the tissue she'd been shredding. "This isn't about Adam. Or the wedding, really. It's about . . ." She sniffled. "I'm really, really sorry, Alexis."

"For what?" Alexis asked, pulling the mangled tissue away from Roxie's fidgeting fingers and handing her a fresh one.

Her sister's eyes met hers. "For putting you through this. I know it can't be easy watching me and Adam getting married."

Alexis's stomach dropped, just slightly. Oh dear. This talk.

"I was so worried you wouldn't come," Roxie whispered. "And the worst part is, I wouldn't have blamed you, not even a little bit. Not after what we did."

Alexis felt tears prick at the backs of her eyes. "You didn't do anything. You fell in love. Even I could see that."

"We hurt you," Roxie countered.

"You did," Alexis acknowledged. "But it's been a long time, honey. I've had time to get over it."

"Are you sure?"

Alexis opened her mouth and then shut it. Was she sure? Just a few weeks ago, she'd been miserable. Hell, the fact that Roxie was pregnant with Adam's child had been enough to send the normally deliberate, regimented Alexis into a spiral of self-doubt and online dating.

And yet now that she was here, now that it was actually happening, Alexis was a little shocked to realize just how little she cared.

Well, she cared.

But she cared as a big sister who was excited about her little sister's big day.

Not as the bitter ex-girlfriend who'd been passed over for someone prettier and more charming and likable.

Because while Roxie was all of those things . . . sweet and soft and completely adorable, Alexis was realizing that maybe that was okay.

She was realizing that Roxie wasn't better than her, just different. That just because Roxie was Adam's dream girl, it didn't mean that Alexis couldn't be someone else's dream girl, just by being herself.

It didn't mean she couldn't be Logan's dream girl.

There it was.

The thought was as right as it was forbidden, but now wasn't the time to deal with whatever was simmering between her and Logan. Now was the time to finally make things right with her little sister so she could marry the man of her dreams in peace.

"I'm really happy for you," Alexis said, wrapping her sister in a hug. "Really."

Roxie hugged her back with a small sigh of relief. "Does this mean we can get back to normal?"

"What do you mean?" Alexis asked, pulling back and adjusting one of her sister's waves so that it curled just so against her shoulder.

"I miss how close we were when we were younger," Roxie said. "There's been a rift between us, and I get it. I mean, the rift was about Adam, and I'm not sure there's any way we could have avoided that, given the circumstances. I just wish there was a way we could get back to where we were."

"We will," Alexis said confidently. "I guess I just needed time."

Roxie's smile was sly. "Or you needed Logan."

Alexis froze. "Logan is—"

Roxie laughed. "You know what? Don't finish that sentence. I love you to death, but I have the feeling you're about to say something that's utter nonsense."

"I don't do nonsense," Alexis replied, her tone slightly grumpy.

"Of course not," Roxie said as she rummaged around on the vanity for her lip gloss. "But some advice?"

"No, thanks."

Roxie rolled her eyes as she dabbed on the gloss.

"That man is crazy about you, but he's careful about showing it. That tells me he knows you. Knows that you're a flight risk, and he's being cautious."

"Okay, yeah, we're not doing this," Alexis muttered, even as Roxie's words gave her butterflies. She reached for her sister's arm. "Come on—let's get you downstairs."

"Wait, I haven't given my advice yet!" Roxie said, dodging Alexis's grasp.

"Fine," Alexis said, giving a panicked glance at the time. She'd never had a bride be late before, and she'd be damned if she started with her own sister.

Roxie stepped toward her, placing both hands gently on Alexis's cheeks, as though trying to still Alexis's worrying—about everything.

"You need to trust this man," Roxie said. "I know it's not your thing, I know you like to be in control, but I think it's time you give up a little control so that you can get something even better in return."

"I don't know if there is anything better than control," Alexis said, only half joking.

"Trust me—there is," Roxie said confidently. "And Logan Harris is the one to show it to you."

"But—"

Roxie held up a hand. "Nope. I'm currently closed to objections. Just promise me you'll think about it. And Alexis?"

"Hmm?"

Her sister's smile was soft and beautiful. "Take me downstairs to get married."

Chapter Twenty-Six

"L OGAN! PUT THAT BACK. They haven't served the cupcakes yet," Alexis said, swiping the key-lime cupcake currently ensnared in his hand.

He lifted it out of reach, catching her against him when she stumbled just slightly in her stiletto sandals as she made a grab for the dessert.

"You did that on purpose," she said accusatorially, her hands finding his chest.

Logan smiled and looked down at her, painfully attractive in the gray suit and moss-green tie that matched her dress almost perfectly. Heather or Brooke must have given him a heads-up on her dress color.

"Did what?" he asked.

"You keep finding ways to ensure we touch," she accused. "First at the pool, now this."

"Is that so?" he said, his hand palming her back for a moment longer than necessary as she righted herself.

She held out an expectant hand. "Give me the cupcake."

"You said yourself there's no traditional cake cutting," he said.

"That doesn't mean you can just go making a muck of the display," she said, jabbing an explanatory finger at the table. "Look, now there's an empty spot in the tower and everyone will think it's fair game."

"Relax, I got permission."

Her eyes narrowed. "From whom?"

"The bride and that cute wedding planner."

Alexis's eyes narrowed further, and he laughed. "What, you thought you could be the only cute wedding planner?"

"Of course not," she muttered. "Heather and Brooke are gorgeous. And Summer is . . ."

"Cute," he said with a smirk as he took a bite of cupcake.

"Fine, yes, she's freaking adorable," Alexis all but snarled. "Are you trying to make me jealous again?"

Logan reached for her elbow, moving her out of the way of a tipsy older couple doing what seemed to be an odd blend of the chicken dance and the twist.

"What do you mean *again*?"

Alexis moved slightly closer to him, the champagne she'd had making her bold. "*Dr.* Valentine," Alexis couldn't help from saying.

"Hey, women aren't the only ones who fantasize about hot doctors," he said.

She pinched his arm slightly just above his elbow and he grinned down at her. "You know, for someone who's made every effort to keep me at a distance, you certainly seem to be fishing for dangerous conversational topics tonight. What's gotten into you?"

Alexis glanced out at the dance floor where her friends and family were dancing their hearts out to varying degrees of coordination. "Weddings," Alexis said simply. "Weddings have gotten into me."

"You deal in weddings all day, every day," he said, finishing off the cupcake. "But this one's different, isn't it? Because of your sister."

"She looks happy, doesn't she?" Alexis said, her eyes finding Roxie and Adam, who were at the center of the dance floor, alternating between holding on to each other and flailing around to a Destiny's Child song Alexis hadn't heard in years.

"She does," Logan said. "*They* do."

Alexis said nothing for a moment, waiting to see if there was any pang at the mention of Adam.

But just as during the ceremony when she'd watched her ex-boyfriend exchange vows with Roxie, she felt only a bittersweet sort of emotion. Not so much for the man, but for the moment.

For years, Alexis had been mastering the art of emotionally separating herself from weddings.

Sure, she got teary now and then, but it was her job to keep her wits about her, to think, rather than feel, on the off chance something went awry in the logistics.

But tonight, Alexis hadn't been the one to ensure the wedding went off without a hitch. Tonight she'd been there as a guest.

As a *sister*.

And as a result, she was feeling all the feels.

Namely, an acute awareness of how badly she wanted that for herself.

It sounded strange, given her career choice, but until she'd seen her sister slip that ring on Adam's finger, looking at him like he was the only other person who existed in the whole world, Alexis hadn't realized just how much she wanted to get married.

She also hadn't realized just how far she'd strayed from her girlhood dreams.

Once upon a time, she'd wanted it all. The career, the perfect home, the perfect husband, the baby, the social life.

Then *life* had happened. Her perfect guy fell for her sister, and she'd responded by letting herself get utterly, totally consumed in her career. A job couldn't hurt you the way a guy could, no matter how much you loved your company.

And yet something was shifting. Tonight she realized she wanted a boyfriend, a husband, a family, not as a way of catching up to her sister or proving to the world that she'd moved on from Adam, but because she wanted somebody to love.

And she wanted somebody to love her the way that Adam loved Roxie.

"I think I need one of those cupcakes," she said.

"That's not what you need."

"It's not?" She glanced up at the strong line of his jaw, longed to run a finger along it.

"Nope."

"All right, I'll bite. What do I need?"

Logan held up his hand in what was becoming an increasingly familiar—and dear—gesture. "Dance with me."

She was already shaking her head. "I don't dance."

"It's always the ones who don't dance that need to the most."

"Logan—"

Just then the music changed, the first notes of Etta James's classic "At Last" coming through the speakers.

"Even better," he said softly as he pulled her onto the dance floor. "Now you don't have to dance so much as hold on to me and sway."

"Another excuse for us to touch," she said quietly. "Shocker."

"One day, Alexis," he said, drawing her close, "you're going to ask me to touch you."

She shivered a little as his hand found her lower back. "Is that so?"

"It is."

"I haven't decided," she said quickly. "About tonight."

"The night's young yet," he whispered against her ear as he pulled her all the way in. "Plenty of time."

Alexis tried to think of another snappy retort, but then Etta's gorgeous, lusty voice started singing about love coming along, about lonely days being over, and Alexis found she didn't want to push him away.

Not physically, not emotionally.

She wanted to be held by this man who'd been so unwaveringly there for her every step of the way. A man who, if she was being perfectly honest, she hadn't treated nearly as well as he deserved.

Logan was a good dancer, and she let him lead her in a gentle sway that was more of a hug than it was a dance, more of an embrace than it was movement.

Her eyes closed as his chin brushed her hair, his

thumb lightly rubbing along her knuckles as he held her hand.

Alexis was surprised to find her eyes watering, although she wasn't sure why. Out of the sheer perfection of the moment, perhaps.

The realization that nobody had ever got her like this man did. And it wasn't just that he understood her.

It's that he understood her, rough edges, jaded coolness, and all, and stood by her anyway.

Trust this man, Roxie had said.

She hadn't understood exactly what her sister had meant until now. Of course she trusted Logan. He owned half her company, he had keys to her apartment, he'd be there in an instant if she needed anything, *ever*.

But that wasn't what Roxie had been talking about.

She'd meant for Alexis to trust Logan with her heart—to trust that he wouldn't hurt her.

"You're so different this weekend," she heard herself whisper.

He pulled back slightly and looked at her. "I'm still me."

"I know. I didn't mean it like that; I just meant that there's this whole other side of you. You're charming and a little bossy and . . ."

She looked away, embarrassed, but he lifted their joined hands, using the side of his thumb to nudge her face back around toward his. "And what?"

Alexis laughed nervously. "Hot. You're a little bit hot when you're like this."

He didn't smile back, but his eyes were warm as they scanned her face.

Her breath caught as whatever he was feeling flitted across his face. But it was gone before she could identify it, and she had the strangest sense that she'd missed something important—vital.

The song came to an end much, much too soon and Logan released her long before she was ready.

"All right, Alexis," he said, his face back to being easy, affable Logan. "Now we can get you your cupcake."

Alexis reached out and grabbed his hand before he could walk away.

He glanced down at their linked fingers, then back up at her face, lifting his eyebrows in question.

Trust him.

Alexis swallowed. She just didn't know if she could. But she knew that she wanted to try.

She lifted her chin, faking confidence she didn't feel in what she was about to do.

"I think I'd prefer to eat the cupcake in my room. If you'd care to join me?"

Chapter Twenty-Seven

LOGAN STARED AT HER for several long beats, and for a terrible minute, she was afraid he was going to say no. That maybe this had all been some horrible game on his part, and all he'd really wanted was for her to capitulate, not to actually kiss her.

Not with as much of a hot mess as she was.

But just when she was ready to go running off the dance floor and stuff her face with humiliation cupcakes, Logan took two steps forward, diving his hand into her hair, which she'd left loose as a nod to New Alexis.

His fingers tugged her hair just firmly enough to get her attention, the intensity on his face belying the happy music and tipsy wedding attendees too lost in Queen's anthem to give them much notice.

"Be sure, Alexis," he said, sounding more British and alpha than ever. "Be very sure, because if I kiss you now, I won't stop. I won't stop until I've kissed you everywhere and until you're asking me to do it again and again and again."

Her eyes closed as he ran a thumb along her jaw-line, and she didn't know what was hotter, his touch or his gaze.

"Be sure," he said again.

"Yes," she whispered. "I'm sure."

She expected him to kiss her then and there, audience be damned. She wanted it.

Instead he made a low growling noise of satisfaction in his throat before he set a hand against the small of her back and led her off the dance floor.

Alexis was so dazed about what she'd just done—about what she was about to do—that she didn't immediately realize what he was doing until he'd stopped touching her.

She watched as he commandeered a bottle of champagne and two flutes from the bartender, dropping a twenty in the tip jar before he nodded toward the cupcake table.

"Grab two of those."

"You want cupcakes now?" she asked.

"No, I want cupcakes after," he said with a wink.

Oh. Okay then.

She could get behind that. She even did one better. She grabbed two cupcakes in each hand, two of each flavor, not caring in the least how it would look to everyone when she waltzed out of her sister's wedding a little early with a handful of cupcakes and expensive champagne.

Alexis wouldn't go quite so far as to say the bride and groom owed her, but . . . sort of.

Somehow they managed to get out of the room without running into her parents, and when they got into the elevator, Alexis heard a happy, high-pitched giggle and was a little surprised to realize it came from her.

"Are we really doing this?" she asked, glancing up at Logan, whose eyes were locked on the ascending numbers of the elevator, obviously impatient to get to their floor.

He glanced at her, his eyes smiling. "Absolutely."

She waited for the panic to set in, but . . . nothing. This was right. She knew it down to her bones.

Once they were inside her hotel room, Logan's impatience seemed to slow, and she tried not to stomp her foot at the way he took his time wrapping a hand towel around the neck of the champagne bottle and popping it open with deliberate movements, opening her laptop to turn on music.

She set the cupcakes aside and sat on the bed, preparing to take her sandals off, but he shook his head.

"Don't. Leave them. Leave all of it."

She went all melty at the quiet command in his voice and obeyed, letting him pull her to her feet before he handed her a glass of the champagne.

"I've waited a long time for this, Alexis Morgan. And I fully intend to take my fucking time."

She shivered as he clinked their glasses together, and she took a sip of the delicious champagne, holding his gaze the whole time, telling him as best she knew how that she wanted this, too.

"There we are," he said quietly, apparently seeing what he needed to on her face.

She took another sip, let him take the glass aside, setting it on the dresser before he reached for her.

His hands cupped her face, and her eyes closed as his thumbs ran along her cheekbones.

Slowly, his face lowered to hers, and when his lips melted against hers, it was perfect. More than perfect, because their other kisses had the element of surprise or exploration, but this one . . . this kiss was about claiming.

He was claiming her as his for the night, and she claimed him right back as her hands lifted, sinking into his hair.

Logan moved closer, nudging her lips even further apart in a deliciously wet, open-mouthed kiss.

When he finally pulled back, her breathing was ragged, her brain feeling wonderfully addled.

He pulled her hair to one side, tugging it to expose her neck to his mouth, and she moaned when his lips trailed over the exposed skin of her throat.

He took his time, lips moving up and down, his teeth nipping as his tongue soothed until she was clawing helplessly at his shoulders.

"More," she whispered.

"You want me to touch you?" he murmured, kissing her mouth again.

She nodded.

He pulled back and kicked his shoes to the side before capturing her gaze with his. "Take my jacket off, Alexis."

She blinked a little, surprised at how much his bossiness turned her on, as well as how badly she wanted to get him out of his clothes.

Her hands lifted to his shoulders as she eased the

suit jacket away from his perfectly shaped upper body. She set it on the bed and glanced back.

"Now the tie," he commanded.

She swallowed, fingers faltering just slightly as she loosened the knot and slowly pulled the tie off, adding that to his jacket.

He opened his mouth again, but she stepped closer, pressing her lips against his as she ran her hands greedily over his torso.

"Let me guess," she said, before her teeth pulled at his bottom lip. "You want this shirt off?"

His breathing was a little ragged now, and she smiled, finding that she enjoyed the control nearly as much as she enjoyed being bossed around.

Alexis took her time with his buttons, delighted to see that he'd forgone an undershirt, likely due to the Florida heat.

She tugged the shirt from the waistband of his pants so she could get at the last buttons, then rested her hands on his bare waist, feeling the hard contours of his ribs beneath her fingers.

"Logan," she whispered, pressing her mouth to the center of his chest.

"Christ," he muttered, his hands lifting to her face, tilting it back so he could plunder her mouth with a kiss.

The kiss turned into a battle of tongues and touching, and she pushed his shirt off his shoulders at the same time his fingers found the zipper of her strapless dress and pulled it slowly to its lowest point at the small of her back.

They both froze for a second as gravity did its

thing, the dress pooling to her feet with no straps or zipper to hold it up.

He moved back slightly, and she prepared herself for the stab of embarrassment at the fact that Logan Harris was seeing her naked.

It was a hundred times more intimate than any other man seeing her naked, and yet also a hundred times more right, she realized.

The way his head tilted down to see her, the way his eyes worshipped her was perhaps the hottest thing she'd ever seen.

"I've imagined this a thousand times," he said huskily.

"Why, because I'm not wearing a bra?" she asked, feeling the need to lighten the mood. She'd hardly needed one—she wasn't exactly big up top, and the front of the dress had been plenty padded.

"No," he said, as his hands trailed up her side. "Because it's you."

Then his hands closed over her breasts, and Alexis forgot all about lightening the mood. She only wanted this moment to happen over and over, to feel Logan's palms cup her breasts, to feel his fingers toy with her nipples for tonight and every night to follow.

He seemed to know instinctively that she was sensitive, never being the type to tolerate rough play at her breasts, and this thumbs rotated over her nipples with just the right amount of pressure, his uneven breathing telling her he was enjoying it every bit as much as she was.

Logan bent, his tongue flicking lightly over her nipple, and her head fell back with a sharp cry. Over and over he licked her, his tongue warm and wet and teasing until he finally eased one taut tip into his mouth and sucked her as his hands palmed her ass and pulled her hips forward.

"More," she said, grinding herself against him shamelessly. "I want more."

Logan straightened, pushing her gently backward until her knees hit the back of the bed. She sat, intending to try again with removing her shoes, but he caught her hand, lifted it to his mouth, his lips fluttering over her inner wrist. "Leave them."

Then he was on his knees before her, his fingers sliding into the sides of her underwear, pulling them down her legs with unabashed intention.

"Logan," she said, feeling suddenly shy.

He met her eyes as he tossed the underwear aside. "My rules, Alexis."

"Since when?" she challenged.

He rested his hand on her stomach and gave her a wicked grin. "Since always."

Then he pushed her back, the element of surprise on his side as she landed on her elbows on the soft mattress and he moved more completely between her thighs, his palms rubbing up the inside of her legs as he spread her open to him.

He traced a finger up her inner thigh, his gaze flicking back to hers at the exact second he dragged his index finger down her seam.

His eyes locked on hers, somehow so much hotter, given his glasses. Clark Kent had a very, very naughty side.

She cried out, and he did it again, pressing further

this time, spreading her open as his finger worked to spread her moisture everywhere.

"Jesus," he muttered, reaching his other hand down to the fly of his pants and adjusting himself before he returned his attention fully to her, his hands spreading her even further open.

He surprised her then, his hands reaching for hers, pulling them toward him and resting them palm down on the comforter, pressing down. "You'll want to hold on, darling."

The second his head dropped, his tongue parting her in delicious invasion, she knew what he meant.

Logan was good at this. Really good.

Her fingers clenched and unclenched over and over again at the comforter, but it didn't do anything to help with the sweet torture of his mouth between her legs.

Again, the man seemed to know her, knowing that she wanted just one finger inside her, gently stroking, knowing that she liked it best when he used the flat of his tongue to move up and down against her sensitive bud with relentless wet strokes.

She tried to keep her hands on the blanket, she really did, but when he quickened his pace just slightly, finding the exact rhythm that had her exploding into his mouth, her hands found the back of his head, her fingers gripping his hair hard as ecstasy rocked her body.

Time seemed to stop, and when she finally stopped shuddering, she found him watching her, his eyes daring her to be embarrassed about the way she lay splayed out before him, or the way his mouth glistened from the moisture of her.

"Thought so," he said smugly, even though she hadn't said a word. At least she didn't think so. Who knew what she'd been moaning midorgasm.

Logan stood, his hand unbuckling and removing his belt as he went to her bag in the corner of the room.

"What are you doing?" she asked. She had to try twice to get the question out, because her throat was so dry.

In response he walked back to the bed, tossed a strip of condom wrappers beside her. *How had he known they were in there?*

"Open one of those," he said, as he bent to pull off his socks, before unzipping his pants.

"Thought you wanted to take your time?" she teased, reaching for a condom as she scooted up the bed.

"Changed my mind," he said, shoving his pants and briefs down his legs, unabashed about the way his cock sprang free, long and thick and rock hard.

"Oh?" she said, unable to look away from him.

He gave her a smug look. "Unless you want me to wait."

Alexis could only shake her head.

He held her gaze as he pulled the condom from her hand, his gaze still on hers as he rolled it on.

She felt the tiniest bit of discomfort at just how confident he was in bed. It signaled a man with plenty of experience. Jealousy clawed at her chest, just a little bit.

He came onto the bed beside her, one hand lifting to remove his glasses, and she caught his wrist.

Logan looked at her curiously.

"Can you leave them on?" she asked shyly. "Or is that weird for you?"

He smiled and bent down to kiss her. "You mean are they going to go flying off if I fuck you too rough? Nah, we should be fine."

Alexis felt a fresh rush of moisture between her legs at his dirty mouth. Just because her breasts liked it gentle didn't mean all of her did.

"Out of curiosity," he said, as he slowly rolled her to her back, his elbows resting on the bed on either side of her head, "do you have a glasses fetish?"

"Not that I'm aware of," she said, spreading her legs so he could settle between them. Alexis caught his face between her hands. "I just want to know that it's you. I don't want to forget for one moment who's inside me."

"Ah, Alexis."

His expression turned tender. He captured her mouth in another kiss as his cock nudged past her folds. Her breath caught. This was happening. It was really happening.

And God how she wanted it.

"That's it," he whispered as she opened her thighs further to accommodate him. "Open to me, baby."

She did.

And he slid inside with zero hesitancy, burying himself to the hilt as though he'd been made to claim her, and she to receive him.

Alexis felt a split second of pure shock, and then there was pleasure. Only deep, rolling pleasure as he eased out, then thrust back in, harder this time, driving her up toward the headboard.

She reached her hands upward to brace herself on the headboard, her eyes opening and meeting his in challenge.

"Yes," he whispered, bending his mouth to her neck.

And then he began to fuck her, hard and purposeful, but not fast. He wanted to make it last. She sensed the moment he got close, knew it in the way his breath quickened, and then he'd slow again, his hips moving in indolent circles as he took her in lazy, hard strokes, only to quicken once more as though he was having a private war between body and brain.

She knew the moment his body won out over his mind.

His hands reached up for hers, his fingers crushing hers as his hips began pumping with purpose.

Logan's chest rubbed against her breasts, their sweat-soaked skin making the sensation almost too arousing to bear, especially with the way she was stretched around him, the way each stroke pressed his body more firmly against her clit.

On purpose, she realized, as she opened her eyes and found him watching her, eyes burning hot behind the glasses. He wasn't going over the edge without her, which was fine because she wasn't going without him, either.

She lifted her head, her tongue dragging over his throat. "I want you. I want you to come inside me."

His eyes closed and he let out a guttural groan. "Damn you, Alexis."

He screwed her even harder, his pace relentless,

and Alexis went over the edge of ecstasy as she cried his name.

"Yes," he said. "Fuck, yes."

And then he came with a vicious roar, driving her even further toward the headboard, even as his arms held her head protectively, face buried in the crook of her neck.

As her orgasm cooled from fireworks to smoldering embers, she turned her head, kissing his ear since it was the only part of him she could reach.

In the past, this was the point where she'd start trying to figure out her extraction plan—brainstorming the least awkward way to get out of bed, and into the bathroom, and out of his life.

But this wasn't just any guy. He wasn't an easy lay. He wasn't just someone to scratch the itch.

It was Logan.

And the reality of sleeping with Logan was as wonderful as it was utterly terrifying.

Chapter Twenty-Eight

THE FIRST THING LOGAN did the morning after sleeping with Alexis was reach for her, desperate for a reminder that what they'd done—what they'd done all night long—hadn't been a dream.

His eyes flew open when his hand found cool sheets instead of warm woman, and he sat bolt upright, trying to get his bearings.

The comforter was at the foot of the bed when it'd been kicked somewhere around round two. The champagne glasses were half-empty from when they'd been consumed around the same time.

He smiled when he saw the empty cupcake wrappers. Those had been the rewards for the third and final round.

Logan dragged his hands down his face. Hell, he hadn't fucked like that since . . . ever.

Still, the temptation to gloat was tempered somewhat by the missing Alexis, and he swung his legs over the side of the bed with the intent of finding coffee and woman.

But which first?

Coffee. He needed caffeine to deal with the missing woman.

He was just picking up the phone to call room service when he heard it—running water in the bathroom.

He breathed out a sigh of relief, dropping the phone and reversing his decision on the order.

Woman, then coffee.

The door wasn't shut all the way, and he nudged it open to a face full of steam. Alexis liked her showers hot, apparently. Just like she liked her sex.

The hotel shower was an enormous, glass-enclosed affair, but Alexis had her back to him, her face to the stream, and she didn't see him approaching.

Through the fog of the glass, he could just make out the outline of her perfect, small ass, and he shook his head ruefully as he realized round three wasn't the final after all.

He was definitely up for round four.

Hell, he wondered if there was even such a thing as a limit when it came to his want of Alexis Morgan.

Logan had done a shit ton of fantasizing about sleeping with her over the years, and the fantasies didn't even come close.

Now the real battle began: figuring out how to keep her.

She spun around in surprise as he eased open the door, but instead of freaking out about her privacy being invaded, she smiled in invitation.

"Morning," she said huskily, moving aside to make room for him beneath the stream. He barely withheld his wince. She *really* liked it hot.

But then her slim arms wrapped around him from behind, her hard nipples pressing into his back. "You're not in here because you have to hurry, are you? What time's your flight?"

Just like that, reality crashed around Logan, and he realized he'd have to implement phase two of his plan a bit ahead of schedule.

"Actually," he said, turning slowly and wrapping his arms around her. "I was thinking of staying for a few more days."

She blinked up at him in surprise, her dark lashes spiky, the faintest amount of makeup remnants beneath her eyes. "Staying?"

"I could use the vacation before things start to gear up with NumberSync and before I tackle the headache of transferring some of my clients to a new accountant."

"Right, of course," she said. "Well, I'm sure a room will be available. I imagine they're not as busy during the week, and most everyone else from the wedding will be leaving today . . ."

"Including you?" he asked quietly.

She lifted her hand, wiping water out of her eye. "My flight's not until three, but . . . yeah. Including me."

"Or . . ." he said, his hands sliding over her waist and down to her butt, cupping her and pulling her forward and against his already hardening length. "You could stay."

"Stay."

She said the word slowly, as though in the process of sorting through how she felt about it.

Sort it out, Alexis. And while you're at it, how about you sort through how you feel about me.

"I can't stay," she said.

But there was the slightest hesitancy in her words, as though they were coming from a script she'd written years ago and was struggling to recall.

"Why not?" he countered, knowing that right now she needed to work through the logistics before she could even access her emotions.

"Well, the Belles—"

"Will be fine. You don't have any midweek weddings scheduled, and Brooke and Heather can deal with any prep work for your Saturday wedding."

"How do you know I don't have any midweek weddings?"

He lifted his shoulders guiltily, and she laughed. "Of course. Heather and Brooke told you. This was always part of the plan, wasn't it?"

"Always," he said, taking advantage of her smile to kiss her.

She gave a small sigh when he pulled back. "Logan, what we did last night was—well, I don't even know that there's a word, but I need some time to think—"

"No you don't," he said firmly. "I mean, sure, you do, and I'll respect that, but just give me two more days of not thinking. Two more days of sex and sunshine and of being Logan and Alexis as lovers, not Logan and Alexis as we were before."

"And what about when we go back?" she said warily. "What will we be then?"

"We'll figure it out," he said easily, knowing he couldn't rush her too far, too fast.

She let out a little groan and rested her forehead on his shoulder. "I can't believe how much I want to say yes."

Logan closed his eyes in relief. "So say yes," he said, his hands closing around her shoulders and pulling her back slightly so he could meet her eyes. "Say yes to two days. Harmless. We'll fly back on Tuesday morning, and whatever happens on Wednesday will be your call."

She searched his face. "Really? You'll give me time to sort things out when we get back? You won't expect us to be all . . . coupley?"

He swallowed a little nervously at the thought that his plan would fail. That he'd seduce the hell out of her this weekend only to have her think of the whole thing as some sordid fling. "Sure," he managed. "The ball will be in your court as soon as we get back to the city."

Her fingers trailed down the center of his chest, pausing when they got to his waist, as her expression turned impish.

"And what did you have in mind in the meantime?"

"Well," he said, his voice coming out a little harsh when her hand drifted lower. "I did think our time at the pool was a bit rushed."

"Mmm," she said, her palm wrapping around his cock. "It was. So pool time, what else?"

"We could, ah—I heard someone mention boat cruises," he said.

"I like boats," she said, her hand pumping him in a slow stroke.

"Yeah?" he managed.

Alexis nodded as she leaned into him, her lips sucking at his neck as she sped up her movements, stroking his cock in slick, hot strokes. "So pool and a boat."

"And meals," he said, eyes squeezed shut. "I've heard there's a great restaurant across the street."

"Pool, boat, and restaurant," she said huskily, dragging her lips across his chest in openmouthed kisses. "There's just one problem with all those things."

"Yeah?" he grunted.

Alexis pulled back and gave him a naughty look. "All of those activities require us leaving this room."

And then she gave him a glimpse of heaven as she lowered to her knees, planting a kiss to the tip of his cock.

"I was wrong about something, you know," she said.

His hands tangled in her wet hair. "What's that?"

She wrapped a hand around him, poising him at her lips as she looked up his body. "I don't need you to be wearing the glasses to know it's you. I'd know the feel of you anywhere."

She licked him. "And the taste."

Logan let out something between a groan and an oath as Alexis took him all the way into her mouth, her lips closing even as her eyes stayed locked on his as she bobbed slowly on his cock, her perfect mouth somehow knowing exactly how he liked it as she alternated between sweet sucking and languid licking from tip to base.

"Alexis," he ground out, his hips pumping of their own volition as she sucked him harder. "I'm getting close."

She responded by putting her hands on his hips, holding him still as her mouth moved faster, the wicked gleam in her eyes telling him that was exactly what she wanted.

The thought of coming in Alexis Morgan's prim and proper mouth was the culmination of every fantasy he'd ever had, and he couldn't say no. There was no way he could say no.

He leaned back slightly, one hand gathering her hair in a tight grip before he slapped his other hand against the wall behind him, knowing he'd need something to hold on to when he went over the edge.

She ran her tongue along the underside of him, gripping his balls with her hand, and Logan lost it, his harsh cries echoing through the steamy glass shower as she greedily sucked down every damn drop of him.

"God," he whispered, when he finally managed to find words.

He held out a shaky hand to help her up, which she accepted before wiping her lips daintily. "Logan Harris, I dare say you're almost as delicious as the cupcakes."

"Almost?" he whispered.

She laughed as she reached for the shampoo bottle. "Well, look on the bright side. You've got two whole days to figure out how to take first place."

Chapter Twenty-Nine

A LEXIS HAD ALWAYS ENJOYED packing for a trip. There was something soothing in the orderliness of it all. Of selecting travel-friendly outfits and versatile accessories. The folding and rolling and the little burst of satisfaction when your travel hair dryer fit just so alongside your Tory Burch flats.

To say nothing of all the potential of the trip ahead.

Unpacking, on the other hand, was another beast entirely.

For starters, everything was either dirty or wrinkled, which meant that laundry and dry cleaning loomed, even after your suitcase was empty.

And then there was the arduous task of putting away all the little things. The bracelets back in the jewelry box, the shoes back on the shoe rack that seemed to have shrunk in the time you were gone. Then there was making mental notes of which travel toiletries needed replenishing for next time. Then the backbreaking task of shoving the suitcase back under the bed, all while trying to remember how you got it out in the first place.

The only reward of unpacking was that little jolt of relief one got from being home. The promise of routine, after days of suitcase living and restaurant food and airports.

Alexis gave her suitcase one last kick to get it all the way under the bed, and dropped the last dirty shirt into the laundry pile, and then waited . . .

Waited for the usual sense of relief.

She frowned when it didn't come.

Where was the happiness that she'd get to sleep in her own bed tonight? The elation that tomorrow she could get back to her schedule of early morning yoga, followed by oatmeal with blueberries, and then a jam-packed day of Belles business?

Generally speaking, Alexis wasn't even sure she liked vacations. Sure, she'd taken the odd long weekend here and there, the occasional beach vacation with a friend from college, but mostly, she stuck around New York, having discovered over the years that she got more joy over watching a bride find her perfect dress than she did sipping frozen cocktails by the pool.

But as she stared at her apartment, she felt only regret that her time in Florida was over.

Not because of Florida itself, but because of . . .

Logan.

Two days with him—well, four, if you count the wedding festivities—had been a good deal more pleasurable than two whole weeks lying in the sand and sun *without* him.

She scratched her nose in dismay. Oh dear.

They hadn't flown home together, since they'd booked flights separately. She'd left Naples early that morning and had landed in New York even before his later plane had taken off.

The entire flight home, she'd told herself that it was a good thing. That it was much better for him to see her off in a cab from Florida than for them to have to awkwardly separate at JFK, going to their respective apartments.

This way, they could draw a clean line. Florida time equals hookup time.

New York time equals back to normal.

Her lips pursed. Normal sounded awful.

Normal didn't involve long walks on the beach, or cocktails at sunset, or long, languid nights between the sheets . . .

Normal didn't involve Logan.

Or rather it did, but it involved Logan as her accountant.

Not as her lover.

Alexis shook her head and went to the refrigerator. She'd arranged for groceries to be delivered earlier and was relieved to see that Jessie had put them away as asked.

But as she reached for the chicken breast and spinach she'd intended to put together for a nice, light dinner, she felt only boredom.

She dropped both on the counter, resting her hands on the cool surface. "Get it together, Morgan. This is what you asked for. A fling only."

Still, it had stung a little just how easily he'd acquiesced. This morning when he'd helped load her suitcase into the cab, she'd been expecting—hoping for—a good-bye kiss.

Instead he'd pecked her cheek. *See you Thursday, Alexis.*

Thursday.

When he'd come by, and she'd make them coffee, and they'd discuss the Belles' business and profit margins and whether or not to backfill Heather's position as Alexis's assistant.

There would be no kissing. No touching. No naked time.

Of course, there'd also be no chance of upsetting the status quo. Everything would remain in order and as it was. It was one thing to mix business with a little bit of sorely needed pleasure—it was something else entirely to mix it with something resembling love.

"No," she muttered. "We're not doing that. If Logan can follow the rules, you can follow the rules."

She picked up the chicken, only to be distracted by her cell phone ringing.

Her heart jumped a bit in excitement. Objectively she knew Logan was still on the plane, but it didn't stop her from hoping.

She ran back into the bedroom, fetching her iPhone from the nightstand only to groan at the caller ID. Definitely not Logan.

"Hi, Mom," she said, pleased that her voice only conveyed about half the weariness she felt at the prospect of talking to her mother.

"Hi, Lexie honey!"

Alexis's eyebrows lifted. Honey? Also, was that . . . happiness she heard in her mother's voice?

She decided to test the theory. "How are you?"

"Oh, I'm fine, just fine."

Alexis's mouth dropped open, not only at the words, but at the slight smugness in her mom's tone.

Cecily Morgan was never fine, and yet . . . here she was. More than fine, if she was reading between the lines.

"What's new?" she asked cautiously.

Her mom gave a low chuckle. "You're asking if Dan Berger wanted to see me again after spending all the rehearsal flirting, aren't you?"

Alexis wrinkled her nose in confusion. "Dan Berger. Like . . . Roxie's godfather?"

Daniel Berger and his wife, Cynthia, had been two of her parents' closest friends growing up, although as far as Alexis knew, they hadn't seen as much of them after the divorce. Especially not after Cynthia passed away a couple years earlier from breast cancer.

In all honesty, Alexis had been a bit surprised to see him invited to the wedding, but then he was Roxie's godfather, not Alexis's.

"Yes, Lexie, that Dan Berger," her mom said with exaggerated patience. "He took me to dinner last night, and we're going to a movie this evening. It's so nice to spend time with a gentleman after so many years with your father."

Alexis was pretty sure she heard the silent *The heathen!* that was tacked onto the end of that sentence.

"That's great, Mom. You sound really happy."

"Well, of course I'm happy. It's nice to have a companion."

Alexis felt a little stab of annoyance. "I'm not

disagreeing, but there are sources of happiness other than a man, Mother."

Cecily made a scoffing noise. "Oh, please, dear. You're telling me you're not happier with your Logan than you are without him?"

Her mother couldn't possibly have known how close that careless comment ripped at Alexis.

When would Alexis learn? When would she learn that she was not the sort of woman that made men lose their head? Not the kind that they fought to keep around.

She'd do well to remember that. To remember that it was one thing to let loose and have a bit of fun, but a whole other thing to lose her head.

Or far worse, her heart.

"Logan and I aren't serious," she said quietly.

"Oh, nonsense. I saw the way he looked at you all weekend. Even that idiot harpy Tawny picked up on it."

"I'm not saying he and I didn't have some fun over the weekend, but we're not . . . he's not . . ."

"Well, you'd best lock that down, honey. A good-looking guy with that, and that accent. If you don't, some other girl who's more—"

"Who's more what?" Alexis interrupted angrily. "Who's prettier? More biddable? More likable? More lovable? Someone more like Roxie?"

"Alexis." Her mother's voice was gently chiding and maybe a little surprised.

"Please. Like you haven't thought it a million times," Alexis muttered.

"Of course I haven't!"

"Then why are you so determined to make sure I

have a man?" Alexis said, years' worth of bitterness bubbling up out of nowhere. "Why not just be happy for me as I am?"

"You think I'm worried for my happiness? I'm worried about yours."

"I *am* happy!" Alexis said, shouting now. "Not everyone needs a man. Not everyone's entire sense of self-worth has to do with getting a man to ask her to the movies!"

There was a shocked moment of silence.

"Well. I suppose I deserve that," Cecily said stiffly.

"I'm sorry, Mom," Alexis said, lowering herself to her kitchen table and rubbing at her forehead. "It's just that it hurts, a little, to never be enough in your eyes. My dreams aren't your dreams, and I get that, but it doesn't mean I don't want you to be proud of me."

"I am proud of you," her mom said, sounding horrified. "Is that what you think? That I'm not proud?"

"I think you'd be prouder if I had a ring on my finger," Alexis said, deciding that if she was going to be honest, she might as well go all the way.

"It's not that," her mom said. "It's just . . . I hurt for you. After what happened with Adam. It destroyed me a little, knowing my two girls loved the same boy."

Alexis was surprised to realize the memory didn't hurt as much as it once had. "It didn't seem that way. It almost seemed like you thought I deserved it. Earned it, somehow."

"Lexie." Her mom sounded devastated. "I couldn't be more proud of what you've accomplished. It's just that you forget I watched you when you were a little girl, playing with dolls, the way you'd play house. Even the way you doted on your father, bringing him his whisky every night, careful not to spill a drop, just because it made him happy. It's not about serving a man, sweetheart. It's about coming home to someone special at the end of a long day. It's about having a family."

Alexis felt her eyes burn at her mom's words. At the undeniable truth of them. "Yeah, well. I was young then. I'm not so sure everyone's cut out for a family."

"Don't think that," Cecily said stubbornly. "Now, that Logan fellow, he—"

"Isn't here," Alexis interrupted. "He's my friend and my business partner, but we're not going to be seeing each other anymore. Not like that."

"But why?"

Because I can't afford to care more than I already do. People leave. They move on.

She'd weathered Adam leaving. But Logan leaving?

Loving Logan and not having him love her back?

She couldn't. She wouldn't.

"Alexis . . ."

There was a knock at her door.

"Hold on, Mom," she said, pushing back from the table. "Someone's at the door."

Probably one of the girls. They were the only ones with a key.

She froze when she opened the door. No, it wasn't *only* the girls who had a key.

A very sexy Brit had one as well. And currently he was watching her with an unreadable look behind those glasses, suitcase in one hand, briefcase in the other. God how she loved that damn briefcase.

"Logan," she whispered.

Her mom laughed happily in her ear. "I knew it!"

"Alexis," he said with a nod. "May I come in?"

She moved aside, trying to control her foolish, elated heart as he stepped past her.

"Mom," Alexis said, her eyes never leaving Logan. "I'll call you back."

"Oh, take your time, dear," her mom said in a knowing tone. "Take your time."

Chapter Thirty

ALEXIS LET HER HAND fall to her side after ending the call with her mother, the other hand still on the doorknob.

She was annoyed to realize she felt . . . nervous. Not a feeling she was accustomed to, and certainly not with Logan.

Logan, on the other hand, seemed completely unfazed as he wheeled his bag into the corner of the room where it would be out of the way, and set his briefcase beside it.

He was wearing a white dress shirt and khaki pants, much as he had for most of their time in Florida, although he'd added a blazer, which he shrugged out of now, placing it on the back of her kitchen chair.

"What are you doing here?" she asked, registering that he'd obviously come straight from the airport.

In response, he walked toward her, not meeting her eyes as he plucked the phone out of her hand and set it carefully on the table.

Only then did he give her his attention—his *full* attention.

Their gazes collided and held for several moments. Then a few moments more.

She wasn't sure who moved first, but in the next instant, they were all over each other.

His fingers tangled in her hair, hers clutching at the shirt at his waist, pulling him closer as his mouth slammed down on hers.

The kiss was messy, a little bit desperate, and she loved every moment of its imperfection. Had it really only been a few hours since they'd made love at dawn?

It felt like forever since she'd tasted him, since he'd touched her, and she burned with the need for his hands and mouth to be on her, all over her.

She needed *him*, she realized.

"What are you doing here?" she asked again when he pulled back to nuzzle her jaw hungrily.

In response, his hand slid down from its grip on her hair to cup her breast possessively, his thumb rubbing over the sensitive center.

Alexis's head fell back with a gasp. "*Oh.*"

His hands found the hem of her shirt, tugging it upward, and she lifted her arms to help him.

The second she did, his hands went to her back, flicking open her bra clasp.

His tongue laved over her nipple before the bra hit the floor, and Alexis gripped his head, holding him to her greedily.

"More," she gasped, as his tongue flicked again and again. "More."

His mouth closed around her, sucking even as his hand slid down her stomach, under the waistband of her yoga pants.

"This is what I wanted to do that first night," he whispered, as his fingers stroked her softly over her underwear. "You don't know how badly I wanted to find out if you were wet for me."

"I was," she whimpered.

"Oh yes?" His finger slicked under the elastic of her panties. "And now?"

She didn't respond. She didn't have to; her body answered for her. She was most definitely wet for this man.

He groaned as his fingers explored her, rolling over her clit as he slid two fingers inside her.

It was as though her body were his to control, and for the first time in her life, Alexis wasn't at all sure that she wanted control. Not when his fingers pumped into her with the perfect amount of finesse and roughness, just the way she needed it.

He lifted his head from her breast, straightening so that he could meet her eyes, even as his fingers never stopped their relentless stroking.

He wanted to watch, she realized. Wanted to see her face when she went over the edge.

She wanted it, too, she realized. For right now, just in this moment, she wanted to be vulnerable for him, and she let go, embracing the orgasm that was encroaching.

"That's it," he said in his deliciously precise accent. "That's it, Alexis."

It was her name on his lips that did it, and she

cried out, clamping down around his fingers, her forehead dropping to his shoulder as she let herself unravel all over him.

She couldn't think. Wasn't sure she wanted to.

Alexis closed her eyes, expecting a moment—needing a moment.

Logan didn't give her one.

He eased his fingers away from her gently, but that was where the gentleness stopped.

Before she realized what was happening, he'd shoved her toward the table, turning her and bending her forward.

The rasp of his zipper was followed by his hands sliding into her pants, shoving them down along with her underwear, a heartbeat before he thrust inside her.

Logan let out a harsh groan, thrusting into her twice more with firm, punishing strokes before his hands slid from their grip on her hips, coming forward until they covered her hands where they rested on the table.

It was unexpectedly intimate, being taken from behind in her own kitchen, his big hands covering hers, his fingers twining with hers as he moved inside her.

"I need you," he said, releasing one of her hands to press his against her back, easing her closer to the table. "I need you just like this. Give it to me."

Alexis gave it to him. She arched her back and moved her hips to meet his thrusts with little pants of want.

Logan's orgasm was every bit as explosive as hers had been. She knew it in the way his fingers dug into her skin, knew it in the desperate panic as he growled her name and pumped into her one last time before his body seized up and then shuddered behind her.

The moment was everything. So much more than anything they'd had in Florida, because it was here, at home. It was *them*.

Logan and Alexis.

It was real and important.

Too much, Alexis realized in panic as her weakened body collapsed to the table. It was too damn much.

And it terrified her.

Chapter Thirty-One

YES, I UNDERSTAND, ELLEN, and I'm going to do absolutely everything I can to make sure that the flowers get here, but you have to understand that Mother Nature is perhaps the one lady who doesn't care in the slightest about money and prestige."

Logan watched in amusement as the woman he'd been obsessed with for a good eight years paced around her living room. Her cell phone had been glued to her ear for more than an hour, even though it was nearly nine o'clock on a Thursday night, well past regular working hours.

He couldn't hear Ellen's response to Alexis's words, but the high-pitched chirps he heard coming from Alexis's phone said that Ellen the disgruntled bride didn't like her answer.

"I understand," Alexis soothed gently. "But we knew that getting flowers from the florist in your hometown was going to make things potentially difficult, and I'm afraid the flooding has done just that . . .

Yes, of course I'll call them. I'll do that right now, and we'll get this figured out."

Logan shook his head as he closed the bridal magazine he'd been flipping through disinterestedly and looked at his watch.

He'd known that the wedding-planner business came with plenty of annoyances, but his experience had been entirely in the realm of the Belles' finances, loans, and so on. In the past week, he'd gotten a whole new perspective of the type of bullshit Alexis dealt with, much of it after-hours.

The woman was doing too much. She needed more people. Brooke and Heather were great, but they were increasingly overworked, too, with ten-hour days, not to mention the busy weekends. And as far as he knew, Jessie was pitching in as Alexis's assistant, but that wasn't the same as a full-time wedding planner. If Alexis didn't hire someone new or start saying no to a few more clients, she'd break. Both herself and her team.

No wonder the woman had been so tightly wound for so many years. She had to be.

"Yes, I'll call you tomorrow," she was saying as she tapped something into her iPad with one finger. "Yes, of course, first thing, my top priority."

Hearing that the conversation was winding down, Logan stood and went to the kitchen, pouring them both a glass of the open bottle of merlot on her counter.

He listened as she said her farewells, then approached with the glass of wine.

"Thanks," she murmured, not glancing up as she

accepted the wine with one hand, continually typing with the other on her iPad.

The second she finished that, she reached once again for her phone, distractedly taking a sip of wine as she scrolled through her phone's contact list.

Then she set the wineglass aside, and Logan watched in disbelief as she prepared to make another phone call.

His hand closed on her wrist. "Alexis. No."

Her eyes flicked up. "What?"

He smiled. "It's nearly nine, darling. Let's go get a bite to eat."

"I have work to do," she said, easing her hand away from him.

"It can wait until tomorrow."

She glared at him. "No, Logan, actually it can't."

"Alexis, I'm hungry, and I've been listening to you talk for the better part of three hours. I wouldn't mind—I've worked some late hours myself—but we've already missed the show we were intending to see and the dinner reservations. At the very least let's get a burger."

"We can order in," she said, glancing back at her phone.

"You need to get out of the house, step away for a moment."

"What I need is for you to not tell me what to do." There was no mistaking the anger in her tone.

Well, that was just fine. He was a little angry, too. "You could have called," he said in a clipped voice. "You might have told me you were off schedule, and I could have made other arrangements for the evening.

It's not as though I have nothing else I could be doing right now—I'm a business owner, too, in case you didn't remember." *Actually a multibusiness owner, with an offer to take on a third*, the small, petty voice in his head reminded him.

"I forgot to call you," she said, her attention already back on the phone.

Unbelievable.

"You forgot." His voice was low and angry now, too, and she apparently realized it, because she glanced up, before sighing.

"Look, I'm sorry, all right? I should have called and told you that it was going to be a late night. I won't be offended if you want to head home."

He laughed and rubbed a hand over his hair. "You won't be *offended*?"

Alexis flung her arms to the sides in exasperation. "What is it you want me to say, Logan? I already said sorry, but this is my life, okay? Lots of long hours."

"Yes, all right. But they don't have to be *this* long."

"Meaning?"

"You're going to burn out if you keep at this pace."

She stilled. "Excuse me? You have issues with the way I run my business?"

Our business, he wanted to correct. But then, that wasn't fair. He was a *silent* partner. As a business owner, he didn't particularly care how she ran the Belles. She'd course correct before doing permanent damage to the bottom line. But from a personal perspective, he couldn't sit back and watch.

And more than that, nor would he tolerate it. Here he was, ready to break his parents' hearts for her. Ready to choose her over people who loved him, wanted him around.

And she couldn't even make time for *dinner*?

He was angry. Brutally so. And yet he tried once more to make it work. To make her *see*.

"Alexis, be sensible. You're exhausted, you're tense . . . can you really tell me you're happy right now?"

"I don't need *happy*," she said, turning aside.

"Of course you do," he said, puzzled.

"No, I really don't." She spun back toward him. "I need *safe*. This business is my life. Without it I have nothing. Do you get me? Nothing."

"Okay, well now that is quite a bit of bullshit," he said angrily, stepping toward her. "Is that what you think? That you're all alone?"

She sighed and waved her hand. "Yeah, I know I have the Belles, and—"

"No," he bit out angrily. "You have me."

"For now," she said, her voice tired. "But I can't afford to think short-term."

"Short-term?" he said incredulously. "Does eight fucking years feel short-term?"

She frowned. "What are you talking about? We've been dating, or whatever we've been doing, for a week."

"Only because you've been damned blind," he roared.

Well, bloody hell. There it was.

Alexis took a step back. "What?"

Logan could only stare at her as the truth settled around him like an ice-cold blanket. "I'm wasting my time, aren't I? After all this, after the past few weeks, after Florida, after *all this time*, you don't see me."

"I don't follow."

"Yes you do," he said, bowing his head, very close to being defeated. "You understand exactly what I'm trying to say here; you just don't *want* to understand it. Because you're scared."

"My business is important to me," she said quietly. "You know that."

"Yes. And I respect that," he said. "But what I need to know, Alexis, is whether it is the *most* important thing."

"What are you really asking?" she asked flatly.

"Is it more important than me?"

Her eyes watered. "You're asking me to choose. That's not fair."

"I know." Logan let his chin drop to his chest for a moment and took a deep breath. "I do know that I'm not being fair, but Alexis, you're not being *brave*, and I suppose I'm rushing you, but I don't think I can take any more."

"What are you saying?"

He lifted his eyes and met hers. "You care about me. I know you do."

"What do you want from me, Logan?"

"I want a woman I don't have to jump through hoops for just to get her attention. A woman I don't have to follow to *Florida* to seduce. I want a woman who doesn't look right through me for the better part of a decade. I want a woman who cares about me like I care about her. Who respects me just as I do her."

Alexis made a desperate sound. "Logan. I need more time. Just give me time to sort it all out. It's new."

"It shouldn't be new," he said. "I should have made

my move before now, but I'm realizing it wouldn't have made a difference, would it? I love you with *everything*, and you won't give me even a little bit of *something*."

And I have people in England who do love me. Just like that, the reality settled in. He could stay here, waiting for a woman who might never open to him.

Or he could go home to his waiting family. People who *did* love him.

Alexis's eyes went wide at his proclamation, but that was it. Logan had dropped the biggest truth of his heart—he *loved* her—and Alexis didn't even move, much less speak.

Logan gave a faint smile, even though he felt ready to crack. "I figured as much."

Slowly he leaned down, setting the wineglass lightly on her end table, too afraid he'd crush it with frustration and ache if he didn't.

He turned to go, and finally, Alexis moved. "Logan, wait."

He didn't. "For how long, Alexis?" he asked, pulling his coat off the back of her chair. "How much longer am I to wait? A few minutes? Another hour? Days? Should I give you months? A few more years, perhaps."

She shook her head in frustration. "*Wait.*"

Logan jerked open the door before looking once more at the woman he loved. "Sorry, Alexis. I think I'm done waiting."

Chapter Thirty-Two

"Yes, I realize I'm letting you know early," Logan said curtly as he placed a pair of oxfords into the suitcase. "I'd have thought you'd be happy that I decided to take over the company ahead of schedule." After Logan had stormed out of Alexis's apartment, he'd spent the rest of the night getting piss drunk at a bar, debated calling up an old flame to take the edge off, and had finally given his father a call, hungover but resolved, and told James Harris he was ready to assume the reins of Harris Services just as soon as his father would allow it. An announcement that he'd thought, based on their earlier conversations, would have been met with much more excitement—or as close as his buttoned-up father could come to that emotion—than he was currently experiencing.

"I'm happy," his father said quietly. "I'm just a little befuddled as to what brought on this sudden change of heart. I want to make sure you're doing it for the right reasons."

"I am."

"Son—"

"Dad. Please. You're getting your way. I'm coming home. Let's leave it at that."

"When I told—when I asked—you to come home, I'd hoped it was because you wanted to, son. But I can't help but think you're running from something rather than toward something."

Logan shut his eyes. "Did Mum put you up to this? She already spent an hour trying to talk about my *feelings* without actually saying the word *feelings*. Shall we do that here as well?"

Logan's father cleared his throat nervously, as Logan knew he would.

The Harris family didn't do feelings, and the patriarch was the least of all of them equipped to even try.

"There's nothing here for me," Logan said quietly. "Nothing that I can't take care of from London."

It burned a little to say that outright. Leaving Alexis out of it, it wouldn't be easy to leave New York. The city itself felt like a part of him, but Logan had perhaps underestimated the role that the other people in his life played. His accounting clients. His college friends.

Most recently, and most especially, his family at the Belles.

Too late he was realizing that he was more than an accountant and a silent partner, just as they were more than employees and spouses of employees to him.

Saying good-bye to Josh would be especially difficult, and he wasn't up for it today.

Monday. He'd say his farewells on Monday.

The day after that, he'd fly from JFK to Heathrow without looking back.

As for Alexis . . .

He couldn't go there. Not yet. Perhaps someday she'd simply be a painful part of his past, the way that Adam was a painful part of her past.

But he wouldn't close himself off the way that she'd let herself be closed off.

Alexis had been left alone too long, had let her scars form too thickly, until nothing, not even the fiercest love, could cut through.

Not even *his* love.

"I'll see you in a few days, Dad."

"Logan."

"I gotta go," he said curtly. "I have a few things to take care of."

"All right," his father said quietly. "I love you, son."

Logan's eyebrows lifted in surprise. "I love you, too."

They hung up, and Logan glanced down at the phone. It was the second time in less than twenty-four hours he'd said the words. This time, however, had been a hell of a lot less painful. This time, his heart hadn't been ripped out at the silence that followed.

He felt a little bad about not telling his father the whole story. But he just couldn't right now. He didn't want to talk. He didn't want anyone to tell him that he'd acted hastily. That you don't wait eight long years for a woman and then decide in the span of one evening to give up on her.

But a man had limits, and Thursday night had been his.

It was the simplest moments that were the most

telling, he was realizing. Those everyday moments when you realized what was most important to a person.

For Alexis, that would always be the Belles. Because that was safe.

The Belles wouldn't hurt her.

He got it. He did. He understood her, which was the worst part of it all. It was because he knew her that he'd had to walk away.

But his heart hadn't been able to take another minute of abuse or neglect.

Reluctantly, Logan looked down at his phone again, knowing he had one more phone call to make that would be a hell of a lot harder than the one he'd made to his father.

He dialed the number for his attorney and waited patiently for the receptionist to put him through.

"Mr. Harris," his lawyer, Georgia Lewis, said in her low, melodic voice. "It's been a while. What can I do for you?"

For a split second, Logan was tempted to slam the phone down. To reverse everything and go back to where he'd been just a few months ago.

But he couldn't go back.

And he no longer had anything left to lose.

"Morning, Georgia," he said. "I'd like to talk to you about starting the process of selling my share in a company."

"Ah, sure," she said, clearly a little caught off guard. "Which one?"

Logan adjusted his glasses. "The Wedding Belles."

Chapter Thirty-Three

W HAT DO YOU MEAN he wants to sell?" Alexis practically screeched into the phone, skidding to a halt in the middle of the opulent hotel lobby where she was meeting with a bride and her sister in twenty minutes.

"I just got the call from his attorney this morning," her lawyer said gently. "Apparently he's decided to pursue other interests. Mr. Harris is under the impression that you'd be interested in buying his shares."

Alexis realized her knees were shaky.

Logan wanted to sell his stake in the Belles?

"Excuse me," someone said, bumping into her.

She dazedly moved to a small seating area and lowered to the couch, wondering how many more blows she could take.

Apparently Logan had decided it wasn't enough to end their personal relationship. Now he was severing all professional ties as well.

He was giving up on their business?

Damn you, Logan.

The man was being ridiculously stubborn. He hadn't returned a single text or phone call, and when she'd gone to his apartment, his doorman had told her he wasn't home, and even though Alexis had suspected he was lying, she'd slunk off with her tail between her legs.

Her friends were no help. She wouldn't go so far as to say they were taking sides, but she definitely got the sense that everyone was protecting Logan.

From her.

It hurt, even as she understood.

"Ms. Morgan, you still there?" her lawyer asked.

"Yeah, Mike, I'm here," she said, wrapping her free arm around her waist as though trying to hold herself together.

"What should I tell Mr. Harris's attorney? Are you interested in buying him out? I know when we first started working together, owning your company out-right was the long-term plan."

Yes, but that was before, Alexis wanted to argue. Before I knew that Logan was vital to the Belles.

But even that didn't seem quite right, Alexis realized with a frown. Logan was an important behind-the-scenes part of the company's beginnings, certainly, but was he vital to the Belles' future?

Or was he vital to her?

"If you're not interested, or aren't in a financial place to take over the entirety of the company, I'm sure we can work with their team," her lawyer was saying. "I got the impression that this isn't a fast-cash move on Mr. Harris's part. Perhaps they'd be amenable to a payment plan, or you taking over the company in smaller portions over time. Perhaps from the bank—"

"No, I want it," she interrupted. "Money's not the issue; I just . . ."

"You didn't know he was planning to sell?" Mike asked kindly.

"No," she admitted. "Although I think I probably should have."

"Why don't you take a couple days to think about this," he said. "Ms. Lewis indicated they were in no rush."

She swallowed her bitterness. So no rush to vacate her professional life, then, just her personal one.

"Thanks, Mike," she said. "I'll be in touch."

Alexis hung up her phone, and realizing she still had a few minutes before her next meeting, she pulled out her laptop to tackle a few emails.

In the days since her fight with Logan, the Belles had been the only thing holding her together. To say that she'd recovered from her postvacation work funk was an understatement.

Alexis had hurled herself into all things weddings.

Other people's weddings, that is.

Lord knew there wouldn't be one of her own on the near horizon. She hadn't been able to bring herself to go on another date after her second kiss with Logan, and she couldn't bring herself to reopen any of her dating apps.

It didn't seem to matter what she did. The more she threw herself into work, the more happiness seemed to elude her, which frustrated her to no end.

She'd just have to try harder. Work harder to get

back to that place she'd been before, where the Belles had been enough to make her happy.

Before he'd decided that their perfectly fine relationship was no longer enough and decided to ruin *everything*.

Alexis swallowed and slowly closed her laptop. She stood, making her way toward the main bar area where she'd be meeting her bride.

She could do this. It would hurt for a while, but she'd heal, just as she had with Adam.

But then Logan was so much more than Adam. And this pain was so much worse.

She frowned when she recognized the familiar faces in the bar, but it wasn't her bride.

"Hey," she said as Heather and Brooke watched her approach, with nervous expressions. "What's going on? Where's Melody?"

"Had to cancel," Brooke said, gesturing for the chair across from the love seat where she and Heather sat. "We were there when Jessie got the call, and decided to . . ."

"Hijack the meeting," Heather finished.

Alexis narrowed her eyes but sat down. "I already told you. I'm not ready to talk about it, and I'd ask you both to—"

"Respect your privacy," Heather cut in. "Yeah, we know. But here's the thing, Morgan, you don't need privacy right now. You need a kick in the ass."

Alexis blinked in shock. "Excuse me?"

"Yeah. You heard me," Heather said, lifting her chin. "You're being an absolute—"

"What Heather means to say," Brooke broke in

diplomatically, "is that we think you don't quite grasp the full situation."

"As it relates to . . . which wedding?"

Heather threw her hands up. "I told you. Hopeless."

Brooke leaned forward, her expression earnest. "Alexis, honey, there's something you need to know. Something big."

Alexis's heart began to pound. She could put her head in the sand all she wanted, but she knew this was about Logan.

And from the expressions on her friends' faces, it most definitely wasn't good news.

"Tell me," she said quietly.

It was Heather who spoke up, her voice gentler than before. "Logan's moving back to London."

Alexis felt like her friend had kicked her in the solar plexus. "Sorry?"

"His father is retiring and wants him to come run the company. His parents sprung it on him a few weeks ago, and he was torn. Between family loyalty and . . ."

"Me," she whispered.

"I think he cares about you a great deal," Brooke said softly.

Alexis's eyes closed. "He does."

He loves me.

She hadn't let those words sink in, not really, at least until this moment.

She'd both hoped and feared that they'd been said in the heat of the moment, but she let the truth roll over her now.

Logan Harris loved her. Had perhaps always loved her.

And he was moving to England.

"When?" she asked.

"Before we answer any specifics, we have to know," Heather said. "Do you love him back? Even a little?"

Her eyes watered. "I don't know. I do . . . he's so important, but so are the Belles, and the company is safer—"

"Whoa. Back up. Explain," Heather said.

Alexis opened her mouth to explain all the reasons why a company was more reliable than a person, why there was nothing wrong with a woman choosing a career over a man, why she shouldn't be expected to fall all over herself just because Logan had decided it was time for her to come to heel.

And then she realized . . .

They were all excuses. All sad, pathetic defenses for the one real truth.

"I don't want to get hurt," she whispered. "If I care too much, he'll hurt me."

"More than it hurt to know that he's leaving the continent?" Brooke asked, surprising Alexis by taking a turn at bad cop.

She opened her mouth, but no words came out.

"Alexis," Heather said. "Is this really what you want? We all love the Belles, but the Belles over everything . . . is that enough?"

"It makes me happy," Alexis said stubbornly. "I've been nothing but happy in the eight years since . . ."

Since . . .

Since she'd met Logan in that bar.

Alexis sat back slowly, the truth settling over her in an epiphany that left her feeling dazed.

"Oh no," she whispered.

All this time, she'd thought it was the Belles itself that had saved her back then. She thought it was the Belles that she'd been living for.

It had never been her company.

Yes, she loved her company; yes, the business was incredibly dear to her; yes, work would always be a pivotal point in her life.

But it wasn't her whole life.

It wasn't even the center of her life.

That had always been Logan. Logan, who'd been her rock, her friend, her partner, her . . . love.

She loved Logan. She had always loved Logan, from the very beginning.

"Oh my God," she whispered even quieter.

"She's having her moment," Heather whispered out of the corner of her mouth to Brooke.

"I certainly am," Alexis said, standing and feeling more purposeful than she ever had. "And one of you is going to tell me where I can find Logan. Right now."

Chapter Thirty-Four

W HERE IS HE?" ALEXIS asked the second Josh
opened the front door of his and Heather's
apartment.

"Hello to you, too," Josh said amiably. "Can I get
you something?" he asked, holding up his Coke can.

"Yes," she said with a pleasant smile. "You can
get me your business partner, who's also *my* business
partner, who I know is hiding out here."

She raised her voice on that last part, looking
around the apartment that Josh and Logan had con-
verted into their work space for NumberSync.

There was no sign of Logan.

"Where is he?" she asked again. "Heather said he's
here, but he's not answering his phone."

"Perhaps because it's midday on a Monday," Josh
interrupted. "This is just a guess, but perhaps he's . . .
busy?"

"Spare me the bullshit. I know he's got a plane
to catch tomorrow, and I know he came here to say
good-bye to you."

Josh took a sip of his Coke. "He did. Since I'm not the one with my head up my ass," he added under his breath.

Alexis surprised herself by laughing. "Well played, Tanner. And I deserve that, really I do. But it's really important that I talk to him."

"About . . . ?"

"Respectfully, not your business," she said, adjusting her purse strap on her shoulder.

"Respectfully," Josh countered, his greenish eyes suddenly a good deal less friendly than usual, "you ripped his heart out last time you saw him, so you'll understand why I don't just hand over the GPS coordinates of his current location so you can do it all over again."

Alexis sucked in a breath. "I don't want to hurt him, Josh. I *never* wanted to hurt him, and I know I did; I just want to fix it."

"How?" Josh's eyes were narrowed.

"What, you, like, want to hear my speech?" she snapped, losing patience with Josh's determination to be Logan's guard dog. She pushed into the apartment, and Josh reluctantly let her.

"I know I would."

Alexis spun around at the wonderfully familiar voice. This whole time, her friends had been right. That damn accent was sexy.

Her heart seemed too full for her chest when she saw him. "Logan. You *are* here." She shot an accusing glance over her shoulder at Josh.

"I was in the loo," Logan said. "What do you want?"

She started to smile at the word *loo*, but her smile slipped at the cold tone. "I need to talk to you."

"Ah," he said, crossing his arms. "Your barrister spoke with you, then."

"Is it just me or is it *extra* British up in here today?" Josh muttered.

"Josh," Alexis said mildly, without looking away from Logan. "Could you do me a huge favor and get lost?"

He let out a startled laugh. "Oh, I'm sorry. I guess I thought for a second that I lived here."

Logan's eyes flicked away from hers for a moment, issuing a silent request to his friend, and she heard Josh sigh. "Fine. I'll be in the other room, music turned up. But Alexis, I swear to God—"

"Tanner," Logan said in a quiet but firm tone.

Josh glared, but he finally left the room, muttering something to Logan as he passed, before closing the door on his way out.

They were alone, and some of Alexis's former bravado slipped as she looked into Logan's cold, removed eyes, so different from the warm, friendly ones she knew so well, and realized she had an uphill battle ahead of her.

"I don't actually have a speech," she said quietly. "I mean, I tried to come up with one, but mostly I was too busy trying to get to you before it was too late, and I guess I just figured that I'd . . . I don't know. Wing it."

He gave a slight smile. "This should be good. I don't know that you've winged anything in your entire life."

"Too true," she said on a nervous exhale. "I find spontaneity far too risky, but I realized something today."

"What?" he asked in a bored tone.

"I realized that if anyone's worth the risk, it's you."

He stilled a little at that, his hand reaching up to adjust his glasses. "You'll have to do a good deal better than that, Alexis."

"I know," she said, clasping her hands in front of her. "Just give me a sec—"

"I already told you—"

"That you're done waiting for me; yes, I know," she said, talking over him. "But I'm just asking for two minutes. Two minutes to get this out. Okay?"

He hesitated, then gave her a curt nod.

She felt a little flutter of hope. At least he was letting her speak.

Alexis took a step forward but stopped when he tensed. "The first thing I need to say is that I'm so, so sorry about making you feel like you were less important than my job. I never meant to hurt you, but seeing it from your perspective, I realize that it was carelessly cruel of me, and I am sorry."

He said nothing, but she forced herself to forge ahead. "About the business thing, I accept your offer. I'll buy your half of the Belles, become the outright owner."

He didn't move. "*That's* what you came here to tell me?"

She held up a hand. "Hold on. There's an ultimatum. What I'm trying to tell you is that I'm okay forgoing being partners in business, but only if we can be partners in another way."

"Wait. I'm offering you your own company, which by the way, is the only thing you've ever wanted, and you're issuing an ultimatum?"

"It's not the only thing I've ever wanted," she whispered, her eyes filling.

"No?"

She shook her head, trying to gather her thoughts, trying to figure out what would make him stay.

But all her words failed her.

The one time she finally needed it, and Alexis's trademark control was nowhere to be found.

Love did this, she realized. It made you weak and clumsy and babbling and . . .

Alive.

"Don't go," she said, her voice breaking as she walked toward him. "Please don't go to London, Logan. I know that's unbearably selfish, I know you love your family and they love you, but . . ."

"But what?" he asked a bit earnestly.

She tried, but nothing came out.

Logan sighed and started to move past her. "It's too little too late, Alexis."

Uh-lex-iss.

"Wait," she said desperately, grabbing his arm.

He shook her off. "I already told you, I'm done waiting. I'm done holding your hand as you take baby steps. I'm done—"

"You can't be done!" she yelled.

He went perfectly still at her outburst, his eyes flaring with what she thought might be hope.

"I know I'm supposed to grovel right now, but I don't know how. The only thing I know is that all this time I've thought that the past eight years have been wonderful because of the Belles, and that's true, but only partially true."

"Alexis—"

Her heart plummeted, and stubbornness settled in. The same stubbornness that had driven her to build a company out of nothing, but this time she was prepared to fight harder than ever before, because this was more important.

"No wait," she said desperately. "I need to finish."

He gave a resigned nod. "All right. That's fair."

It wasn't much. He seemed almost . . . tolerant. But it was something.

But she had something better.

"I love you," she said on a hiccuping sob. "I love you so much, Logan Harris."

His eyes went dark and then maybe, maybe just a little bit watery.

She took advantage of his silence, even though her own eyes were *well* past watery.

"The past few years have been wonderful because of you," she forged ahead. "I think . . . I think I've loved you since that very first day at that bar, and what's more . . . I think you've known it. Haven't you?"

His smile was fleeting. "I was fairly certain. Hopeful."

"And you waited for me," she said quietly. "All this time, you waited for me to figure it out."

"And nearly died in the process," he grumbled.

Alexis dropped her purse to the floor before easing toward him, her hands lifting to his chest, fingers pulling at the fabric of his shirt as she held him close.

"Tell me I'm not too late," she whispered urgently, staring at the button of his shirt. "Tell me we have a chance and that we can make up for lost time, and that I can make it up to you, and—"

Logan's mouth took hers a split second before his hands found her waist, pulling her toward him until her hands were crushed between them, her mouth fused all the way with his.

He kissed her on and on, his mouth both urgent and tender before he pulled back slightly, raining kisses over her cheeks. "You don't know how long I've waited to hear you say all that," he said quietly.

She laughed. "A few years, I imagine."

He pulled back and met her eyes. "Eight years, four months, and twelve days."

Alexis blinked. "What?"

"Since the very day I met you," he said, touching a finger to her lips.

Alexis melted. "Logan—"

He interrupted her. "The night we met, you asked me what I was doing making my offer. Why I was offering my inheritance to a woman I'd just met in a bar."

"You said it was because you believed in the business."

"I didn't give a shit about the Belles, at least not right then. And you knew it. You said there was another reason, and you wanted to know what it was, remember?"

She gave a watery smile. "I do. And you said that if I accepted your offer, that maybe someday you'd tell me."

He smiled down at her, his hands cupping her face. "Ask me again. Ask me the reason."

"Why did you offer a woman you'd just met your entire inheritance?" she asked.

His lips pressed to the center of her forehead. "Because you weren't a woman I'd just met. From the very moment I saw you, I knew. I knew you were the woman I loved."

"I can't decide if that's nuts or romantic," Alexis said with a little laugh.

His lips trailed over her cheek, finding the sensitive skin of her ear. "When we tell the story to our chubby children, we're absolutely going with romantic."

Children.

Her children.

Her children with Logan.

"Yes," she whispered.

"Yes to what?"

"All of it," she said, pulling his head down to hers. "I say yes to all of it."

Epilogue

Eight Months Later

AFTER AN EXHAUSTING TUESDAY, Alexis was just on her way to meet Logan at their favorite French bistro around the corner from their apartment when her phone buzzed with a text message.

Change of plans. Meet me at 97th and Amsterdam for a predinner drink?

Alexis wrinkled her nose in confusion. That was all the way up toward Harlem and not at all convenient to their dinner location. But then, Logan had been steadily working to build out his NumberSync team, so perhaps he'd met with a potential candidate up that way.

Alexis checked email on the cab ride up, feeling both grateful and slightly stressed by the sheer magnitude of messages that she couldn't keep up with.

There had been at least four new client requests just that afternoon, all of which would have been perfect fits for the Belles' clientele if they had any availability whatsoever, which they didn't. She, Heather, and Brooke were all booked out for months, not just with weekend weddings, but weekday weddings as well. If this kept up, she'd have to look at hiring someone else.

It was still important to her to keep the business small and intimate, but surely one or two more wedding planners couldn't hurt. She set her phone back in her purse, figuring she'd talk it over with Logan over drinks.

She smiled when she realized she'd be asking her boyfriend rather than her business partner. The paperwork had been finalized just a few months earlier. Alexis had accepted Logan's offer to buy his half of the company.

She'd been the sole owner of the Wedding Belles for all of a month. And then promptly sold two-thirds of it. A third to Heather, a third to Brooke.

It felt good. *More* than good. Her professional life had never been better.

But more importantly, neither had her personal life. She and Logan were going strong, eight months in, and though he was no longer her partner on paper, he was her partner in all the important ways.

The cab pulled to a stop at the designated address, and Alexis paid the driver with a distracted thank-you, her instincts buzzing with a sense of foreboding as she stepped onto the curb.

Her heart flipped in her chest as she realized why the address of the bar had seemed vaguely familiar.

It was the bar where they first met.

Alexis felt a smile dawn on her face as she walked

toward the front door of the dive bar, knowing she'd be out of place in her pencil skirt and gray pumps, and caring not in the least.

It was mostly empty, being relatively early on a Tuesday, and Alexis spotted Logan immediately at the bar. He still insisted on wearing suits most every day though he didn't have to anymore, and she gave a little happy sigh that the man with the broad shoulders and dark brown hair was all hers.

He hadn't seen her yet, but just as she was about to approach him, inspiration struck, and she walked toward another seat instead.

The one she'd been sitting in that very first day she'd met him.

She forced herself not to look his way but couldn't quite hide her smile as the memories washed over her.

"Can I get you something to drink?" the short black-haired bartender asked. It was a different bartender from before, of course, but Alexis ordered the same drink she had then.

"Pinot grigio," she said.

"I don't think that's on happy hour," said the sexy British voice beside her.

Alexis turned to see Logan grinning down at her, and she leaned toward him with a conspiratorial smile. "It's okay. I can afford it."

"Oh yeah?" he asked, sitting beside her, beer in hand.

She nodded confidently. "Yup. Own my own company with a couple friends of mine."

"Is that so?" he said with a smile. "Want to tell me about it?"

"Some other time, maybe," she said. "Can I buy you dinner?"

Logan smiled. "Can't. Meeting my girlfriend later."

Alexis shrugged. "No problem. Excuse me, miss, can I get some food?" she said, getting the bartender's attention. "I'd like the burger, medium, with Swiss. Fish and chips, extra tartar, and . . . the chicken club."

The bartender gave them a curious look as she placed Alexis's wine in front of her. "Sure. No problem."

"So what's with the trip down memory lane?" Alexis asked, spinning her barstool slightly toward Logan.

He leaned toward her, his eyes twinkling behind his glasses. "I'd like to make you an offer, Alexis Morgan."

She smiled, remembering those same words from all those years ago. "What kind of offer?" she said, repeating her line.

This time, there was no Wedding Belles proposal for him to gesture to.

Instead, he reached into his suit pocket, pulled out a Tiffany blue box. Set it in front of her.

Alexis's breath caught. "Logan."

He leaned toward her slightly and whispered, "You'll understand why I don't get down on one knee in this place, right? There are peanut shells."

She let out a happy laugh as she reached for the box with a shaking hand.

Inside was a glittering solitaire. Utterly classic. Utterly her.

"Marry me?" he whispered.

Her eyes watered when she saw his were wet.

"Yes," she said, cupping his face. "A million yeses."

She heard a sniffle that she thought might be the bartender, or maybe it was herself, and she slipped the ring on her finger.

The second she did, Logan caught her face with one hand, turning it toward his so he could seal the engagement with a kiss.

"I love you," he whispered.

"I love you, too. So much."

"I hope you don't mind me proposing in perhaps the least romantic place in Manhattan." Logan reached for her left hand, looking down at the ring. "I just figured that we started our first partnership here. Made sense to start the second one, too."

"I'm not going to get a call from my lawyer saying you want to dissolve this one in a few years, am I?" she teased.

"Sorry, sweetheart. You're stuck with me on this one."

"Forever?" she asked hopefully.

Logan smiled tenderly, pulling her close for another kiss. "Forever and always."

Acknowledgments

OH GOSH. I CONFESS that I've been sitting here staring at the word *Acknowledgments* a little shell-shocked, because it's hitting home that this isn't just the end of me writing the story of Logan and Alexis.

It's the end of writing The Wedding Belles!

Coming to the end of a series is always a little bittersweet. On one hand, writing a book is hard, writing a series is even harder, so there's always that tiny sense of relief that maybe, just *maybe* you'll now be able to shower before noon and eat something besides Doritos for lunch.

On the other hand, the bigger hand, there's the not-so-minor heartache of saying good-bye to your characters. Brooke, Heather, and Alexis (and Jessie!) feel a bit like family. And their respective men, well . . . is it vain to say sometimes I create my own book boyfriends? Whenever I'm in the Upper West Side of the city and pass Seventy-Third Street, I think of the Belles, imagining that they're in there planning the next Kardashian wedding or something.

Oh wow. Moving on before I start to get weird(er) about this!

Every time I get to the acknowledgments of my books I wince a little, because it's so darn difficult to really, truly express in words how much the crafting of a book is a group process! I used to think you wrote the book, ran spell check, slapped a cover on it, uploaded it to Amazon or shipped it to Barnes & Noble, and that was that. Oh, how cute and naïve I was!

Writing a book isn't a golf game, it's a football game. Team sport all the way, and *this* team was absolutely amazing.

First huge shout-out goes to my editor, Elana Cohen, who I'm pretty sure was almost as invested in the Belles as I was, laughing and crying along with me the whole way as we made these characters fall in love and then go through the absolute *wringer*. Thank you for all your time and HEART.

Next, Kristi Yanta. Oh man. I started to type "my fabulous beta reader," but that's just plain insufficient. You are SO much more than a beta reader. You go above and beyond every time—and don't think for one second that I don't notice and appreciate it! I sometimes think of my books as "our books" because I absolutely could not do them without you. You're like . . . my Obi-Wan.

For Marla Daniels, I know we didn't get to work together for very long on these books, but I can't tell you how much I appreciate you stepping in and picking up this series as though it'd been your baby since the very beginning.

Kristin Roth, I hope you know how amazing you are! I never knew copyedits could be sexy, but man did you rock these. It's not every day that someone can combine sterling attention to detail with a gentle touch, and I really appreciate how deft you were in handling all my author quirks and nudging me toward better word choices.

Christine Masters, don't for one second think that I don't have my eye on you, noticing everything you do (in a non-creepy fashion). Thanks for always ensuring things go to production with nothing less than perfection.

Wow, okay, and that was just on the editorial side!

For Melissa Gramstad, for making sure this book got into as many hands as possible, and to the cover design team, because, COME ON, how gorgeous are the Wedding Belles covers, am I right?

Next up, for "my people." For my amazing assistant, Lisa Filipe . . . sometimes I don't even know how I get to tomorrow without you. Same goes for my agent, Nicole Resciniti, who lets me call her at the crack of dawn, before she's had her coffee, any time I have a random idea or thought.

My street team . . . oh my gosh, you guys, I know we're small, but WE ARE MIGHTY. I don't thank you enough, but know that every day I'm like, "Thank GOODNESS" for those ladies.

For my handful of UK readers who let me bug them with questions on Logan. Heart you guys.

For ALL my readers, because your enthusiasm and

support gets me through every day when I'd rather floss all day than write another word.

Last, never ever least, my beloved friends and family. Especially my husband, Anthony. I wouldn't have had the guts to start this journey without your insistence, nor the ability to get where I am now without your sacrifice and support. For all the times you patiently make me dinner while I'm on deadline, and maybe don't get a thank-you because I'm living inside my head, know that it's YOU who are in my heart and who inspires each and every happy ending.